WITCH IN RETROGRADE

Midlife Spirit Guides Book 1

WENDY WANG

Cover Designed by Deranged Doctor Designs

Proofreading by Indie Edits with Jeanine

2.1.22

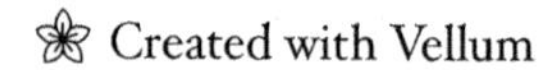

CHAPTER 1

Sarah Jane Prentice got into her 10-year-old Volvo 740 wagon after work and immediately felt a chill despite the 75-degree heat of late September. She glanced at the passenger seat.

"Geez Jessica!" Sarah Jane pressed her hand to her heart. "I need to put a bell on you. You scared the crap out of me."

The spirit gave her a sly smile and shrugged her translucent shoulders. Sarah Jane sensed the pleasure it gave the spirit and couldn't really blame her for it. After all, being dead was hard when almost no one could hear or see you. Sometimes people could sense spirit energy, or in the case of Sarah Jane, see spirits, but they were rare.

Sarah Jane put the key in the ignition but didn't start the car. "Don't you have somewhere else to hang out?

I'm already late." Her coworkers swarmed into the police department parking lot, ready to head home after a long day. She tipped her head and gave one of her fellow homicide squad members, Rob Rodriguez, a smile. He gave her a brief wave, completely unaware of the clingy ghost next to her. Jessica had been haunting her for nearly eleven months now since her body turned up dumped off a running trail. Since the spirit realized Sarah Jane, the detective at the scene, could see her.

The radio clicked on, and metal music blared inside the Volvo's cabin. "Come on," Sarah Jane said, her irritation and patience beyond their breaking point. "I am so not in the mood for this." The spirit continued flipping through stations like Sarah Jane wasn't even there.

"Stop it," Sarah Jane snapped and twisted the knob of the radio until it clicked off.

"Geez, you're just like my mother." The spirit's voice drifted through Sarah Jane's head.

She finally glared over at the apparition. Jessica had been nineteen when she died. They'd found her near a barely flowing creek bed, posed like a goddess from a greek statue, wearing a toga-like dress. But today the ghost wore a pair of ripped jeans and a faded blue T-shirt that read, *You smell like drama and a headache.*

The words on her T-shirt changed almost every time she appeared to Sarah Jane, and she had to admit, she liked the young woman's snarky sense of humor. Had the ghost owned a T-shirt like it when she was alive? When she was in a better mood, Sarah Jane would ask her. Jessica folded her nearly translucent arms across her chest and sunk down in her seat. Her long dark hair hung like a curtain covering her face, and Sarah Jane had to resist the urge to tuck it behind Jessica's ear so she could see her better, the way she would've done with her own daughter Selena.

Jessica reminded Sarah Jane a lot of her daughter. Same dark eyes, same dark hair. Although Selena's calm demeanor and kindness shone in her face. She also exuded a maturity that Jessica didn't. Her husband Dan had always called Selena their old soul. Maybe she did have an old soul, or maybe it was because Selena was the only girl, stuck between two brothers. Or maybe because she was part of a family of witches, Sarah Jane and Dan had tried to instill a sense of responsibility for the world in all their children at a very young age.

"I'm sorry I'm so grumpy." Sarah Jane's shoulders sagged under the weight of everything she'd had to deal with lately. "It's been a really hard day. And I'm not in the mood for your music. If you'd like to listen to a little classical or some folk rock..."

The spirit huffed. "Thanks, I'll pass."

It always fascinated Sarah Jane how a spirit carried habits and mannerisms into death. She watched the spirit's chest rise and fall as if she were taking a breath. Did the spirit have to work at it to make her body (if you could call it that) move that way? There were always so many questions in her head about spirit life.

"So, what made today so hard?" Jessica pushed her hair out of her eyes and fidgeted with a small tear in the leather passenger seat.

"You know what," Sarah Jane said softly. "Your mother came to see me. Those days are the hardest, because I have nothing new to tell her about your case. And the day's about to get even harder because..." She blew out a heavy breath dreading the words. "It's my 49th birthday. And my family insists on giving me a party even though I told them I don't want one this year."

"At least you can still talk to your family," Jessica grumbled. "Do you know how much it sucks to go home and see my mother? I can't touch her. Or talk to her in any meaningful way. I can't tell her I'm okay-ish."

"I can only imagine how difficult that is. I'm sorry." Sarah Jane pivoted in her seat to face the spirit. She glanced around the parking lot of the police station, no one seemed to notice her talking to an empty seat. "I'm doing everything I can to find the man who killed you. Once I do, you'll be able to move on, and I will personally let your mother know that you're in a better place when that happens. I swear I will."

"Yeah." Jessica's voice cracked, and she shrugged. "Whatever."

"You know it would help if you could give me a

description. Or better yet, tell me where he is. Tell me where he kept you for those five days, and I will go get him right this minute and make sure he never does this to another girl."

The spirit hugged her arms around her body, and a stricken expression crossed her pretty, oval face. "I've told you a million times, I don't remember."

Jessica's voice dropped to a whisper. The sound skittered across Sarah Jane's senses. The spirit began to flicker as if she had suddenly lost all the energy it took to power her apparition.

"Wait. Don't. I know it's scary," Sarah Jane said even though a part of her wanted the ghost to disappear. Her family was already going to be pissed at her for being late. "There are techniques I can use to help you remember."

"No." Jessica vanished. Sarah Jane slapped the top of the console between the seats and sat back, defeated. There was no point trying to call Jessica back; she wouldn't come. Sarah Jane had been trying for the past eleven months to get Jessica to discuss her murder, but it wasn't working, and she knew the spirit wouldn't move on until her case was solved.

Sarah Jane pinched the bridge of her nose and then massaged her forehead. The headache she'd had most of the day lingered just beneath the surface despite the two Excedrin she had popped earlier. Her phone chimed, letting her know she had a new text. She dug it out of the pocket of her tote bag.

Amykins: *Where are you? Everybody's here.*

She frowned at the text from her younger sister Amy and quickly jotted off her reply.

Sarah Jane: *I'm leaving work now.*

The phone rang in her hand, and she almost dropped it in surprise. Her sister's name appeared on the screen. She pressed the icon to answer. "What's up, Amy?"

"Since you're going to be late anyway, can you stop at Safeway?"

"Why? Can't you send one of the kids out? Ask Dalton to go." Sarah Jane knew her twenty-three-year-old son was probably the first to arrive at the house, and he probably brought his laundry.

She heard her sister's loud sigh.

Sarah Jane found herself giving in. It seemed easier than resisting after this miserable day. And, after all, how could she argue with her younger sister, who had sacrificed so much when Sarah Jane's husband Dan had gotten sick. Amy had moved in as soon as the diagnosis came and practically held their family together for almost three years. She cooked meals for Sarah Jane's two youngest children who were still in middle and high school at the time. She schlepped Dan to every appointment he had because Sarah Jane had to work.

Dan had long-term disability through his company, but it wasn't enough to allow Sarah Jane to quit her job.

She'd had better health insurance even though he worked at an up-and-coming software company for the healthcare industry, and she couldn't afford to lose her job. So, Amy came to her rescue.

Sometimes Sarah Jane wished she could've talked Dan into cashing out some of his 401k so she could stay home with him, but he wouldn't hear of it.

"That's our retirement, baby," he had told her. "I'm going to get better, and then we'll need that money so we can travel the world."

Only he hadn't gotten better. And eleven months ago, while she was on the job hiking a popular walking and bike trail that ran along the waterway into the heart of San Jose to examine the body of a young woman who had been murdered and dumped, he died peacefully in his sleep in the hospital bed they'd set up in the living room.

Sarah Jane sighed, the weight of all she carried heavy on her shoulders. She sensed Amy waiting on the other end of the line. "So, what do you want from Safeway?" She tried not to sound put-upon.

"Could you pick up some more chocolate ice cream?"

"Amy, come on. You know I don't even eat ice cream." Sarah Jane gritted her teeth.

"You don't eat it, but everybody else does, including your children," Amy scolded. Sarah Jane closed her eyes and pressed her lips together tightly so she wouldn't say anything mean and counted to ten.

"Fine," Sarah Jane finally said quietly. "How much do you need?"

"If you could get two containers of Breyers chocolate, that would be great."

"All right. I'll be home in a bit."

"Thank you so much," Amy said in a singsong voice. Sarah Jane ended the call and tossed her phone onto the empty passenger seat. She turned the key in the ignition and when she put the car into reverse, Jessica's voice drifted through her head.

"Happy birthday, Sarah Jane."

CHAPTER 2

The long crack extended from the fractured glass in the upper corner of the mirror, distorting his image and cutting him in half. The break had happened a long time ago. His mother had gotten angry about something, he couldn't even remember what now, and she had thrown a heavy quartz crystal obelisk at his head. He'd ducked, and the mirror bore the brunt of her anger.

Alive, she seemed to have two moods, hateful bitch or guilt-wielding mama bear. Now that she was dead, he was the one in control. All it took was a flash of a bundle of sage or a shake of the box of salt in her direction to keep her spirit in line.

He leaned a little to the left of the crack to get a better look at himself, then flipped up the collar of his light gray oxford, wrapped the solid black tie around his neck, and tied it with a Half Windsor knot. When he finished, he straightened the tie and inspected his handiwork in the mirror. He liked to look his best at work; it made hunting easier.

After tucking his shirt tails into his black trousers, he buckled his matching leather belt, then put on his freshly shined, lace-up shoes. Impressions were everything. Not that it would matter at five-foot-eight and a hundred and forty-five pounds soaking wet. Most people barely noticed him, especially in the uniform. It didn't stop him from raising a hand, giving a brief salute to the women on campus when he passed them on his rounds.

He liked to look them in the eye. If one of them smiled back at him, he made a mental note of her face, her body, and whether she could be part of a future project or not. If he saw her again, he'd make some excuse to talk to her, to get a feel for her. If she passed that test, then the real quest to include her would begin. The women were always interested when he told them about his art. Well, most of the time. Sometimes the ones that showed little interest were actually his favorites. Then he'd embark on a campaign to convince his potential subject to participate in one of his projects.

So far, he'd completed eight, and he was almost finished with his ninth project. Soon he'd go on the prowl for just the right media for his next masterpiece. It might take weeks or even months to gather what he needed, as it had for this current work in progress.

He heard the metallic squeaking of a bed coming from the back of the house and made a mental note to shore up the insulation again.

His mother's ghostly voice drifted through his head. "That's what happens when you give them too much freedom." She appeared in the mirror as if she were standing behind him. If he turned, he might see her; he might not. It really just depended on her mood.

"Stop it, Mother. I know what you're trying to do."

"What? I'm trying to protect my baby boy. If someone hears her..."

"No one's going to hear her. I've cast a muffling spell. If any noise does get through, the neighbors will think it's the television or something."

His mother scowled, and her ample jowl shook. "Your hubris will be your downfall. Mark my words."

"Sure, Mother, whatever." He turned away from her image and quickly ran a brush through his short dark hair, then set his baseball cap with the security company's logo just right. He took one last look, pleased with himself, then headed out of his room to deal with the noise problem.

He headed for the kitchen at the back of the house on the main level, then passed through the defunct beauty salon his mother had set up illegally twenty-five years ago. That's where he learned how to shampoo for his mother and watched her style, clip, and curl the hair of the women who entered through their back door. She had only one styling chair and two pink vinyl reclining chairs pushed up against sinks with matching pink bowls. One day, the old dryer chair finally shorted out. The damn thing had nearly caught on fire and smoked up the place. His mother had pushed the ruined dryer into a corner, unplugged it, and covered it with a black cloth. He'd never moved it.

The smell of burnt plastic sometimes surfaced on rainy days, even though, after the disaster, his mother had made him scrub the place from top to bottom. He pulled his key ring from his pocket and slipped the key into the deadbolt leading to the secret room he'd built off the salon.

She screamed as soon as he entered the room. It surprised him that she had any voice left at all. She liked to scream a lot. He closed the door quickly behind him and flipped on the overhead light. She struggled against her bindings, handcuffs that held her to the cot.

"Sweetie, we talked about this," he said. "The more you fight, the more difficult it will be to put you in the installation. You want to live forever, don't you?"

Her chest heaved up and down, but she grew quiet.

"Please let me go." Her raspy voice sounded painful. "Please, I swear to God I won't tell anybody about you. Or this place. Please, just let me go."

He sat on the bed next to her and stroked her cheek. "You are my Artemis. How can I let you go?"

"My name is Haley, not Artemis. Haley Brooks."

"Oh, my beauty. My Artemis. You only have a little longer. I promise. You'll be free tonight."

"Wait." She looked at him with a quizzical expression. "You're going to let me go?"

"Yes. I have to let you go so the world can see you, can see my Artemis the way I see you. Your voice sounds terrible. Would you like some water?"

She grimaced, and her throat undulated when she swallowed. She frowned and nodded her head.

"I thought so," he said. "I'll be right back with a bottle of water and a fresh diaper. Can't have you heading out into the world with a diaper rash, can we?"

She wept softly.

"There, there, my love, my beauty, my masterpiece." He stroked her hair. "The world is going to love you as much as I do."

CHAPTER 3

Dread rolled over Sarah Jane like a thick wave of fog once she turned onto her street and slowed the Volvo down to approach the fifty-eight-year-old ranch-style house she now shared with her youngest son, Larkin, and her sister. It had been over twenty years since she and Dan bought the house with a down payment his mother had given them.

"The worst house in the best neighborhood," he'd told her because it had needed so much work. His sheer enthusiasm for all the plans he had for making it the best house on the block had infected her. And so, she'd agreed to take out what seemed like an enormous mortgage at the time because she believed in him. Believed in them.

Maybe it was all the changes they'd made together, but when Dan was alive, the house emanated magic. It called to her after the terrible days she'd have dealing with murder and the depravity of humans. The house beckoned her home, offering comfort and love.

Now a dark energy had swallowed it up. Where Dan had been the center, almost pulsating with light and love for his family, for the world, she was the dark side of the heart. She's the one who looked into the abyss nearly every day.

"You should quit. You could do something else," Dan had said to her on too many occasions to count.

"I'm good at it," Sarah Jane would counter. "And it might be hard, but at least I get the satisfaction of putting some horrible person away. And I like helping people."

"You could help people in other ways," she remembered him saying one particularly difficult night. Then, he kissed her on her temple. "You just have to believe you can. It's like you're determined to solve every murder on behalf of your mother. You should let it go."

She'd shrugged at him. "There's nothing to let go. We know who killed my mother. My goal is to make sure that all the other families whose loved one is murdered has answers too."

She pushed away the memory and parked her car next to her sister Susanna's silver minivan. A quick glance in the rearview mirror at the street, and she knew all her family had come. Dread tightened its grip around her heart. She grabbed the bag of ice cream and headed inside.

"I'm home," she called once inside the foyer. She glanced at the closed French doors leading to the study on her left. Through the darkened window panes she could see the outline of Dan's desk and the tall bookcases lining the walls, all still untouched in the eleven months he'd been gone.

Originally it had been their formal living room, but since they weren't formal people, Dan turned it into his office. One of these days, she'd need to go in there and go through everything. All the papers and files. And the books! What would she do with all those books? She couldn't bear the thought now, so she put on her blinders—as she always did when it came to dealing with what was left over from Dan's life—and slipped off her shoes. She shoved them underneath the bench near the front door next to her youngest son's Converse high tops. A long row of shoes belonging to her visiting sisters, her daughter, her other son, and even her grandmother reinforced what she already knew. Nobody respected her wish not to celebrate her birthday today.

The familiar clicking of toenails on the hardwood floor drew her attention, and she looked up to find her son's ten-year-old pit bull lumbering toward her. The brown and white dog bonked his blocky head against her leg, and his hind end wiggled with each wag of his tail.

"Hey, Petey." She scrubbed behind his ears. His eyes

shut, and his mouth opened with his tongue lolling to one side. "Who's the best boy?" She scrubbed harder. "Who's the best boy?"

At least the dog loved her. Something warm rubbed up against the back of her legs, then jumped up on the bench in front of her. Her sister's familiar. A long-haired white cat with one blue eye and one green eye stared at her curiously.

"Hi, Coal." She held out a fist for the cat. Coal gave it a long sniff before he finally rubbed his cheek against the side of her hand as if to say, "You may now pet me, human." Sarah Jane gave him a good scratch behind the ears.

"Well, that took you long enough." Her youngest sister Amy appeared from around the corner with a blue gingham dish towel draped over one shoulder. She'd clipped her long, blond hair up high on the back of her head and strands of it poked out, reminding Sarah Jane of a rooster. Amy took the bag of ice cream from Sarah Jane and wrinkled her delicate nose.

"You smell like death. That spirit's been with you again. You should just let me get rid of her," Amy said.

"No." The word came out a little too forcefully, and Sarah Jane's cheeks flooded with heat. "I need her. She's going to remember something, and I'll be able to solve her case. Then she'll move on without any help from a spell."

Sarah Jane peeled off her black suit jacket.

Amy shrugged casually. "You should go take a shower. Gran is here, and you know how she feels about anything related to death."

"You'll feel that way too when you're ninety-two. Anyway, I haven't seen a reaper creeping around looking for a ghost, so I don't think Gran is in any danger," Sarah Jane quipped.

"Fine." Her sister twisted her lips with familiar disapproval.

"What's up with you?"

"Nothing." She turned and disappeared through the door leading to the kitchen. Sarah Jane knew better, though. It took a lot for Amy to get riled about anything, but she shook it off for now. They would have it out later when there weren't almost a dozen people in her house. Sarah Jane didn't have the energy for a scene tonight, so she took a deep breath and centered herself, then headed into the kitchen.

They were all there, just as she expected, gathered around the long farmhouse table that broke up the space of the kitchen and the adjoining family room. Her four sisters, Susanna, Cass, Rainey, and Amy. Her grandmother. And her three kids, Dalton, Selena, and Larkin.

"SJ!" Susanna called, grinning until her green eyes became half-moons. Her grandmother, who had nicknames for them all, had always called her sister Susanna, smiley eyes.

"We were beginning to think you were never going to

come home. I saved you a seat." She patted the chair between her and Selena.

"Thank you." Sarah Jane gave her sister a weary smile. "I'm going to get a plate first. I'm starving. I didn't have time for lunch today."

"Of course," Susanna said.

A huge spread was laid out on the kitchen island, including barbecued chicken, macaroni and cheese, her grandmother's potato rolls, a large green salad over-flowing with vegetables from her grandmother's garden, a pot of fresh green beans, and an uncut chocolate birthday cake that Amy had made from scratch and decorated herself. Two unlit candles perched on top. The numbers four and nine.

Sarah Jane's jaw tightened with dismay. She wasn't sure what upset her more, the cake—which her sister knew she didn't eat because at her age any sweet thing settled around her middle—or the numbered candles and what they represented. One year till fifty. She and Dan had always said they'd go to Hawaii for her fiftieth. Just the two of them. A second honeymoon. But now, that would never happen. She scowled at the cake and helped herself to a chicken breast, green beans, and a plate of salad with no dressing, then took the seat between her sister and daughter.

The conversation around her ceased, and after the third bite of food, she could feel her family's eyes on her. She dropped her fork next to her plate and glanced around at all their faces. They had already finished their dinner, with forks resting on their plates or beside them. Sarah Jane wiped her mouth with her napkin and folded her arms on the table. Her gaze settled on her sister Cass, who stared at her with her lips twisted in anger.

"What?"

"Nothing." Cass shifted in her chair.

Of her four sisters, Cass could be the most contrary. Her grandmother always blamed it on her red hair. But Sarah Jane knew it was mostly the trauma of their childhood that had made her sister so tough. It had been a miracle that any of them had survived their parents' relationship. And when their mother died, Cass, who'd been ten at the time, took it the hardest. She didn't just have a chip on her shoulder, she lived behind a wall of chips and wielded words like a blunt instrument.

"Clearly it is something, Cassiopeia." Sarah Jane rarely used her sister's full name unless she wanted to get under her skin. The thing about her family was no matter how old they got, how mature they got, they all knew how to push each other's buttons. Buttons that acted like a time machine. Suddenly they were all children again, freshly traumatized and trying to figure out the world without parents.

"It's just..." Cass narrowed her dark green eyes. "You knew we were having a party. And yet you left work late. Then you took forever to get ice cream."

"I left work late because I have a case."

"You always have a case," Cass said.

"Well, maybe Amy didn't tell you all, but I really didn't want a party this year. And as usual, my wishes weren't taken into consideration. So, excuse me for not rushing home."

Susanna gently touched Sarah Jane's arm. "We just wanted to cheer you up, sweetie." Always the peace-maker. Susanna hated it when any of them fought. She had spent a lot of their childhood and teenage years putting herself between Sarah Jane and Cass especially. "We feel you need your family right now. I know you don't think you do but—"

"Aunt Susanna's right." Dalton piped up from the end of the table. Sarah Jane's mouth sagged open.

Some days he looked so much like his father, except for his eyes. He had definitely inherited the Prentice green eyes, but everything else was Dan—his silky, dark, brown hair, the square of his jaw, and broadness of his shoulders.

"You always worked a lot. Dad never seemed to mind. He always told us the work you were doing was important."

Something else unsaid lingered in the air, swirling around her older son's head. She could almost hear the echo of his feelings—*why was your work so much more important than us?* But he would never say such a thing out loud.

"I swear to the goddess, Mom, you've done nothing

this year except push us away even more. Work is just an excuse."

His words lodged in her heart like a bee's stinger, spreading pain through her body with each beat. She folded her napkin and threw it across her plate, unable to look any of them in the eye.

"It hasn't even been a year since he died. You just don't understand. None of you." From the corner of her eye, Sarah Jane saw her grandmother tilt her head and furrow her brow. Her breath caught in her throat. Her grandmother had lost her husband when she was younger than Sarah Jane. "Except maybe you, Gran." She pushed her plate away and stood up. "I didn't want any of this. And I'm sorry, Cass, if you're pissed because I didn't meet some timetable you had in your head. But somebody else could have gotten the ice cream, and I would've gotten here sooner. I have completely lost my appetite, so if you'll excuse me, I'm done."

"What about the cake?" Amy said, sounding alarmed. "It's double chocolate. Your favorite."

Sarah Jane shook her head. A weary smile crossed her lips. "Double chocolate was Dan's favorite, not mine."

"But...but you have to blow out the candles and make a wish," Amy continued.

Sarah Jane bit her tongue so she wouldn't say something cruel. "Cut the cake without me. You know I don't eat sugar anyway. And as far as wishes go... I don't have any this year."

She stopped before she left the room and kissed her grandmother on the cheek. "Sorry, Gran."

Her grandmother grabbed one of her hands, holding her in place. "I'll light a candle for you, Sunny Girl." Her grandmother gave her hand a gentle squeeze. "I'm afraid the only way out of all this darkness inside you is through. But that means you have to keep moving. You can't stay here buried in your grief. Otherwise, all that negative energy will sprout roots and freeze you to the spot. You understand?"

Sarah Jane blinked hard. She gave her grandmother a quick nod, not trusting her voice. Her grandmother's grip fell away, and Sarah Jane rushed upstairs before the first tears began to fall.

CHAPTER 4

Sarah Jane closed her bedroom door and peeled off the rest of her unofficial uniform—a brightly colored blouse, pink in this case, that was supposed to convey authority and approachability and black pants that matched the suit jacket she'd left downstairs. She left the clothes on the floor like a trail of breadcrumbs.

These days she barely spent time in the room beyond sleeping. The only reason it didn't resemble a teenage boy's cave was because Amy insisted on cleaning it. Almost daily her sister picked up Sarah Jane's clothes, hung them up in the closet or put them in the laundry hamper, then made the bed. The duvet and pillows made that part easy on her sister, and Sarah Jane tried not to think too much about how she sometimes felt she took advantage of Amy's generosity and love for her. But at the same time, she knew if Amy didn't make her daily sweep, there would be a permanently unmade bed and hardly a path between the piles of clothes. She sighed and made a half-hearted attempt at order by picking up her pants and draping them over the armchair in the corner of the room. Then she headed into the master bathroom for a quick shower.

She turned the brushed nickel handle until water gushed from the shower head then adjusted the temperature. While she waited for the water to get hot, she released the neat bun at the base of her skull and ran a brush through her long mahogany hair, ignoring the silver streaks that sprouted from her side part and framed her oval face. Ever since the first hot flash surprised her fourteen months ago, she found her neck sweaty nearly all the time and rarely wore her hair down now. It might be easier to manage if she just chopped it all off short. She leaned in close to the mirror but couldn't imagine her long locks gone. Most of her makeup had smudged off throughout the day, and what hadn't, settled in the lines around her eyes.

"You look like a raccoon," a soft voice echoed through her head. How many times had Dan said that to her when she'd arrived home so whipped, she just wanted to fall into bed? She closed her eyes and pictured him; his soft, brown eyes and dark, salt and pepper hair. The scruff of a beard she liked to run her fingers over. She could almost feel his strong, warm hands on her shoulders, standing behind her, peering at her reflection.

"Do I look old?"

"No way. You don't look a day over thirty-five."

"Liar. You know lying to a witch is a serious offense."

"Who's lying?" She felt his lips on her neck.

The sound of a hissing cat stirred her from her memories, and Sarah Jane opened her eyes. She just about jumped out of her skin at the sight of the ghost in the mirror. She pressed her hand against her chest.

Sarah Jane rounded on the spirit of Jessica King. "Sweet goddess, would you at least announce yourself?"

The cat perched in the doorway and hissed at the apparition again. She knew her sister meant well by sending Coal to check on her, but she shooed the cat away. "Go on now, Coal. This is none of your business, and you can tell your mother that." She closed the bathroom door, and her gaze shifted to the spirit.

"We had an agreement." Sarah Jane crossed her arms over her chest, thankful she hadn't taken off her bra and underwear yet. "You were not going to follow me into this house. My son and sister live here, and they are both just as sensitive to spirits as I am. I won't have you scaring my son."

The spirit sat down on the toilet seat and crossed her legs. "Oh, for Christ's sake. I'm not here to scare your son." She still wore ripped jeans, but her T-shirt had changed again. This time it read, *It's all fun and games until a redhead gets angry*.

Sarah Jane narrowed her eyes. "Are you spying on me?"

"What? No. Why?"

"Because I just had a..." From the way the spirit stared at her, Sarah Jane could tell she had no clue that she just had a fight with her sister—a redhead. "Never mind. Why are you breaking the rules?"

"Are you going to put me in jail?" Jessica chided.

"I might put you in spirit jail if you don't watch yourself. I won't hesitate to burn you out of here with some sage and keep you out with salt and black tourmaline."

The spirit raised her hands in surrender. "Fine. Sorry. I just came to tell you he's killed again."

"What? So you know where he is?"

"No, not exactly. It's her energy I felt more than his. It's like we're all connected," Jessica's spirit said.

"What do you mean? How many are you connected to?"

"More than two. You need to widen your search."

"It's been months, and you're just now telling me this?"

"He hasn't killed anyone else since me, I mean, besides her. I've got to go."

"No, wait." Instinctively, Sarah Jane reached out to stop her from leaving as if the ghost was a mortal. The spirit just wafted in front of her like a cloud. "You have to tell me where she is. Maybe I can still catch him in the act."

"Get some sleep, Sarah Jane. You look like shit... And tomorrow's going to be a bitch of a day." Jessica flickered for a second and then vanished.

"Dammit. Come back." Sarah Jane waited for a minute or two, but the spirit had slipped off to wherever it was she went when they weren't together. How the hell was she supposed to sleep now?

She grabbed a pair of sweatpants off the chair in the corner and gave them a sniff. She'd only worn them once this week. She fished a T-shirt out of a drawer—one of Dan's Stanford T-shirts that she just couldn't bear to part with—and slipped it over her head. She put on her running shoes and slipped down the hall as quietly as she could to grab her purse from the bench in the foyer. Once she retrieved her cell phone, she headed back to her bedroom and gave her partner, Mia Johnson, a call.

Mia picked up on the second ring. "I know you are not calling me during your birthday party."

"The party's a bust," Sarah Jane said. "I did have a visitor though."

"Who?" Mia asked. In the background, Sarah Jane could hear Mia's two kids jabbering about spaghetti. "Anthony put that down." Mia scolded. "Stop playing with your food and eat it please." Then she came back on the line. "Sorry about that. We're in the middle of dinner."

"No," Sarah Jane said. "I'm sorry. I should've realized. It's just, Jessica King came to visit me at my house."

Mia had been in homicide for almost a year when Sarah Jane decided to tell her the truth about who she really was and what she could do. Learning that Sarah Jane was a witch had both intrigued and frightened Mia, but it had been easy enough to prove because Mia's dead grandmother liked to show up every once in a while to keep an eye on her granddaughter.

Telling Mia was a turning point of sorts for Sarah Jane. It was a relief to have an ally. She'd been in the department for almost 15 years, and while some of her squad definitely thought she was weird—Robert Rodriguez for example—none of them knew the truth about her and her abilities. Except Mia.

"Does she usually visit you at home?" Mia asked, her voice full of caution.

"No. Generally, I don't allow it. But she had something important to tell me. He's back. He's killed again."

Mia gasped. "Oh my God. Does she know where he is?"

"She says she doesn't. She says she just knows he's killed because she's connected to the other girl. But she couldn't tell me how. She also said there were more than just the two of them."

"And you believe her?" Mia asked, unable to keep the mix of shock and excitement out of her voice.

"I don't know. I mean, I checked VICAP after Jessica was killed."

"Maybe we need to check again."

"Yeah, that's what I was thinking. I'm going back to the office."

"Tonight? It's almost eight o'clock. Don't do that."

"Why?"

"Because it's your birthday, Sarah Jane. And because it won't make a damn difference until somebody finds her body. And since Jessica can't tell us where that is..."

"I know. I just..."

"I feel the same way, but there's really nothing we can do. Yet."

Sarah Jane took a deep breath and sat down on the bed. "I hate this. It's like I have this knowledge, and I can't do anything with it."

"I know. Why don't you try to get some rest? Take a hot shower. Watch some trash TV, or go to bed early. Anything to get your mind off it."

"Sure," Sarah Jane said. "I'll get to the squad room early tomorrow after my run."

"Sounds good. I'll see you then."

The line went dead, and Sarah Jane flopped back across the bed. Then scooted over to Dan's side. The pillow had long stopped smelling like him, but that didn't keep her from putting it to her nose and breathing it in.

"Why don't you talk to me?" she whispered against the striped cotton. "It's like open season for every other ghost with me. Where are you?" Salty tears slipped down her cheeks making an itchy trail. "Please. If you can hear me, Dan, please come see me. I need your help. I need your wisdom."

She hugged the pillow tighter and cried. After a bit, the tears wouldn't come anymore, and she curled up on her side and fell asleep.

CHAPTER 5

Sarah Jane's feet pounded on the trail, keeping time to the thoughts running through her head. Jessica had ignored her pleas first thing this morning to lead her to the new girl's body. Another girl had died, and Jessica said she'd find more victims out there. Her stomach flip-flopped with visions of what she might have missed.

Poor Jessica. She and any other possible victims (if Jessica was right) were the ones who'd gotten the shaft. Sarah Jane hadn't been on her game in the weeks after Dan died. Maybe she'd come back to work too soon, but she just couldn't stay home. Everywhere she looked there were reminders of him. Still, how could she have missed more than one victim? If the new body was discovered today—she had a feeling it would be, and her feelings about this sort of thing were rarely wrong—her lieutenant would want her to take point on the case, but she didn't know if that was the right thing to do. Begging off would be tricky, though. She'd worked really hard for the past ten years to show her lieutenant she could count on her. Just the thought of losing ground in her career at this point made her feel sick.

A shout came from behind. “Left.” A guy wearing khaki pants and a black jacket with reflective tape on the back and sleeves whizzed past her on a bicycle. She slowed down to walk and another jogger passed her. Her left knee ached. Time for a new pair of shoes. The five-mile run before work each morning tore through the brand she needed for support.

Up ahead, she spotted Jessica leaning against a tree just off the paved trail. The ghost wore a pair of black jeans and a form-fitting purple T-shirt with the words, *Running Sucks*, in large white letters along with a graphic of a pair of running shoes. Sarah Jane sped up a little before the ghost changed her mind and disappeared.

“Good morning.” Sarah Jane stopped on the trail and pretended to stretch against the tree where the spirit waited. “Do you have some news for me?”

“You look like shit. Did you get *any* sleep last night?”

“Do you really care?”

Jessica shrugged. “Not really, I guess. Just making conversation.”

“Great,” Sarah Jane whispered and glanced over her shoulder at two more bicyclists heading to work at this hour of the morning. “Maybe we can keep these visits contained to my car then.”

Jessica scowled. “Yeah, whatever. I guess I do have some news. About a minute ago a runner found her body. It wasn't that far from where he dumped me. Near the creek again. I guess he likes water.”

“That's great.” Sarah Jane reached for her cell phone in the leg pocket of her joggers.

“Shouldn’t you wait until they call you? I mean how will you explain that you knew where she was?”

Sarah Jane paused and glanced down at her phone. The spirit was right, she needed to wait. An impossible task but the right thing to do. “Dammit.” Sarah Jane tucked her phone back into place.

“She's there. Scared. I'm hoping you can see her too. She seems way more traumatized than I was.”

“We'll see about that.” It was on the tip of her tongue to tell the spirit she was still traumatized, but she thought better of it because she still needed Jessica's help. Sarah Jane's face heated unexpectedly, and she fanned herself with the hem of her T-shirt.

“What's up with you?” Jessica asked.

“Nothing. I'm just hot. I've been running,” Sarah Jane snapped. “Can you go wait with her? Until I can get there.”

“Sure. It's not like I have anything better to do.” Jessica disappeared.

“Right.” Sarah Jane ignored the ache in her knee. It

had been acting up a lot more than usual lately. She shook out the tight muscles in her leg and walked the rest of the trail back to the parking lot. Even with her knee, she was in better shape than most of the detectives on her team. All mostly in their forties and fifties, they'd let themselves go soft around the middle and suffered from bad backs. Not to mention poor diets.

Once Sarah Jane reached the parking lot, she opened the back tailgate door of her Volvo wagon and reached into the cooler she kept in the back for her after-exercise water. She'd put six new bottles in it just two days ago, but this morning it came up empty.

"Dammit, Larkin," she whispered. She didn't want to think about what he and his friends had refilled it with when she let him borrow the car the other night. While Larkin was basically a good kid, he was still a teenager. And that meant parties, beer, and maybe even drugs.

He could have at least replaced her water bottles, she grumbled to herself. She shut the lid to the cooler and checked her watch. 6:17 am. She still had enough time to stop at a convenience store before she headed into the station to take a shower and change. She climbed into the driver's seat and put the car in gear. She'd read Larkin the riot act once she got home, but for now, she needed to stop for something to drink. Her throat felt as dry as ash.

She went to a gas station not that far from the park and scanned the parking lot when she arrived. Everything appeared normal, although, surprisingly, the store didn't seem busy at this time of the morning. Her son Dalton had a phrase for this constant checking of her location; he called it her cop protocol. Assess all threats.

She liked to think of it as assessing the energy of a place, getting a lay of the land, so she knew what to expect. To Sarah Jane, it was more of a witch thing than a cop thing because she'd been doing it most of her life. The lone car parked on the side of the building probably belonged to the employee. She pulled into a space right up front.

"Don't go in there." Jessica's whispered advice slithered through Sarah Jane's head, and the temperature in the car dropped fifteen degrees. She shivered and glanced at the rearview mirror. The spirit sat in the backseat. She wore her hair in a long braid wrapped around her head, and Sarah Jane could make out the black lettering on her pale gray T-shirt. It read, *Kiss Me I'm Dead*, above a stylized skull.

"What are you talking about?" Sarah Jane glanced around the parking lot and peered through the large, brightly-lit front windows.

"You go in there, and your life is going to change, and not in a good way. Trust me on this."

Sarah Jane shot her a skeptical look. "So, you're a fortune teller now? I'm not sensing anything, and my intuition is pretty on point about this sort of thing."

"Whatever." The spirit rolled her eyes. "Don't blame

me later when everything goes to shit." Jessica disappeared.

For a second, Sarah Jane doubted her abilities, which happened frequently lately. It seemed every spell she touched these days went sideways, but her ability to talk to the dead and sense the energy around her seemed intact. "You're being ridiculous. Just stop it," she said aloud then hopped out of the car.

A doorbell rang when she entered the building. She immediately greeted the attendant sitting behind the counter with a perfunctory wave. "Good morning."

The middle-aged man looked up from his book, his dark eyes warm with recognition. "Morning."

She knew to head to the coolers along the back wall. An array of beverages, ranging from beer to soda to water and, of course, juice and milk, filled the shelves. The cool air slapped her in the face when she opened the door and reached inside to pull out a liter-sized bottle of water. She lingered for a moment, letting the chill wrap around her head and shoulders. She pressed the plastic bottle against her cheek.

"I'm sorry to bother you, but could you hand me a water?" A woman's voice startled Sarah Jane, and she pulled her head out of the cooler. A short, buxom woman stared at her with a wide, expectant grin on her round face. Her curled black hair just brushed the tops of her shoulders, and her red suit complemented her golden-brown skin. She looked as if she were dressed to go to church with her two-inch heels and red hat complete with a red satin ribbon and matching feather. Sarah Jane's senses tingled with prickly warm energy, and she studied the woman for a moment, trying to figure out where the feeling was coming from.

"Wow. You're really put together for this time of the morning," Sarah Jane blurted.

"Why, thank you." The woman smoothed her hands over her suit jacket. "I'm a big believer in looking your best to make you feel your best."

"I can see that." Sarah Jane nodded.

"Looks like you've been running this morning," the woman said. "Now that's a habit I never could get into. I'd rather walk. Much easier on the knees, especially at our age." The woman nudged Sarah Jane with her elbow.

"Right. I didn't realize it was so obvious." Sarah Jane found herself drawn to the woman's soft, warm energy emanating like a tiny sun.

"Not to be rude, but the athletic pants sort of give it away and you're all sweaty and red-faced. Unless it's that time of life for you..."

Sarah Jane's face heated again, stretching down her neck. She twisted the water bottle in her hand. "So..." She cleared her throat. "Do you live around here?"

"Not exactly. I've been called here to help—"

The doorbell rang again, and shouting drew Sarah Jane's attention.

"Excuse me." Sarah Jane stood up on her tiptoes to

get a better look at the commotion. A beanpole of a man wearing a hoodie pulled up over his head waved a gun around.

"Shit," Sarah Jane muttered. Out of habit, her hand went to her hip but came up empty. Her gun was still locked up in the gun safe in her car. All she had on her was her badge, her driver's license, a credit card, and her phone. She turned to the woman and ordered, "Stay here."

The woman in red nodded, her brown eyes large, round saucers.

Sarah Jane crept along an aisle to better assess the situation. She crouched down below the height of the shelves with chips and cookies, and when she got to the end, she stopped and peered around the corner.

The punk leaned over the counter. His spittle flew when he yelled, "Just give me all the cash and open the safe, man. If you want to go home to your kids, you'll do as I say."

"What are we going to do?"

Sarah Jane almost jumped to the ceiling at the sound of the woman's whisper right behind her. She glared at her. "Ma'am, I need you to get down on the floor and stay put."

"Maybe we should go talk to him." She gestured to the front counter. "I think he's just high. And probably scared out of his mind. I mean who sticks up a convenience store at six o'clock in the morning. He must be suffering something pretty awful. Desperate. You know?"

"Yeah. I'm sure that's it." Sarah Jane tried not to roll her eyes at the woman's kind conjecture, but she'd seen enough jackasses like this one when she was a patrol officer to know he probably was high and the only thing he had on his mind was getting money for a fix. "Now, please just get down."

The woman held her hands up in surrender. She squatted down next to the cookies and gave them a wistful look. Sarah Jane squatted next to her and jotted off a quick text to her squad. Hopefully, one of them would respond. They were all probably on their way to the station house.

Sarah Jane: *Robbery in progress at Chevron Station on Scott. Not that far from San Tomas Aquino Creek Park.*

Mia Johnson, the youngest person on the squad at 34, texted back first.

Mia Johnson: *Are you okay?*

Rob Rodriguez: *Call 911.*

Sarah Jane gritted her teeth.

Sarah Jane: *Trying not to let him know I'm here, yet. Glad to see you have my back, Rodriguez.*

Mia Johnson: *Don't do anything stupid, even if you have your weapon on you.*

John Waterson, a third member of her team, joined in. At 59, John was the most seasoned detective in the division.

John Waterson: *I'll call it in. I agree with Mia. Wait for backup SJ.*

Sarah Jane: *Thanks John. Don't worry about me. There's only one other customer in the store, and she's with me.*

The screaming punk got louder.

Sarah Jane: *Gotta go.*

Sarah Jane peeked around the corner again. The woman in red stood in the middle of the checkout area, only a few feet away from him. She leaned one way, then the other, as if to get a better look. A moment later, she turned to Sarah Jane with a grin on her face and waved for her to come closer.

"What the hell?" Sarah Jane mouthed. She pointed to the floor in front of her and gritted her teeth, then mouthed, "Get over here."

The attendant wept and packed a plastic bag. "Just take this. Please. That's all I have access to."

"I don't believe you!"

"Why? There's a sticker on the door right there that says we don't have more than a hundred dollars in the drawer, and the clerk can't open the safe," the clerk pleaded.

The punk paced back and forth. He banged the gun against his forehead. He kicked a display in front of him, sending a box of candy bars skittering across the floor.

Sarah Jane took two deep breaths and stepped out from behind the shelf with her hands up. "Hey, kid. He's not lying. That's all they have on the premises. If you're smart, you'll take the money and go."

"That's right," the woman in red said, "You can't get blood out of a turnip."

Sarah Jane's jaw tightened. The last thing she needed was well intentioned 'help'.

The punk turned and jumped a little at the sight of her. "Where the hell did you come from?" He aimed the weapon at her, his hand shaking a little.

"You don't want to do that, son." Sarah Jane took a step closer to him. She lowered her voice. "I've already called the police. They'll be here any second, and you should know, I'm a police officer. Shooting me will not do you any favors."

"You're right about that," the woman chimed in. "Although I don't think he could really shoot you. That gun looks like a toy. Just look at the tip."

Sarah Jane gritted her teeth and refused to engage with the woman.

"Just take a closer look." The woman pointed at the gun. "It's too shiny, and I think he broke off the orange tip that toy guns have to make them look less real. If they really want them to look less real, they should just make them rainbow colored, if you ask me."

"Ma'am, no one asked you. I told you to get down and stay down," Sarah Jane snapped.

"Who the hell are you talking to?" The punk furrowed his brow with confusion. The sallow color of his skin and his grayish broken teeth confirmed her thoughts. He was a meth head.

Sarah Jane looked from the punk to the woman. Only she'd disappeared. Good. Maybe she'd finally listened.

"I'm talking to you." Sarah Jane directed her attention back to him. She focused on the gun's barrel. A bit of orange plastic still clung to the inside. What the hell? The woman was right?

"Is that a toy gun?" Anger lived near the surface these days. Blame it on grief or going through menopause, she didn't care, but she could go from zero to rage in sixty seconds. This jackass pointing a toy gun at her and the clerk enraged her. The look on the punk's face told her all she needed.

"Are you freaking kidding me?" She marched forward and grabbed the weapon out of his hand. The plastic weighed hardly a few ounces. She had to make herself toss it to the ground instead of beating the crap out of him with it.

"Oh shit." He bolted for the door. His shoe connected with one of the candy bars, his feet slipped out from under him, and he landed hard on his back. Sarah Jane seized her opportunity and jumped on top of him. He squirmed underneath her like a live wire, but she put her full weight onto his hips and got hold of one of his arms. The words popped into her head, and she focused on turning her intention behind them into a spell. She'd taught her kids from an early age that any word, any idea, any wish could be a spell. To be careful with their thoughts, because paired with focus, real magic could happen.

"Be still!" Sarah Jane uttered the spell aloud. The air around her sizzled and crackled. Something popped next to her ear, and a whiff of ozone stung her nose.

A second later, stars exploded in her vision when his free hand punched her in the face, striking her cheekbone. The flash of pain took her breath away, and he wriggled out from under her. She shook her head, holding onto her face for a moment. Her spell had failed. It was such a simple incantation. How had she not manifested it? She turned her head and looked through the glass front door as everything unfolded.

The kid rushed out of the store into six uniformed cops holding their weapons on him. He skidded to a stop and threw his arms in the air.

A moment later, Mia Johnson walked through the door.

"Geez, Sarah Jane." Mia kneeled next to her, her dark braids pinned away from her face. Her pale pink blouse and dark tan suit looked stylish this morning. "You sure know how to start the day off right."

Sarah Jane laughed. "This is exactly how I like to start my day. With a run and a black eye. What are you doing here?"

"I was already at the station when I got your text, so I headed over to make sure you were okay."

"Thanks."

Mia offered her a hand and helped Sarah Jane to her feet. "So... it looks like your..."—she lowered her voice to a whisper—"spirit friend was right. We've got a body."

"Are you kidding me?"

"Nope. We should get you looked at to make sure you don't have a concussion, then we can head over there."

"I'm fine. I just need to change."

"You sure?"

"Yeah. He didn't knock me out. I swear." Sarah Jane held up her hands. "There's one thing we need to do before we get out of here. There's another customer here. I need to make sure she's all right."

"Okay." Mia turned to the clerk. "Sir, are you all right?"

The clerk gave her a squeamish look. "Yes, I think so. Although, I'm done with this job. It's not worth it."

Mia gave him an understanding nod.

Sarah Jane walked up and down every aisle. Checked the storeroom and the bathroom but found no sign of the woman in red.

She walked back to the clerk, ignoring his trembling hands for a moment. "Did you see what happened to the other woman that was here?"

He lifted a brow with a curious look on his face.

"What other woman? You were the only one in the store when that kid came in."

"Are you sure?"

"Yes, positive," he said.

Mia gently took her arm. "Okay, sounds like maybe he hit you harder than you think."

"No. It's not that." Sarah Jane gave the store one more look. Maybe the woman had just been a spirit. She ran into random spirits a lot. The original owner of this store sometimes appeared to her and couldn't stop complaining about his son selling the business. She shook off the thoughts. They had a body, and that took precedence. "It was probably... Never mind. I've got my clothes in the car. Let me just get changed, and we'll head over there."

"It's a good thing you've got your sneakers with you. From the location of the body, it looks like we're going to have to hike a ways." Mia stared down at her phone.

"I know." Sarah Jane jingled her car keys in her hand. "Jessica told me."

CHAPTER 6

By the time Sarah Jane and Mia arrived on the scene, uniformed officers had started cordoning off part of the bike path. Sergeant John Alford, the officer in charge of the scene, greeted her and Mia once they signed in and collected nitrile gloves. Sarah Jane had worked with the lanky officer on many cases and gave him a nod.

"What have we got, Sergeant?" Sarah Jane donned her pair of gloves.

"Female, approximately eighteen to twenty-one. No identification. She's been posed and appears to have been strangled." His mouth twisted with the grim words. "Just like Jessica King."

"So, the scene is similar," Sarah Jane mused. "Is the coroner here yet?"

"No, ma'am. Not yet. Good thing you got your walking shoes on. She's off the path."

"Down near the water," Sarah Jane said.

"Yes, ma'am." He cocked his head, giving her a curious look. "How'd you know?"

"You said it was like the King case, so..." She shrugged. "That's where we found her. If I recall correctly."

"Right." The sergeant nodded. "I've yellow-taped fifty yards out in every direction from the body."

"Great. Start a grid search and have your men comb through and look for anything out of place. Mark it. Video it. Also..." She glanced over at the crowd beginning to gather by the tape closest to the bike path. They were mostly moms with strollers, walkers, or runners. Those on bikes appeared to be in too much of a hurry to stop. "Make sure to film the crowd. If it gets to be too much, push the tape back."

"Captain Carter already told me we can't shut down the path because some people use it to ride to work, and we don't have a safe way to direct them onto the street."

"Fine." Sarah Jane tried not to roll her eyes in front of the sergeant. Her captain had only one thing in mind when he gave those orders. Politics. She was sure of it. Captain Chris Washington was young for his position and ambitious. He loved it when things reflected well on him—like when his homicide squad solved high-profile cases—but when one of his people's actions made him look bad in the eyes of the public, he would raise hell. The last thing she wanted today was to piss off her captain. She didn't need the headache.

"Don't close the path completely. Push the tape as far away as you can from the entrance to the scene and only let those on bikes through. The joggers and the moms will have to get their exercise later."

"You got it." The sergeant gave her a quick nod. "Anything else?"

"That's it for now. Just let me or Detective Johnson," Sarah Jane said while jerking a thumb toward Mia, "know immediately if you find anything."

"Yes, ma'am. The body's this way." The sergeant gestured toward a thick grove of trees separating the paved path from the river running through the city of San Jose. He signaled to one of his officers.

"Hey, Sergeant, when I'm done at the river, I want to talk to the man who found her. The runner?" Sarah Jane looked straight into his narrow, bony face.

"Runner didn't really find her. His dog did," the sergeant said. "He ran into a homeless guy in the woods when he went to fetch the dog. The homeless guy told him there was a dead girl by the water. He went to check it out, and sure enough, there was a dead girl."

"Okay. I want to talk to them both then," Sarah Jane said.

"That's going to be tricky. The homeless guy disappeared."

"Well, that's just great," Sarah Jane grumbled. "Get a description of him from the runner. Then assemble some people to check the encampments close by."

"Yes, ma'am." The sergeant didn't look thrilled with the order, but he didn't argue. Instead, he handed them over to the officer and headed back toward the trail.

After a few minutes of pushing through the thick underbrush, the trees opened onto the banks of a river that, because of the drought, had diminished to barely a trickle in places.

Someone had covered the young woman's body with a tarp. Which was a good thing because Sarah Jane already had a premonition of the Channel 4 news chopper on its way. It wouldn't take very long before they were hovering over her crime scene. She had no doubt—no doubt at all—that they already knew the murder was similar to Jessica King's because somebody couldn't (or she often suspected wouldn't) keep their mouth shut. And she often suspected some people inside her department would happily divulge information on a case for a little extra money.

"Hey, Ingalls." Sarah Jane motioned to a stocky officer with a thick red mustache standing close by. "Do we have a tent on the way?"

"Yes, ma'am." The officer nodded. "It should be here momentarily."

"Good." Sarah Jane spotted Jessica hovering alone in the tree line with a bored expression on her pale gossamer face. The ghost would have to wait until Sarah Jane finished with the crime scene's assessment. She had too much to handle right now to even attempt to deal with Jessica's concerns. Maybe she'd tell her the dead girl's spirit had been freaked out by all the policemen. Maybe she'd been drawn back home to her parents, or goddess forbid, the place where the guy had murdered her. Sarah Jane knelt down next to the body and peeled back the tarp. She couldn't touch the girl yet; the coroner always had first dibs on the body, but from a cursory glance, a dark purple ligature mark spanned the circumference of the young woman's throat and seemed the most likely cause of death.

Leaf litter and sticks clung to her long, dark hair, and she wore a toga-like dress almost identical to the one Jessica had worn. Sarah Jane looked over the corpse from head to toe, and the oddest thing to her was the bow and arrow in the girl's hands. The killer had taken care to wrap one hand around the bow and then place an arrow between two fingers in her other hand. Almost as if she were readying herself to hunt.

"This just gets weirder and weirder, doesn't it?" Mia stooped down next to the body. "What do you think that bow and arrow is about?"

"I don't know. She's dressed almost like a goddess." Sarah Jane stared down at the body but for a moment didn't see it, the connection. Her mind whirred with her mother's bedtime stories about the different goddesses from around the world. Sarah Jane had loved all the mythology, especially the Greek gods and goddesses.

"Remember how we thought when we first found Jessica that she must've been to a toga party on her college campus?" Sarah Jane began. The seed of a thought bloomed in her mind.

"Yeah." Mia narrowed her eyes.

"And we decided—mainly because Jessica told me she wouldn't be caught dead at any sort of college party with a theme—that he dressed her postmortem."

"Uh huh." Mia furrowed her dark brows. "Where are you going with this?"

"I should've seen it before. He's dressing them like goddesses. The bow and arrow. She's either Diana or Artemis—goddess of the hunt. Although, I suppose, technically, togas are Roman, so she may be posed as Diana. I don't remember finding any weapons with Jessica's body, do you?"

Mia gave her an open mouth stare. "It's been a while. I'd have to check the file. How do you know that stuff about goddesses?"

"My mother taught me." Sarah Jane shrugged. "She thought it was an important part of my training..." Sarah Jane dropped her voice to a whisper, "as a witch."

Mia nodded and glanced around the crime scene as if to check how close the other officers were. "Of course." Mia had done an admirable job of accepting Sarah Jane as a witch. But sometimes parts of her life, like rituals or the mention of coven meetings, appeared to make her partner uncomfortable, so she tried to keep it to a minimum. Sarah Jane chocked it up to Mia's strict religious upbringing. It took Mia a long time (and Sarah Jane answering a lot of questions) for Mia to not show signs of trepidation when Sarah Jane used magic, or her psychic medium abilities to help her solve a case. "So why do you think he's dressing them this way?"

"I don't know. Maybe as homage." Sarah Jane swept her gaze around the crime scene. The forensic techs, newly arrived in the last few minutes, had wasted no time starting their work, and the uniformed officers were still searching for evidence in a grid pattern and dropping markers. The coroner and her techs burst through the tree line carrying a stretcher and a body bag. Sarah Jane heard her internal clock ticking. They didn't have much time left before the body would be swept off to the morgue. She closed her eyes for a moment and tried to sense spirit energy.

"You looking for me?" Jessica's voice filtered through her head, and a chill settled around her shoulders. Sarah Jane opened her eyes and Jessica had moved from the tree, appearing now on the opposite side of the body, facing her.

"Hey, Mia, don't freak out," Sarah Jane began. She looked her partner in the eye. "Jessica's here, and I'm going to pretend to talk to you, but I'll really be talking to her. You okay with that?"

Mia glanced around with newfound anxiety displayed in her wide, dark eyes and the wrinkles around her mouth caused by a frown. "Is she next to me?" Mia looked ready to bolt. This is what freaked her out about Sarah Jane's witchcraft. It wasn't that she didn't believe in her friend and colleague's superpowers; she just didn't understand them.

"No. She's on the other side of the body. She's not going to come near you. Right, Jessica?" Sarah Jane gritted her teeth and gave the spirit a pointed look.

"She can't see me so... there's no point in me following her around."

"Do you have some information, or are you just here to entertain me with your sunny personality?" Sarah Jane said.

"The girl was gone when I got here. I don't know what happened to her."

"What about that connection you said you had?" Sarah Jane said. "What happened to that?"

"I can feel her terror, but that's about it. It's not like I have a window into her consciousness."

"Great." Sarah Jane shifted, putting one knee on the ground. She was going to end up stiff tonight if she didn't get off the cold ground soon; she could feel it starting in her hips. "Anything else you might want to add?"

"Yeah. The homeless guy that found her? He stole the gold necklace she was wearing."

"But he's not the one who killed her, right?"

"No, he wasn't."

"Thanks. Did you get a good look at him at least?"

"Yeah, I did. You find him, and I can ID him."

"Great. Don't wander too far."

"I live to serve. Oh, wait. No. I'm dead so not really sure what my purpose here is."

Jessica's droll tone grated on Sarah Jane.

"Your purpose here is to help me find the person who killed you, so you can move on to wherever it is you need to go."

"Maybe." Jessica quipped. "Maybe I'm just supposed to hang out with you for the rest of your life."

The thought of being followed around by a nineteen-year-old ghost doling out snark for the rest of her life made Sarah Jane tired. She loved her kids, but some part of her was looking forward to them growing up and moving away. Being haunted by a perpetual teenager was not her idea of a wonderful life.

"No. We're going to find him, and you're going to move on if I have to march you to the afterlife myself."

"Geez, you sound like my mother." Jessica rolled her eyes.

Sarah Jane ignored the spirit and gave Mia a grateful smile. "Thanks for playing along so that I don't look, well, you know, crazy."

"Sure," Mia said, her expression anything but sure. "Anytime."

"We should go hunt down that homeless guy Sergeant Alford mentioned and interview the runner who found her body," Sarah Jane said.

"Good morning, detectives." Bill Grundy, one of the investigators from the medical examiner's office, kneeled next to the body and gave Sarah Jane a smile. He wasn't that much older than her. Although with his nearly all-white hair, he reminded her more of an old man than someone in his early fifties. The last few times she'd seen him, he'd been a lot friendlier than usual. He pointed to the tarp. "I see you've already taken a look at her, Detective Prentice."

"Yeah. She has ligature marks around her neck, but that's about all I could tell without touching her."

"Well, we'll take care of her from here." His dark brown eyes settled on Sarah Jane. "How've you been doing, Detective?"

"Oh, my God. He likes you." Jessica kneeled next to Grundy and grinned. "I know you can feel those vibes coming from him. He reeks of pheromones. I bet he wants to ask you on a date. You should totally go on a date with him. How funny would that be? "

"Um...I'm okay." Sarah Jane shifted from her knee to her feet, ready to stand. To run if necessary. Anything to get away from the uncomfortable weight of his stare and Jessica's running commentary. "How about you? How's your wife?"

"I guess you didn't hear, huh? We're getting divorced.

She decided she's a lesbian. After twenty years of marriage. So... yeah." His smile faded.

"Holy shit!" Jessica snickered. "Can you say awkward?"

Sarah Jane cleared her throat. "That must've been really hard." She tried to ignore the spirit. "I'm so sorry to hear that. But it probably wasn't a snap decision, and it really wasn't about you. She was probably born that way and just couldn't admit it to herself."

"Yeah." Bill's shoulders sagged a little. "She comes from a Catholic family...so."

Why did people tell her stuff like this? Her mind raced, trying to find the right thing to say. Amy or Susanna would've known exactly how to handle this situation. "I'm sure it's been tough."

Bill shifted on his feet. Sarah Jane thought he was becoming uncomfortable too. "Yeah. It has been. She left the kids with me too. Didn't want anything to do with her old life." A painful memory flickered through her head like an old home movie—Bill standing at his wife's car door, as she sat in the driver's seat fumbling to get the keys in the ignition, her round face stoic. "You can leave me Gina, but you can't leave them. They're your kids for Christ's sake. They need you." Gina put the car in reverse and backed out of the driveway leaving Bill standing dumbfounded and wounded in the driveway.

Sarah Jane took a deep breath and tried to hold onto her emotions. "Gosh... I'm so sorry." Sarah Jane flashed a help-me look at Mia, who looked on at the whole conversation with a bemused expression.

"So sorry to hear that, Bill." Mia jumped in. "Could you call us as soon as you fingerprint the vic to let us know if you get an ID on her?"

"Oh, yeah. Sure." He seemed relieved to get back to crime scene mode. "No problem."

"Great. Thanks." Mia got to her feet, dragging Sarah Jane with her. "Well, we have a homeless guy to find and interviews to do. We'll talk to you later."

"Sure. See you, Sarah Jane." Bill held up an awkward wave.

"Uh huh. See you."

As soon as they were out of earshot, Mia let go of Sarah Jane's sleeve. "Have you learned nothing from me?"

"What?"

"That man reeks of lonely-hearts club. You don't ask personal questions you don't want the answers to."

"She's very wise." Jessica appeared next to her, keeping in step with them. "You should listen to her. You have too much baggage of your own to deal with his, too."

Sarah Jane opened her mouth to reply to the spirit, but a strange buzzing sound caught her attention. She turned her head to listen. She knew that sound. It took her a moment to place it, but then she remembered Larkin and his drone. Dan had bought the drone for him because Larkin was interested in photography and wanted to put together aerial photographs for a school project. They'd given it to him on his birthday with one warning. He was not to use it to spy on people.

The drone whizzed overhead, stopped, and hovered near the uncovered body. Her instinct kicked in, and she ran toward Bill. He seemed paralyzed by the sight of the drone hovering fifty feet above their crime scene.

Sarah Jane pointed to the corpse. "Cover her up!" It took a moment to get his attention, so she said it louder. "Bill! Cover her up now." Her command seemed to shake him out of his stupor, and he quickly pulled the tarp over the dead girl. Twenty different officers stopped in their tracks and pulled their weapons.

"No!" Sarah Jane waved frantically at them. "Do not shoot. Martinez. Cho. Follow it. See if you can find the operator. He can't be far. Take some men with you," Sarah Jane barked.

The two officers nodded and gathered up two or three men each, then headed in the direction of the drone.

Mia caught up with her, a little out of breath. "Do you think that was a kid or a news agency?"

"It's hard to say at this point," Sarah Jane said. "Hopefully, the footage won't end up on the six o'clock news, even if an amateur took it and handed it over to one of the news stations."

"Don't forget social media. It could end up on YouTube," Mia chimed in.

"Surely, he wouldn't be stupid enough to put it there. We'd catch him for sure."

"Maybe." Mia shrugged. "We'll ask Stuckey to keep an eye out for the footage when we get back to the squad room."

Stuckey was the most technical of all the detectives. He knew how criminals could use proxy servers to be untraceable shadows on the web. He also knew how to maneuver through the dark web, a place Sarah Jane couldn't bring herself to think about, much less comb through. They had caught their share of stupid people who had posted a brag about getting away with something, but most of it had been petty crimes.

Sarah Jane scanned the sky overhead one last time and then turned to Bill. "I think the best thing would be to get her out of here as quickly as you can," she said. "I'll have some officers help you if you need it. Just let's get her away from any possible prying eyes."

"Sure, thing, Detective." Bill nodded and motioned for his techs to join him. Sarah Jane kept watch as they loaded the young woman into a body bag, then onto a stretcher. "I'll take the bow and arrow since it was on the body. We'll fingerprint it. I'll let you know as soon as I have an ID."

"Thanks, Bill. I appreciate it. We're going to check

with missing persons to see if any reports have been filed on someone with her description."

"Sure thing." Bill nodded. "I'll be in touch." He began to walk away once his techs picked up the stretcher, then he stopped with a thoughtful look on his face before he returned to face Sarah Jane. "I'm sorry if I made things weird, telling you about my wife and all. I know it's not exactly the same thing, but I understand you know what it's like to lose someone you love. Even if mine's not dead."

"I appreciate that, Bill. And you did lose someone, especially since she's cut off contact with her kids. That's pretty serious. I'm glad they have you."

"Yeah, they really are the only thing keeping me going at this point," he said.

"Oh, brother," Jessica muttered.

"Listen, Bill, maybe you should talk to somebody. There's no shame in it. Our kids are great. I love mine, but they can't be the reason that I get up in the morning, and yours can't be either. Because someday, in the not-too-distant future, they're going to leave the nest."

He nodded. His lower lip quivered a little, and he bit it and took a deep breath. "You're right."

"My sister Susanna is a therapist. If you want to talk to somebody, she's great, and she takes our insurance so... just something to think about."

Sarah Jane managed a weak smile. If she had been Amy, Susanna, or Rainey, she probably would've thrown her arms around him and given him a big hug. But hugging was something she reserved for people she loved, and she couldn't have embraced Bill even if she wanted to.

"Thanks, I appreciate that. I might just do that." He sniffled and jerked his thumb toward his techs. "I better get out of here so you can get back to processing the scene."

Sarah Jane nodded. "Take care, Bill."

"You, too." He turned and headed to the path through the woods.

"Yeah, that was pretty pathetic. I don't know why I ever thought you should go out with him."

Sarah Jane glared at Jessica, unable to stop herself. "Have some fucking empathy for once in your life, okay?" Her cheeks and chest heated with a flash of anger.

"Geez. Sorry," Jessica said, but she didn't sound sorry.

"You know what? You're in a time-out."

Jessica made a noise in the back of her throat. "What?"

"You heard me. I don't want to hear from you or see you for the next twenty-four hours," Sarah Jane said. "And don't think I won't resort to doing what it takes to make sure that happens."

"But... but you need me," Jessica said in a small voice.

"Nope. I'm a cop. I'm quite capable of solving this crime all on my own, thanks."

"Yeah, right. We'll see about that." Jessica defiantly crossed her arms. "Good luck finding the girl's spirit without me." She spat out the words and vanished.

Sarah Jane felt the eyes of a uniformed officer who had stopped nearby. He stared at her with an open mouth.

"What?" she snapped. "Get back to work."

His mouth snapped shut, and he scrambled in the opposite direction. Sarah Jane sighed. Mia approached her with caution on her face.

"Everything okay?" Mia asked.

"Everything's fine. Jessica was just being a brat, so I put her in a time-out," Sarah Jane said.

"Is that even possible?" Mia asked. "She's a spirit, not a three-year-old."

"Trust me, it's possible. But it also means we don't have her help."

"Well, we are detectives, so..." Mia shrugged. "I think we'll be okay. We've solved plenty of murders without her."

"You're right. Let's go find that homeless guy. And start tracking down leads," Sarah Jane said.

Mia grinned. "Now you're talking."

CHAPTER 7

"How are we supposed to find him if we don't have a description of him, detective?" Sergeant Alford asked. He had volunteered to come with them to the homeless encampment after questioning the runner who had discovered the body. The only thing the runner could tell him was that the man had the look of a homeless person and wore a brown coat. Other than that, he didn't get close enough to get a good look.

The three of them wandered through the encampment near the river. It appeared almost empty of people, but Sarah Jane knew they weren't alone. She could almost feel some of the residents nearby, watching them, fearful, while others hid inside tents and cardboard boxes guarding their few possessions. Sarah Jane went to the center of the littered area and raised her arms.

"Listen up, everyone. I know you're here. I need to

talk to the man who found the girl's body this morning. You're not in any trouble. But I need to know what you saw." She turned in a circle scanning the space for movement, for any sort of response. "Please. It's really important. It could help me find the man who killed her."

The runner had insisted the homeless guy must've killed the girl, but Sarah Jane knew better after assessing the scene. She may have been held for five days like Jessica, but she was relatively clean and had been dressed and posed with things no homeless person would have with them. And the likelihood of the same homeless person doing it twice just didn't seem possible to her. Still, she needed to talk to the man. She thought about casting a coaxing spell. But after what happened this morning with the punk at the convenience store, she decided against it. It was time to bring her sisters in on the problem with her magic, assuming they were all still speaking to her after her meltdown at the birthday party.

"Okay," Sarah Jane said. "Let's fan out and see if we can find anything or anybody wearing a brown coat who looks suspicious."

"Um, no disrespect, detective, but that's pretty much everybody here," Alford said.

"Sure. Still, we need to look," Sarah Jane said.

The three of them split up, and when Sarah Jane didn't see anyone matching the description, she kept moving up the Guadalupe trail until she came to the next encampment. She counted three in total at the moment. It wouldn't take long before people complained, though, and forced the police to clear out the homeless. Most of the time they ended up losing half the stuff they had collected, including their shelters. It made her sick sometimes to think about how these people were treated, and it also made her angry at herself because she didn't do more.

Some days it felt hard enough just to take care of herself and her family. She had nothing left over for social issues. Even if she really cared about them. Once she reached the next encampment, she made her speech again. More people appeared at the second encampment, this one underneath a bridge.

Something red caught Sarah Jane's eye, and she followed a path between the tents. A young man sat on the hillside near the pylons supporting the bridge. His dark brown hair and thick, long beard hid part of his dirty face, but a few things about him stood out. First, he wore a brown coat just like the runner described. Second, in one hand, he held what looked like a gold necklace. And sitting next to him on the hill was a familiar face—the woman in red. The woman she had spoken to in the convenience store just a few hours ago. The man rocked back and forth talking to her, and she appeared to listen to him calmly, fully focused on him.

Sarah Jane pointed at the woman. "I know you," she said. "I couldn't find you after the robbery to make sure you were okay, and then the clerk said you weren't there at all."

The woman held up her hands. "I can explain." Her dark eyes wide and sincere.

The homeless man stopped talking. Fear washed over his features, and in a flash, he turned and began to climb the steep hill that led to one of the freeways. Although, at this point, Sarah Jane wasn't sure which.

"Wait!" Sarah Jane called after him and began to climb. She had to hold onto clumps of grass to pull herself up the hill. At times like this, she was grateful she still made herself exercise even though part of her really hated it. Her knee began to sing by the time she caught up to him. She grabbed him by the back of his coat and yanked. He flattened himself against the ground and curled his arms underneath himself, bowing his head into the dead grass.

"You're not real. You're not real!" His voice grew louder.

"I am real. Turn over. I'm not going to hurt you," she said.

"He's not going to believe you. Poor soul, he's lost." The woman in red had somehow climbed up the hill and now sat next to him. She stroked the side of his head with the back of her fingers. "It's okay. You're safe. She's not going to hurt you."

"Are you sure?" the man said in a small voice.

"Oh, yes. I won't let her." The woman continued to

stroke his hair. “Shh... Come on, Everett. You can do some real good here.”

He sniffled and rolled onto his back. Sarah Jane leaned one knee against the hill to keep her balance and had no idea how the woman had climbed up in the two-inch heels she wore. She looked spotless. Where grass stains and reddish dirt covered Sarah Jane's suit pants, especially below the knees.

“Everett, my name is Detective Sarah Jane Prentice. I need to ask you some questions. Where did you get the necklace in your hand?”

Everett threw his arm over his eyes and shook his head. “I can't tell you.”

“Okay.” Sarah Jane held up her hands. Then realized that was a bad idea as soon as she began to wobble on the hillside. “Listen. I need you to please come with me. Let's get off this hill to someplace safe. Someplace where you and I can sit and talk. I'll make sure you get some food and a hot shower and some clean clothes. How does that sound?”

Everett peeled his arm away from his face and looked Sarah Jane in the eye. “What kind of food?”

“Just about anything you want... within reason, of course.”

“Can I have a hot roast beef sandwich with blue cheese crumbles from Charlie's Sub shop? I sometimes go through their garbage cans. They have the best roast beef sandwiches,” Everett said.

"Absolutely." Sarah Jane offered her hand. "Can I help you up?"

"No." He held his hands next to his heart, and a flash of gold caught Sarah Jane's attention. "I promised her I wouldn't tell you."

"Okay. No worries. You can keep that necklace, for now, okay?"

Everett lifted himself onto his elbows then pushed himself to his feet.

"That's great. Thank you."

Everett eyed her warily. "A hot roast beef sandwich."

"Absolutely. What about you, ma'am?" Sarah Jane turned her head to give the woman in red a grin. After all, she had been the one to help calm him down. The least she could do was buy the woman a hot roast beef sandwich if she wanted it. A cold pang shot through Sarah Jane's heart. The woman was gone. She carefully glanced around, trying not to fall on her ass and slide down to the bottom of the hill, but there was no sign of her anywhere.

"Where did she go?"

"Where did who go?"

"The woman who was talking to you. The woman in the red suit."

"You could see her?" His muddy brown eyes widened.

"Yes, I could see her. She was talking to you."

"I thought I was the only one who could see her. Her name is Bernice. She's really nice."

"Okay. That still doesn't explain where she went."

He shrugged. "I don't know where she goes. She just comes to visit me sometimes. We talk about things."

"Great," Sarah Jane muttered, unsure of who or what she'd just encountered. "Come on, Everett. Why don't you and I get out of here? We can get some lunch and talk about things too."

"Sure. That would be good," he said and helped her down the hill.

CHAPTER 8

"Who do you think he's talking to?" Mia leaned forward with her elbows on the desk. Sarah Jane stared at the computer monitor in front of them, looking for any signs of the woman in red.

Everett sat at a table in one of the interview rooms. He faced to his right and jabbered on to someone who wasn't there. Every time Sarah Jane mentioned the necklace in his hands, he became agitated and held it close to his chest. She didn't try to take it away from him because she didn't want to upset him more. She needed him to talk to her. But he refused to do that until he had eaten.

Sarah Jane eyed the AV and technology tech, Elton, sitting at the end of the table staring at another monitor. She signaled Mia with her eyes that she couldn't talk about it. Mia tipped her head, clearly not understanding. "What?" Mia mouthed.

"Maybe he's talking to a ghost or his imaginary friend." Sarah Jane gave her an exasperated frown. "Who knows?"

"Right. Who knows?" Mia chuckled then focused on the monitor as if she might see either one of those things.

"I'm going to see if Rodriguez is here with the sandwiches." Sarah Jane rose from her chair, and Mia followed.

They stood in the hallway outside of the AV room near the homicide squad room. Mia touched Sarah Jane's elbow. "You okay?"

"I'm fine. He was talking to a woman though when I found him. The same woman I saw in the convenience store this morning."

"Are you sure? That kid hit you pretty hard." Mia gestured to Sarah Jane's blackening eye. Her face throbbed a little bit, but for the most part, she hadn't thought about the altercation with everything else going on.

"She was there, Mia." Irritation crept into Sarah Jane's voice.

"Okay." Mia held her hands up in surrender. "I'm not trying to make you mad. So, you think she's a... ghost?" Mia whispered the last word.

"I don't know. She didn't seem like it. But that doesn't mean she isn't, I guess," Sarah Jane said. Mia's dark eyes filled with sympathy. Something Sarah Jane hated. "I'm going to text Rodriguez to see where he is."

"Okay. I'll see if I can get Everett to let me look at the necklace."

"Great. Good luck." Sarah Jane gave her a smile.

"Yeah, you, too." Mia snickered. "Tells you a lot that I'd rather deal with the homeless guy than Rodriguez."

"I hear you on that." Sarah Jane grinned and headed toward the squad room.

The modern, brightly lit space looked more like a call center than a homicide squad room. Two rows of low-walled cubicles ran down the center of the space. Each detective had their own cubicle but could easily stand up and speak to their coworkers if needed. A large whiteboard took up one wall and could fold up behind two other whiteboards, almost like an academic classroom.

The names of the detectives and the active cases they were assigned to ran along one side of the main whiteboard. Some of the lists beneath the detectives' names were long. Sarah Jane and Mia frequently worked together, but at any time, the whole squad could be pulled to help work different angles of a case.

They all had their specialties. Stuckey and Ross knew the ins and outs of social media better than anyone else.

Stuckey also loved anything technological and never minded watching hours' worth of video or searching the dark web. Rodriguez was your man if you wanted to deal with an outside entity for records—like a cell phone company, or a power company. If she put in a request to pull phone records, it would take twice as long as Rodriguez. He had the magic touch.

Rodriguez pushed open the glass door to the squad room with his hip and held up two bags of food from Charlie's Sub Shop, a triumphant look on his face.

Rodriguez made her follow him to his cubicle. He put the bags down on his desk, opened one, and pulled out a sandwich and a bag of chips. He handed her the receipt. "You owe me forty-seven bucks."

"Okay. I appreciate you doing this. Let me get my wallet." A minute later, they settled up the bill. She stopped by her desk, dropped off her wallet, and grabbed two pairs of gloves, shoving them in her blazer pocket. Then she took the bags of food to the interview room, stopping only to grab a few sodas from the machine in the break room. It was unusual to eat with a potential suspect, but she hoped it would put Everett at ease. She pushed open the heavy door.

"Food's here." She held up the bags. "I got you a sandwich, too."

"I appreciate that." Mia pulled out the chair next to her and gestured for Sarah Jane to sit.

"How's it going, Everett?" Sarah Jane asked.

"We were just talking about his friend. Bernice," Mia said.

"Oh, great." Sarah Jane took a seat. She opened a bag and handed Everett his roast beef sandwich with blue cheese crumbles, a bag of chips, and one of the sodas.

"Yes. Bernice is my friend, and she comes to see me sometimes. She said I needed to help you. Which is really the only reason I'm here, other than the sandwich of course."

"Of course," Sarah Jane said. She helped herself to a ham and Swiss sandwich and the diet soda. Mia grabbed the other diet soda for herself and popped the top. "So, Everett, where did you get that pretty necklace from?"

"No." Everett squirmed in his seat, suddenly agitated. He turned his face as if he were talking to someone else in the room. "It's mine now. Please don't make me give it to them," he whispered.

For a split second, Sarah Jane wished that she had her sister Susanna's ability to sense thoughts. Maybe if she could listen to the conversation he was having in his head, things might be clearer.

A familiar voice floated through her mind. Bernice's voice. "Everett. We talked about this. You promised you'd help these officers out." The skin on Sarah Jane's broke into goosebumps. He was still talking to Bernice. Sarah Jane glanced around the table for some of the other telltale signs that a ghost was present—a sudden drop in temperature, an eerie energy that made even those who couldn't sense ghosts uncomfortable. Mia opened her bag of chips unfazed. She didn't dare say anything with the cameras rolling.

Everett's features twisted into a pout. "I don't want to."

"You don't want to what, Everett?" Mia asked.

"He doesn't want to give us the necklace. I thought you wanted to help us." Sarah Jane shifted in her chair, trying to make him look her in the face. "Isn't that what your friend would want?"

Everett let out a heavy sigh and put the necklace on the table. "Finders, keepers. You can look at it, but you can't keep it."

"I'll see what I can do," she said, not wanting to make any promises because the necklace did belong to the girl they found, Sarah Jane didn't have much choice in confiscating it as evidence.

He pushed the necklace to her. "Finders keepers."

Sarah Jane nodded and took the gloves from her jacket pocket, pushing one pair toward Mia. She pulled on the gloves and picked up the chain to study the disk pendant with a tiny diamond embedded in it. The gold metal burnished in the warm LED lighting of the room. Sarah Jane flipped over the pendant and ran her thumb across three initials engraved in the back — H & B. She handed it to Mia. "What do you think?"

"Everett, was this necklace around the young woman's neck? The young woman you found."

"No, no, no. I didn't go near her. She was dead. I've seen dead before, and it's... It's scary. I didn't know if she was catching. Sometimes people who die are catching." He shook his head. "Bernice showed me where to find the necklace."

Everett took a big bite of his sandwich and chewed with his mouth open. Sarah Jane tried her best to keep her face neutral.

"That was really nice of her," Mia said.

"So, you didn't get close to her body?" Sarah Jane asked.

Everett shook his head. "No way. I don't like the dead."

"Okay." Sarah Jane said. "Where exactly did you find the necklace?"

"It was in the trees. Before you get to the river. That runner's dog came after me. He wasn't friendly. That's why I ran." Everett crunched on a chip. Then took a long swig of his soda.

"That must've been startling."

"Yeah," Everett said.

"So, you didn't see anyone else besides the runner and his dog. Like down near the girl on the riverbank?" Sarah Jane studied Everett's face. He couldn't have been very old, maybe twenty-five at the most.

"No, I didn't see anybody else. Just her and that runner and his dog."

"Okay. Did Bernice see anyone?" Sarah Jane asked.

"I don't know. You'd have to ask her." Everett shrugged and took another big bite of his sandwich.

"Everett, I need to hold onto this necklace for a little bit."

"No...no. Finders keepers. You promised." He grabbed for the necklace. Sarah Jane pulled it out of his reach and into her lap.

"I never promised, Everett. This doesn't belong to you." Sarah Jane used her best mom voice to show him she was in charge, but also that she understood him. "I need to find out if it belonged to the girl on the riverbank."

He continued to try to get the necklace. "Finders, keepers."

"Everett, stop it. Do you want me to call in an officer to take you to jail?" Sarah Jane asked, her voice full of warning.

Everett settled down. "No."

"Let me do some digging on this necklace. If it turns out that it doesn't belong to our victim, I will do my best to return it to you."

Everett glared at her from beneath his dark bushy brows. "Promise?"

"Yes. I promise... I will do my best."

Everett's agitation subsided, and he picked at his bag of chips. "Okay."

"Thank you. Why don't you finish your sandwich? I'm going to find you a bed for the night, okay?"

Everett shrugged and ate another chip. Sarah Jane and Mia wrapped up their sandwiches and left him alone in the interview room.

CHAPTER 9

Sarah Jane finished her sandwich and hopped to her feet. She glanced over her cubicle wall to Mia's desk. "Can you check on Everett for me? I'm going to make some calls to see if I can find him a bed for the next few nights."

"You don't want to see if the captain will spring for protective custody?" Mia asked. She took the last bite of her ham and cheese.

"He's not really in any danger unless you consider disappearing a danger. I think I can find him a bed for a few days," Sarah Jane said. "It just means I have to call my sister Cass and make up with her."

"Are you ready to do that?" Mia wiped the corners of her mouth with a napkin and rose from her chair.

"Ready as I'll ever be, I guess."

"Okay. I'll check on him. You go make nice."

"Thanks."

Sarah Jane grabbed her phone from her purse and headed out of the building away from listening ears. Once she got to her car, she climbed inside and locked the doors. With a quick scan of her contacts, she found Cass's number and hovered her thumb over the call icon. Her stomach twisted into a knot. As a social worker, Cass was her best hope for finding a bed for Everett on such short notice. Cass also volunteered a couple of nights a week at one of the local shelters. Sarah Jane couldn't stomach having her sister hang up on her, so she opened her sister's contact and pressed the message icon instead.

Sarah Jane: *Do you have a minute?*

She stared at the screen, waiting for an answer. Any answer. Yes. No. Fuck off. Knowing Cass and her ability to hold a grudge, it would likely be the last of those options. It took a few minutes for three dots to appear on the screen.

Spitfire Cass: *What's up?*

Sarah Jane: *I need your help. Professionally, I mean.*

Spitfire Cass: *How so?*

Sarah Jane: *I need a bed at a shelter. Do you have space?*

Spitfire Cass: *Call me now.*

Sarah Jane did as she was told.

Her sister picked up on the first ring. "Are you in trouble?"

"No, of course not. I have a possible witness. He's

homeless, been living along the Guadalupe River trail in one of the encampments. Can you help him?" As bitchy as Cassiopeia Prentice could be, she also had a huge heart, and her entire family knew it.

"Is he in danger? Or is he a danger?"

"Not that I'm aware of. I just can't lose him." Sarah Jane told her sister what she could about her case without crossing any lines regarding confidentiality and ongoing cases, but sharing just enough detail to push her sister's sympathy buttons.

"Get him to the State Street shelter by five, and I'll do my best to get him in."

"I will. I really appreciate this, Cass. And I just wanted to say I'm really sorry that I pissed you off yesterday."

Cass let out a heavy sigh. "That's really not an apology, Sarah Jane. An apology means you take responsibility for your actions. Anyway, it doesn't matter."

Sarah Jane could feel her sister pulling away from her, could picture her in her office surrounded by stacks of folders, outdated pictures of her nieces and nephews, and her diplomas framed and hanging on the dingy gray walls behind her. "Just get him here by five, and we'll go from there."

"Sure thing." Sarah Jane squeezed her eyes shut. The apology she'd offered up was lame, and she knew it. Her sister deserved better than that, but she couldn't quite bring herself to say the right words.

"Oh, there's one more thing. Maybe after we get there, you could do me a favor and cast a spell to keep him from getting lost or disappearing."

"Why can't you cast it yourself?"

"Yeah, I'm having a little trouble with my magic. It's sort of on the fritz."

"On the fritz?" Cass echoed. "What does that even mean?"

"It means every spell I touch these days seems to go to hell. I had a little altercation this morning and tried to cast a spell to subdue a suspect. It totally failed, and he clocked me in the face."

"Holy goddess, Sarah Jane. How long has that been going on?"

"I don't know. A while." Sarah Jane rubbed her forehead, and her shoulders tightened. The last thing she needed was a lecture.

"Have you told Gran or Susanna?"

"No. I don't want to worry them. I'll be fine. It's probably just some sort of blockage. It will pass. In the meantime, can you help me out or not?"

"Does Amy know, at least?"

"I think she suspects."

"Maybe we should have a coven meeting. See if Gran or Susanna can sort out the cause."

"That would be great, but I don't have time for that right now." Sarah Jane scrubbed her forehead a little harder, causing a little pain to travel across her scalp.

"So, will you do it? I really need to keep tabs on him for this case."

"Yeah. Okay."

"Thanks. I really appreciate it."

"Sure. Just be careful out there without your magic, okay? Don't do anything stupid. Black Tourmaline doesn't repel bullets."

"That's what Kevlar vests are for." Sarah Jane couldn't help but smile at her sister's concern. Warmth spread through her chest, and she knew they would be okay. They'd been through too much as a family to let some petty argument get between them. "Anyway, thanks."

"Sure thing."

The line went dead, and Sarah Jane stared down at the phone for a moment. She checked her face in the rearview mirror and jumped a little when she noticed Jessica sitting in the backseat.

"Hi. I thought you were in time-out," Sarah Jane said.

"I thought you'd want to know I sort of found her. She's really messed up, and I don't know how to get her to talk to you."

"Ok. Thanks for letting me know." Sarah Jane shifted in her seat, turning to face the spirit. "I'm sorry I was so hard on you. But the things you said about Bill weren't very nice. I wouldn't put up with that from anybody."

"Yeah, I know. I'm sorry I said them. You were super nice to him when you didn't have to be."

"That's because I work with energy, and you get back what you put out into the world. Do you understand?"

"Sure." Jessica's gaze shifted, and she stared through one of the windows. "I think the only way you're going to be able to connect with her is through your dreams."

"Come on. Please. Don't do that. I really hate that," Sarah Jane pleaded.

"I know. But I don't think there's another way at this point. Sorry." A strange smile crossed Jessica's lips. "See you in your dreams."

"No. Wait." The spirit vanished. "Great. That's all I need," she mumbled.

CHAPTER 10

It was nearly eight by the time Sarah Jane got home. Amy had settled into the recliner in front of the television with her knitting on her lap. She'd been working on a complicated lace shawl for at least six months. Sarah Jane thought it would be easier to buy one, but she knew the needlework was akin to meditation for her sister.

"Hi, SJ," Amy called without looking up from her needles.

"Hey. I'm sorry I'm late. I caught a big case this morning."

"No worries. I saved you a plate. It's in the oven."

"Thanks. I'm not really hungry."

"Sarah Jane, you have to eat something. Did you at least eat lunch today?"

Amy finally looked at her. "Oh, my goddess, Sarah Jane. What happened to your face?"

"Nothing. I got smacked by a punk I was trying to arrest." Sarah Jane touched her eye gingerly and sucked in a breath through her teeth when a sharp pain shot across her cheekbone. "I was actually going to ask if maybe you could speed up the healing so I don't look so scary."

Amy put her knitting aside. "Let me get my oils. Come into the kitchen."

"Thanks." Sarah Jane rubbed the back of her neck and pulled out one of the bar stools at the kitchen island.

Amy retrieved a plastic shoebox full of essential oils, salves, concoctions in roll-on bottles, and tinctures. She examined each bottle and jar until she found exactly what she was looking for, a dark blue bottle with a dropper.

"Here it is." She opened the bottle and doled several drops of the mix onto her fingertips. "This might sting a little."

"No problem. Do you want my eyes open or closed?"

"Closed. I don't want to get any of this in your eye. That would definitely burn."

Sarah Jane nodded, shut her eyes, and lifted her head so her sister could get a better look. Amy gently patted her oil-coated fingertips around Sarah Jane's eye socket and quietly chanted her healing spell three times.

Broken veins, bruises deep, heal your wounds, so you may sleep

In the morn, when you arise, barely a trace will shade your eyes

Warmth spread across Sarah Jane's cheek and eye area, and she breathed in the lavender and rosemary-scented oil mixture. Tears immediately flowed, and Sarah Jane squeezed her eyelid tight.

"Did you get it in your eye?" Amy asked.

"No, it's just strong." Sarah Jane sniffled. "It's fine. Is there arnica in here?"

"Birch."

"I can smell it."

"Just give it a minute."

Sarah Jane nodded, after a few moments, she opened her eyes again. "Where's Larkin?"

"He's upstairs working on his homework." Amy rearranged some of the oils in the box and then put them back into the cabinet. "He asked me for a spirit bag today."

"Why?" Sarah Jane peeled her jacket off and threw it over the back of the barstool next to her.

"He said spirits keep waking him up. Poor thing. I told him I'd have to get some supplies tomorrow, but I'd make him one."

"Did he say who's bothering him? Is it random spirits or...?" She gently touched a finger to her bruises. Already, the soreness was starting to ease.

"He didn't say. Just asked if I could make him one."

"Okay, I'll ask him about it later. Maybe we need to strengthen the protection wards around the house again," Sarah Jane said. "They don't seem to be lasting very long."

Amy shrugged. "That's what happens when you have a house full of psychic mediums. We can attract every spirit within a hundred-mile radius."

"No kidding." Sarah Jane leaned forward resting her elbows on the island. She picked aimlessly at a bowl of fruit in front of her. "If it didn't help me with my job, I'd ask you to make me a spirit bag too."

"Just say the word and I will." Amy cocked her head. "I don't know how you put up with it day after day. It would drive me crazy to be haunted like that."

"I think we're all haunted in some way, aren't we?" Sarah Jane said.

"Maybe."

"I talked to Cass today."

"Good. Did you kiss and make up?" Amy asked.

"Not exactly. But I'm going to go ahead and tell you this because I know if I don't, she will because you know how our family is."

"Yep. What happened?"

"Nothing happened exactly, but I'm having some trouble with my magic. Cass thinks we should have a coven meeting to discuss it."

"Is that how you got that shiner?" Amy pointed to her eye.

"Yeah. I was trying to subdue a guy, and my freezing spell didn't work. The next thing I knew, I was seeing stars." Sarah Jane cast a glance at her sister to see her reaction.

"I see. Well I'm glad you told me. Cass is right. We should get together, lay some hands on you. See if Gran can figure out what's going on. A witch without her full magic is a vulnerable thing."

"I know."

"Then it's settled, I'll call everybody together. Why don't you get your dinner out of the oven and eat?" Amy folded one of the dish towels on the counter. "I'm going back to my knitting."

"I think I'm just going to go to bed. I'm exhausted. It's been a horrendous day."

"All right." Amy reached into the oven and took out the pan covered in aluminum foil. "Sleep well."

"Thanks." Sarah Jane slid off the barstool and headed to her room.

CHAPTER 11

Sarah Jane stared down at the body next to the nearly dry riverbed, trying to glean any information she could that would tell her the identity of the girl. When the girl sat up with a disgusted look, Sarah Jane knew it had to be a dream. Although, a nightmare might have been a better description.

"Who the hell do you think I am?" The girl got onto all fours and started to crawl toward Sarah Jane. "I'm the last girl who died. I'm the next girl who dies. I'm the legion of others you missed. I'm your sister. I'm your daughter. I'm your niece. And we're all dead because of you. Because you screwed it up the first time."

Sarah Jane tried to scramble away, but the girl launched at her, growling, angry, baring her teeth.

"He took my name, and you let him turn me into this...this... Artemis." Her accusation a vicious hiss. The girl beat on her chest and yanked on the toga. The gold disk still hung around her neck and flashed in the sun, blinding Sarah Jane for a moment.

Sarah Jane woke up sweaty, her T-shirt soaked and clinging to her back, and her face, neck, and chest on fire. She threw back the light quilt she slept under and went into the bathroom. Foggy from another bout of interrupted sleep, she held a washcloth under the faucet.

"Mom?" Larkin's panicked voice alerted her immediately. She poked her head outside the bathroom door, holding the cool, wet washcloth in her hands, and found her son in sweatpants and a T-shirt, standing in her doorway, his hazel eyes wide and frightened.

"Hey, sweetie. It's two o'clock in the morning."

"Yeah, I know." He scrubbed his eyes. "There's a ghost in my room."

Sarah Jane wiped her face then draped the washcloth over the back of her neck.

"Well, tell him to go away. You've got school in the morning."

"That never works for me, Mom. And it's not a him, it's a her. She wants to talk to you."

"To me?" Sarah Jane removed the washcloth from her neck. "Is she wearing a toga? Or a snarky T-shirt?"

"What's a toga?" Larkin gave her a befuddled look.

"Never mind. I'll go talk to her. Can you go downstairs and get one of Aunt Amy's spirit bundles for burning and a box of salt? There's also a bowl of crystals on the island. Grab any of them that are solid black."

"How many should I bring you?"

"All of them." Sarah Jane patted him on the arm. "And bring me some matches too. We're going to make your bedroom a ghost-free zone."

"Should I wake up Aunt Amy?"

"No, we can handle this. It's just a ghost, right?"

"Right." Larkin gave her an uneasy look.

She tossed the washcloth into the sink, then headed to Larkin's bedroom. When she rounded the corner into his room, the familiar chill of a ghostly presence slapped her in the face, and she shivered.

"Listen, I know you're still pissed at me, but I told you not to scare..."

The words died on her lips when she came face-to-face with a young woman she'd never seen before. She cocked her head, unsure of her emotions. Usually, when faced with a spirit, she took control of the situation. Tried to be firm but empathetic. The one thing she hated most about seeing spirits is their lack of boundaries. She and her sister constantly fought to keep ghosts at bay.

"Hi. Who are you?"

"I'm Ashlyn." The translucent young woman was not what Sarah Jane expected. Petite, with white-blond hair, her pale eyes fixed Sarah Jane to the spot. "Are you Sarah Jane Prentice?"

Sarah Jane hugged her arms around her body. "I am. Listen, I don't mean to be rude or insensitive to your situation, but I'm a little full up on ghosts at the moment." Sarah Jane began.

"Jessica sent me. Still feeling insensitive?"

"That depends on why she sent you."

"Sorry, but I don't have long. I have to get back because he gets home soon, and he makes us all line up when he gets there and counts us like coins or something to be collected."

"Who is he? And how do you know Jessica?" Sarah Jane took a step closer to the spirit.

The spirit's eyes widened, and she glanced over her shoulder. "I can't stay. I just came to say Haley's not the only one. Don't forget about us."

"Wait, who's Haley?"

"She's the one who sent you the dream. She's pretty pissed and also pretty scared. And she can't leave like I can. I tried to bring her with me, but she couldn't make it past the trophy room. His powers have gotten stronger since his mother died."

"What is the trophy room? More importantly, where is the trophy room?"

"Sorry. Just promise you'll find us."

The spirit disappeared as Larkin entered his room. "Mom? You okay? Where did she go?"

"I don't know," Sarah Jane said softly. The short

conversation swirled through her mind, and so many questions flooded in.

"I got all the stuff you wanted." He stepped closer until his elbow brushed against Sarah Jane's.

"That's great, sweetie. Thank you. Spread the salt along the windowsill. And put at least one crystal in each corner of your room. You're going to have to do the spell."

"Me?" Larkin's mouth fell ajar, and he glared at her flabbergasted.

"Yes, you. You are sixteen years old." She and Dan had made sure all of their children were well-versed in their craft from a young age. "What's the problem here? I know you cast spells all the time."

"Yeah, but that's for little stuff. I never cast when I want to get rid of a ghost. Why can't you cast it?"

"Because this is a great learning opportunity for you."

"Sweet goddess, Mom. Not everything has to be a learning opportunity." Larkin crossed one arm over his chest, his hand latching onto the other.

"Just do it." She hated lying to him, but there was no reason for him to know her magic wasn't working very well. The last thing she wanted was for the spell to screw up. Her son needed protection. "One of the strongest protections you can have is the one you create yourself."

"Yeah, what's the strongest? Why can't we use that?"

"Because you already have it, and it won't protect you from ghosts." She took the bundle of herbs and the book of matches from his hand. “Go ahead and put the crystals down and spread the salt.” She struck one of the matches on the cover and lit the herbs, swirling the bundle around until it began to smoke.

“Take this.” She handed the smoking herbs to him. “You've seen me and Aunt Amy do this a hundred times. You know what to do.”

“Yeah, sure.” He began to walk around his room holding the smudge stick near the ceiling.

“That's great, sweetie. Now concentrate and repeat after me. Spirits be gone, leave this place. You're not welcome in this blessed space.”

Larkin echoed the spell, sounding a little unsure of himself.

“You need to be more forceful. Show them this is your space, and they are not allowed here. Imagine they're...Dalton.”

Larkin snickered, then put more authority in his voice. “Spirits be gone, leave this place. You are not welcome in this blessed space.”

“Better. Now add this, spirits be gone, you're not to stay, the space is sacred, now go away.”

“Should I put it all together?” Larkin asked.

“Yes. Just make sure you use that same voice.”

Larkin repeated the complete spell a couple more times, his voice and demeanor more confident by the end.

"How do you feel? Do you still sense anything?" Sarah Jane gently placed a hand on his shoulder.

"It feels better in here. Not as creepy."

"Good." She gave his shoulder a squeeze. "Now put that out and put it back where you found it. Then go back to bed. We have to get up in a few hours."

"Sure. How do I put it out again?"

"The same way you put out your doobies."

"What's a doobie?"

"You're kidding me, right? I know you smoke pot sometimes. Just don't let me catch you with it. It may be legal, but you still have to be twenty-one."

"Oh my goddess, do you mean weed?"

"Yeah, okay weed."

"I am so not having this conversation with you. And for your information, I rarely smoke. It's bad for your lungs. I prefer gummies."

"I have definitely smelled pot in your room."

"That wasn't me."

"Fine, it wasn't you. Well, just be careful with the gummies, okay? It's easy to eat too many because they're basically candy. And again, not in front of me."

"Fine, not in front of you. Can I go back to bed now?"

"Yeah, sure, hon. Don't forget to put that out. I don't want the house to catch on fire."

"Okay. 'Night, Mom." Larkin left for the kitchen.

Sarah Jane padded down the hall to her room,

flopped onto her bed, and rolled over to stare at the ceiling. The spirit's words took root in her mind, and the questions bloomed, making it nearly impossible to go back to sleep. How was he keeping them? And where the hell was that trophy room?

CHAPTER 12

Sarah Jane arrived at the squad room exhausted and buzzing about the conversation she'd had the night before with the spirit. The minute she walked through the door, Mia stood up and held a printout in her hand. "We got a hit from Missing Persons matching our vic's description."

Sarah Jane crossed to Mia's cubicle without stopping at her own. "That's great. Has Bill Grundy called with results on the fingerprint scan?"

Mia shook her head. She wore her long dark braids in a high ponytail that landed just below her shoulders and as usual looked stylish in a pale gray suit with a dark purple blouse. "Not yet. I'll give him a call as soon as the morgue opens."

"May I?" Sarah Jane gestured to the printout and Mia handed it to her. She scanned the information, the photo of the young woman drawing her eye. "It definitely looks like her." She could see the shadow of the angry, hissing young woman who tore into her in her dream behind the young woman's smiling face. "We'll get a background check and ask Rodriguez to start digging through her social media." Sarah Jane rattled off their next steps, a checklist she kept in her head, mainly for herself. "Then we need to notify next of kin."

"I've already started the background check and set up a murder board in the conference room so we can capture a timeline of her movements on the day she went missing, " Mia said.

"You rock. Thank you. Let's head in there. I have some news to share." Sarah Jane met her partner's dark brown eyes.

"Sure. Something happen last night with you-know-who?"

"Not exactly."

"Ma'am," Rob Rodriguez's tone drew Sarah Jane's attention to the woman standing at the entrance to the homicide squad room. Her angry voice reverberated across the squad room.

"Can I help you?" Roderiguez asked. Sarah Jane took a few cautious steps forward.

"I want to speak to the detective responsible for my daughter's case," the woman said to Rodriguez, who was attempting to shield her from the squad room. Suddenly, her agitated gaze settled on Sarah Jane, and she pushed past him without making contact.

"That's her," the woman said, pointing a finger at Sarah Jane. "That's the one I saw on the video."

"Ma'am," Rodriguez side-stepped and got in front of the woman. He angled his body between her and the cubicles. Sarah Jane set her things down on Mia's desk and headed toward the commotion.

"It's okay, Rodriguez. I'm Detective Sarah Jane Prentice. And you are?"

"My name is Elaine Brooks."

"Okay, Mrs. Brooks. How can I help you? Did you say you saw me on a video?" She exchanged a glance with Rodriguez.

"Yes. A friend of mine sent me a video this morning. Said it was going viral." The woman pulled her phone from her purse and opened an app before she handed it to Sarah Jane.

"Rodriguez." Sarah Jane pushed the phone into his hands, and the look on his face told her everything she needed to know. The drone from yesterday. The one the uniformed officers couldn't find. The operator had posted the drone footage of the crime scene with a clickbait headline. Crap.

"That's my Haley." The woman's lips quivered. She ran her fingers through her thick, curly salt-and-pepper hair, and it stood up in all directions, making her look a little like Sideshow Bob from the Simpsons. Her sharp, blue eyes burned with fear and anger but most of all grief. Sarah Jane had seen that look on parents' and spouses' faces too many times to count in the last thirteen years. Hell, there were some days she saw it on her own face.

"Why don't we go sit and talk somewhere? Is that okay?" Sarah Jane asked.

"Fine," the woman muttered and folded her arms tightly across her chest.

Sarah Jane cut her gaze to Rodriguez. "Can you track that down, please?"

"You got it," he replied. Turning to Haley's mother he gently said, "Ma'am, I'm going to need your phone for a few minutes. Do I have your permission to look through it?"

"Of course, I don't have anything to hide." The woman sniffled.

"Thank you." Rodriguez nodded and walked past Sarah Jane down the aisle of cubicles. From the corner of her eye, she saw him stop at Mia's desk. He said something she couldn't hear, and they both glanced in her direction.

"Let's go this way." Sarah Jane steered the woman toward the room where she'd interviewed Everett for most of yesterday afternoon. The cream-colored walls cast a warm glow in the warm LED lights.

Sarah Jane pulled out one of the molded plastic and metal-framed chairs, and the woman sat down at the dark wood table. She sniffled and dug through her purse, retrieving a small package of Kleenex.

"So, tell me about your daughter. Haley, you said?"

The woman dabbed at her eyes before she spoke, sucking in a deep breath and taking in the interrogation room as if this might be a dream, or rather a nightmare.

"Haley went missing over the weekend. We filed a report with you people, but we haven't heard one word since."

The woman clenched her jaw, and a bright red aura began to emanate around her, and Sarah Jane could feel her anger. The longer she sat, the angrier she became. Angry no one had paid attention to her pleas for help. Angry her daughter might have ended up in a viral video on social media. Angry that the dead girl might actually be her child.

If something happened to one of her kids, Sarah Jane could easily see herself becoming this woman. Maybe even worse.

"And why do you think the girl on the video is Haley?" Sarah Jane asked. "It didn't show much of the victim before she was covered. And honestly, the footage is pretty shaky."

"You're right, it is, but Haley has long brown hair like that girl. And she's been missing, so..." The woman pressed her hand against her mouth as if to hold in the emotions close to the surface.

"Did you bring any pictures of Haley with you?"

The woman nodded and retrieved several photos from her purse. Sarah Jane looked them over. There was no doubt in her mind the girl smiling back at her from the picture was the girl from their crime scene.

"She's beautiful."

"Thank you," Mrs. Brooks whispered.

"Is Haley your only child?"

"Yes."

Sarah Jane touched the corner of one of the photos. The image of Haley walking across a darkened parking lot filled her head. The young woman's long hair flipped over her shoulder every time she looked behind her as if she were checking to see if someone was following her.

Panic fluttered in Sarah Jane's chest, and the hair on the back of her neck stood up. She let the emotion flow through her for a brief moment, trying to determine where it came from. Then, when she lifted her finger from the photo, the panic went away. Had Haley been stalked before she disappeared? Something had put the young woman's senses on high alert.

"May I keep this?"

The woman nodded, and Sarah Jane placed the snapshot on the table.

"When was the last time you talked to Haley?"

"Last Thursday. I called her."

"What did you talk about?"

Mrs. Brooks wrung the tissue in her hands. "Mainly her job, her school schedule, and whether she'd be able to come home for her father's birthday at the end of the month."

"So, she works and goes to school?"

"Yes."

"What does Haley do for work?"

"She works part-time at an auction house in San Francisco a few nights a week and weekends. Mainly in fine art. She wants to be an appraiser when she graduates."

"That's ambitious. Where does she go to school?"

"The University of Santa Clara. She's double majoring in business and art history. Haley loves art. Thankfully, she got a full ride for school because we could never have afforded to send her there."

"It is on the expensive side. My daughter started there as a freshman this fall." Worry stabbed through Sarah Jane's chest. Why hadn't Selena mentioned a missing girl on campus the other night when she was at the house? *Oh right. Because you threw a fit and never talked to her.*

"Her father and I have tried to ground her in reality. The auction house job gave her a chance to work in the industry and have a real job when she graduates."

Sarah Jane nodded. "Sure."

A light knock on the door drew Sarah Jane's attention away from Mrs. Brooks. Mia stuck her head into the interview room, her dark eyes round and full of sympathy. She waved Sarah Jane to the door.

"I need to step out for a moment. Can I get you anything? Soda, coffee, water?"

"No, thank you, I'm fine." Mrs. Brooks continued to fidget with the ragged tissue in her hands.

Sarah Jane closed the door behind her when she left the room and kept her tone quiet. "What's going on?"

"I talked to Bill Grundy. They positively identified the body as Haley Brooks from a fingerprint scan. She's bonded for a company called Harold House Auctions."

Sarah Jane let out a heavy sigh and cast a sorrow-filled glance at the door. "Okay. I don't see any reason to wait on the notification. We'll get the mother to sign a consent form and see if she'll let us search her house, and then we'll get a warrant for Haley's dorm room. We should notify missing persons that it's now a homicide."

"Sure. Let me get a box of tissues and a form, and I'll sit in with you."

"Thanks."

A few moments later, Mia returned, and they both entered the room. The woman's gaze went straight to the box in Mia's hand, and she shrank against her chair. She shook her head.

"Mrs. Brooks, this is my partner, Detective Johnson."

"No." Tears leaked onto Mrs. Brooks's face. "No."

Sarah Jane took the seat next to Mrs. Brooks, and Mia placed the folder and tissue box on the table within the woman's reach before she dragged one of the chairs closer.

"Mrs. Brooks, I'm so sorry to have to tell you this, but the medical examiner has returned an identification on the body of the young woman we found yesterday morning. I'm afraid your daughter was a victim of a homicide."

Sarah Jane placed her hand on the woman's back. The woman let out a terrible keening wail that made Sarah Jane's bones ache. The vibration of energy from the woman's pain prickled against Sarah Jane's fingers. She stayed steady and didn't pull away from the grief-stricken mother even though the woman's body shook violently with cries before she collapsed weeping against Sarah Jane's shoulder.

Mia slipped her hand into the woman's and held it. Every ounce of energy the woman had spilled over onto Sarah Jane. She could get through most days now without crying. Without being paralyzed by the thought of having lost her Dan forever. But on days like today, when someone else's grief flooded through her, it was all she could do to stay upright.

After several moments, Mrs. Brooks cried herself out. She let go of Sarah Jane and Mia, then righted herself in her chair. She grabbed several tissues from the box and blew her nose.

"Maybe I should look at her," Mrs. Brooks said. "Maybe they're wrong."

"They identified her through her fingerprints," Mia said softly.

"And trust me, you don't want to have an image of your daughter in your head the way she is now," Sarah Jane said.

"Do you have children?" Mrs. Brooks asked

"Yes." Sarah Jane nodded.

"So, you know. If it were your daughter, you'd want to see her. Wouldn't you?"

Sharp anxiety stabbed through Sarah Jane's heart at the thought of Selena dead on a slab in the morgue. She would call her daughter later just to touch base.

"No. Actually, I wouldn't. Not like that. Once the M.E. is finished with her body, it'll be released to a funeral home. You should wait until they've taken care of her, for your own sake."

Mrs. Brooks insisted. "You have a daughter?" Her gaze fixed on Sarah Jane, taking her hand.

"I do," Sarah Jane said, feeling the intensity of the woman's pain through her skin.

"You should hold on tight to her." Mrs. Brooks squeezed Sarah Jane's hand until her knuckles turned white. "Hold on as tight as you can because anything could happen."

Flashes of memory spilled from Mrs. Brooks and poured into Sarah Jane's head. Haley Brooks as a small child, beautiful with big, brown eyes and long, dark hair she liked to wear in pigtails. Haley Brooks as an awkward teenager with thick glasses in overalls and Chuck Taylor shoes. Haley Brooks packing to go back to school, worried about getting a prestigious internship.

Sarah Jane squeezed the woman's hand and then gently pulled away. She blinked away the visions.

"Yes, ma'am," Sarah Jane said. The woman broke down and began to weep again. Sarah Jane put an arm around her shoulders, and Mrs. Brooks grabbed onto her as if she were a life preserver. Sarah Jane let her cry until she'd spent all her tears, at least for the moment, and steeled herself again against further onslaught of the woman's emotions.

After a few minutes, Mrs. Brooks's shoulders stopped shaking. She pulled out of Sarah Jane's arms and retrieved more Kleenex. Sarah Jane quickly swiped away her own tears before Mrs. Brooks could notice.

"Do you think you could answer some questions for us?" Sarah Jane asked. She pulled a notepad and pen from her jacket pocket and put them on the table.

Mrs. Brooks nodded. "Of course."

"When did you realize Haley was missing?"

"Her boss called me. Haley didn't show up for work on Sunday, and it's not like Haley to miss work. Besides her schoolwork, her job is extremely important to her."

"And that's when you filed the missing person's report?" Sarah Jane asked.

"I called her roommate first and then talked to all of her friends. None of them had heard from Haley. I called the hospitals and even the city morgue."

"Do you think you can make a list of those friends for me?"

"Of course."

"Can you think of anyone who might want to hurt Haley?"

"No. No...Haley doesn't have a lot of friends, but the ones she has are loyal and love her."

"Did she mention meeting anyone new recently?" Mia asked.

"Not that I recall. Although, she did say there was this guy at work who gave her the creeps."

"Do you remember his name?" Sarah Jane asked.

"She didn't tell me his name. She just said that if he touched her butt one more time, she was going to make a formal complaint against him for sexual harassment."

"Okay. Can you give us the name of her boss?"

"Yes. Angela Friedman. She's the one who called me."

"So, let's keep working on the timeline." Mia pressed her pen tip to the notepad in her hand. "You called Haley's friends on Sunday. And when did you file the report with the police?"

"Sunday night. My husband and I called, and they sent an officer over. We gave him all the information. He made some comment that maybe she has a secret boyfriend we don't know about. Which was ridiculous." Mrs. Brooks's jaw tightened.

"I know that's frustrating," Sarah Jane said. "Did

Haley mention anyone bothering her at school? Or did she feel like someone might be following her?"

"No. Not that I recall." Mrs. Brooks shook her head.

"Aside from the creep at work. What about clients of the auction house? Anyone there take a particular interest in her work? Maybe too much interest?"

"No. She didn't mention anything like that. Everything was going her way."

"How do you mean?"

"Haley is the most determined person I've ever known. I was worried that keeping the job would be too much on top of her schoolwork, but she said, 'No, Mom. I'm making connections that'll pay off in the long run.'" Mrs. Brooks pulled a fresh tissue from the box. "That was my Haley. She always got what she wanted and wasn't afraid to work for it."

"You mentioned a roommate. Did she live in an apartment? Or on campus?"

"She lived in the dorms. Most of her friends have moved into apartments, but Haley's scholarships pay for tuition and room and board fees, and her father and I thought she'd be safer on campus."

"So, she has a car? That she drives to and from work?" Sarah Jane jotted down some notes.

"Yes. A little Honda Civic. She bought it when she was in high school. She was very proud of it."

"How often does she come home?"

"Not very often these days. She's too busy with her studies and work."

"Does she have a boyfriend?"

"No. Haley's too serious about her studies to bother with boys. She always said, 'There'll be time for love later, Mom.'" Mrs. Brooks's voice cracked, and she wiped her nose.

"It would be really helpful if we could go through Haley's room."

"Of course. Although, I don't know what you'll find since she doesn't live with us most of the time."

"We might find more than you think. We'll just need you to sign this consent form." Mia opened the folder, then pushed it with a pen toward Mrs. Brooks. She took the form and looked it over, then scribbled her signature at the bottom.

"Thank you," Sarah Jane said when she slid the form into her folder. "May I ask where your husband is, Mrs. Brooks?"

"He's at work."

"He didn't feel like he needed to come with you today?"

Mrs. Brooks squirmed in her chair and cast her gaze down at the table. "He doesn't know I'm here. If it were up to him, we'd wait until the police contacted us. But...I couldn't wait anymore."

"Sure. Where does your husband work?" Sarah Jane asked.

"Why?"

"It's standard procedure to talk to all the family members."

"Oh, well, my husband's very busy. I'm not sure he'll be able to talk to you at work. He's usually out driving during the day."

"What does he do?" Sarah Jane kept her face neutral, her mind spinning. Why was Mrs. Brooks suddenly throwing up walls?

"He's a local driver for Penguin Trucking. If you really want to talk to him, he's usually home by six-thirty."

"Okay." Mia exchanged a knowing glance with Sarah Jane before jotting down a note. "Thank you. If you wouldn't mind giving me the names of Haley's roommate, dorm number, and her friends, that'd be great."

"Of course." Mrs. Brooks blinked hard and scrubbed her face with a tissue. "Whatever you need."

Sarah Jane turned to Mia. "While you take her information, I'm going to just step out for a moment." She gave Mia a look that said, keep her busy. She smiled and left the room as Mrs. Brooks pulled her phone from her purse and began rattling off names for Mia to record.

Sarah Jane hurried back to Mia's desk and grabbed the missing person's report on Haley Brooks. "I need some help." Rodriguez popped up from his chair; John Waterson and James Stuckey moved their chairs closer to hear.

"What's up, SJ?" John Waterson asked. His short white hair glowed against his tan face, and he pushed his glasses from his long thin nose to the top of his head.

"I need someone to pick up the father of my murder victim. He works at Penguin Trucking."

Waterson removed his glasses and stood up. He smoothed his white oxford, straightened his dark blue tie then slipped his long thin arms into his pale gray suit jacket. "Do you need me to do the notification?"

"No, I'll do that. Just tell him we have some more questions regarding his missing daughter." She handed him the missing person's report.

Waterson looked it over. "Okay. I'll be back in a bit."

"Thanks, John. I'll go stall her mother."

"Yep. Good luck with that." Rodriguez tipped his head at her and took a seat.

❧

ABOUT AN HOUR LATER, WATERSON RETURNED WITH Mr. Brooks in tow and immediately texted Sarah Jane. "Arrived. Meet you at the squad room."

Brooks barely came up to Detective Waterson's shoulders, and his hair looked thin at the crown and too dark to be natural. He couldn't have been more than fifty. And although he was rather lean, he had a potbelly and a redness about his nose that made Sarah Jane wonder about his relationship with alcohol.

"Mr. Brooks, thank you for coming in. I'm Detective Sarah Jane Prentice." She thrust her hand out to shake and waited for him to take it.

He eyed her suspiciously before finally taking Sarah Jane's hand. She opened herself up to his energy, letting it flow through her. His fear and confusion hit her first. Then came the memory. Haley watching him in his workshop as he carved a piece of wood into a bird.

"What should I do, Daddy?"

"First thing you should do is carry that mace your mother got you in your hand, not in your purse." He looked over the top of his glasses, down his bulbous red nose. "Then if he gets too close again, stomp his foot, and kick him in the groin. You knee his nuts, and I promise he will leave you alone forever."

Sarah Jane suppressed the urge to smile at the vision filling her head.

"What's this all about? Did you find Haley?" he asked, his voice full of concern.

"Why don't you come with me, and we can talk a little more." Sarah Jane led him down the hall to the interview room, where his wife waited patiently.

"Jim." Mrs. Brooks straightened in her chair, her fingers tightening around the tissue in her hand. "I told them not to bother you at work."

"What's going on, Elaine? What are you doing here?"

"I just couldn't sit still." She sniffled. "I told you that girl on the video was Haley, and I was right."

"No. I don't believe that." He took a step back and shook his head.

"I'm so sorry to have to tell you this, Mr. Brooks, but we found your daughter's body yesterday morning. And your wife brought us the video. She was right to come in."

"What?" He shook his head, his face reddening. "No, that can't be true."

"I'm sorry, but we identified her from her fingerprints this morning. Why don't you have a seat."

He scrubbed his hand through his hair, and his chest heaved as if he were suddenly short of breath. "I don't believe this. What happened? Who... who did this?"

"That's what we're trying to find out." Sarah Jane pulled out a chair for him, and he sat down holding his upper left arm. He massaged his bicep as if it ached.

"Are you okay, Mr. Brooks?" Sarah Jane noticed the sweat beading on his forehead. She exchanged a glance with Mia.

"No, I'm not okay. You just told me my daughter's dead." His voice broke, and he grunted. He gripped his upper arm tighter. "I can't breathe."

"Mia, call 911. I'm going to get some aspirin from my desk. I'll be right back." Sarah Jane ran down the hall and returned in less than a minute. She shook two aspirin out of the small bottle and gave it to him along with a paper cup full of water.

"Jim, you better not die on me." Mrs. Brooks held

her husband's hand tightly. "Do you hear me? I can't lose you, too."

Mr. Brooks chewed up the aspirin and swallowed the water completely in one gulp. He writhed in pain before finally collapsing in his chair.

"Jim." Mrs. Brooks's voice grew strident, and she shook her husband's hand. "Jim. Can you hear me?"

A few minutes later, two paramedics raced into the room.

"Heart attack, I think," Sarah Jane said. "Mrs. Brooks. Why don't we get out of the way so they can do their job?"

"Come on, Mrs. Brooks." Mia took one of Mrs. Brooks's arms, Sarah Jane took the other, and they gently separated her from her husband. A few minutes later, the paramedics wheeled Mr. Brooks out of the building down to a waiting ambulance. His wife followed behind them, tears and worry etching her face.

"Well, that didn't go exactly the way I planned." Sarah Jane folded her arms across her chest and watched the elevator door close.

"At least we have somewhere to start," Mia said.

"Yeah, we do. Let's pay a visit to Harold House Auctions and see what we can learn about this guy that was harassing her."

"Sure." Mia sighed. "Maybe we'll get lucky."

"Maybe."

CHAPTER 13

Harold House Auctions occupied a warehouse on Battery Street in San Francisco. As soon as the paramedics drove off with Mr. and Mrs. Brooks to the hospital, Sarah Jane and Mia wasted no time driving nearly an hour to drop in on Haley Brooks's most recent employer. Mia took the wheel, and Sarah Jane buckled herself into the passenger seat, determined not to give Haley's killer a New York moment in which to escape into the shadows this time.

Harold House didn't look like any of the auction houses Sarah Jane remembered visiting with Dan twenty years ago when they first bought their house. Inside the industrial building, Harold House was swankier, reminding Sarah Jane of an old English manor house, something she might've seen in a movie. In the mahogany, wood-paneled reception area, a receptionist greeted them. Her dark hair and a bright, pink blouse complemented her pale complexion, and she beamed an open smile she reserved for the typical visitors.

"Good afternoon. Welcome to Harold House Auctions. How can I help you?"

Sarah Jane flashed her badge. Mia drew her blazer back and put her hand on her hip, making the badge clipped to her belt visible.

"I'm Detective Prentice, and this is Detective Johnson with the San Jose Police Department. We're here to see Angela Friedman. Is she in?"

The receptionist's dark brown eyes widened, and she blinked several times as if she didn't know what to do. "Yes. She's in the back dealing with the shipment from an estate."

"Okay." Sarah Jane nodded her head. "Would you please let her know we're here and that we need to speak with her?"

"Of course." The receptionist fumbled with the phone on her desk. A moment later, she dialed a number.

"Ms. Friedman, there are two detectives here to talk to you. Yes, ma'am." The receptionist nodded and hung up the phone. "She wants me to take you back to her office. Is there anything I can get for you? Water? Soda? Coffee?"

"No, thank you," Sarah Jane said.

The receptionist nodded, her eyes bright with false

cheer, and she hopped up from her chair. "Right this way."

Sarah Jane and Mia followed the woman through a door that led to a hallway of modern offices that didn't match the old-world facade of the reception area. They passed a conference room with a large table and a glass wall, and several offices with frosted glass doors. Finally, the receptionist opened the last door on the right and gestured for Sarah Jane and Mia to enter.

"Ms. Friedman will be with you in a moment," the receptionist said.

"Thank you," Sarah Jane replied. The receptionist nodded and left them alone in the small minimalist-styled office. A large glass desk and an office chair that looked more like art than something comfortable to sit in took up half the room. A triptych of abstract paintings hung on the wall behind the desk. The bright, broad strokes of reds, sea blue, yellow, white, and dark navy splashed in a pattern across the three canvases. In a strange way, it reminded Sarah Jane of the ocean. But she wasn't the artist in the family. Her sister Rainey might have been able to help her interpret it better.

"Good morning, or I should say afternoon, I guess." A tall, lanky woman with dark curls brushing the top of her shoulders strode into the room. She wore a pair of jeans, Sketchers, and a dark green T-shirt that set off her olive skin.

"I'm Angela Friedman. Is this about Haley? I've been worried sick about her."

She gestured toward a simple, yellow leather couch and brown, Barcelona-style chairs in the sitting area that took up the other half of her office. "Please have a seat."

Mia smiled at Sarah Jane as if to ask permission, then took a seat while Sarah Jane remained standing. Mia pulled her notebook and pen from her blazer pocket.

Sarah Jane took the lead. "I'm sorry to have to tell you this, but we found Haley's body yesterday morning."

Ms. Friedman sat down hard on the couch, her mouth ajar with disbelief. "Are you sure it's Haley?"

"Yes, ma'am, we're sure," Mia said softly.

Ms. Friedman leaned back on the sofa as if she needed the extra support to stay upright. Her hand drifted to her mouth. "Oh my God. How did she die?"

"She was a victim of a homicide." Sarah Jane carefully watched Ms. Friedman's energy and body language to get a picture of her and her relationship with Haley.

The woman lost all color in her face. "What? No." She shook her head. "That doesn't make any sense. Haley was a nice girl. She...why?" Tears spilled onto her face. "Why would someone kill Haley?"

Sarah Jane finally took a seat in the open chair across from Ms. Friedman. "We're hoping you'll be able to help us with that. When did you last see Haley?"

Several moments passed before Ms. Friedman regained her composure. She got up and searched in a desk drawer for a box of tissues and covered her face with one before she was ready to speak. She returned to the couch and stared at Sarah Jane with watery, dazed eyes.

"Saturday evening. We had an auction, and she volunteered to stay late to help tag some of the things that didn't sell," Ms. Friedman said.

"Do you remember about what time that was?" Mia asked.

"I left around nine thirty because I promised my husband I'd be home at a decent hour. So, I left Haley here to finish up," Ms. Friedman said. "And now I feel sick about it."

"You know what time she left?"

"I can check her timecard," she offered. "If you wait here, I'll go get it."

"Do you mind if I tag along?" Sarah Jane perched on the edge of the chair, ready to get to her feet.

A look of surprise flashed across Ms. Friedman's face, and her gaze bounced between Mia and Sarah Jane before recovering. "No, of course not. Right this way."

She rose from the couch, and Sarah Jane followed her into the hallway to a set of metal double doors. Ms. Friedman punched in a code on the keypad next to the door, and when the light on the keypad turned green, the lock clicked, and she pulled the door open. They entered the large warehouse with huge metal shelves divided into four zones. A pallet loader was parked near the closest of the shelves. Ms. Friedman led Sarah Jane to a standard time clock on the wall. She thumbed through the cards in the holder next to the clock until she found Haley's still in its slot. She studied the card for a moment.

"It looks like she punched out at 11:32 on Saturday night." She handed the card to Sarah Jane.

"May I keep this?"

"I won't be able to pay Haley if you do." Realization clouded her dark eyes, and she stared at the card for a second. "I guess it doesn't matter now, does it?"

"Maybe you can make a copy of it, and I'll take the original with me. You could send the paycheck to her parents."

"Of course." Ms. Friedman sniffled. "I can't believe she's gone. She had such a bright future."

"Why don't we go back to your office and talk about a few things? I have a few more questions."

Ms. Friedman nodded and swiped away the tears that had fallen. "Of course."

A few minutes later, the three of them settled into Ms. Friedman's office again with Sarah Jane and Mia in the chairs and Ms. Friedman on the couch hugging one of the throw pillows.

"So, Angela," Sarah Jane began. "Haley's parents told us someone at work was sexually harassing her. Do you know anything about that?"

The surprise on Angela Friedman's face didn't quite

read true. Angela shook her head. "This is the first I'm hearing about that. I can guarantee you that if someone had been sexually harassing her, I would have taken steps to make sure it stopped. Did her parents mention who it could've been?"

"No, they didn't know his name," Sarah Jane said. "Just that he was someone she worked with. I'm going to need a list of all the male employees, so we can interview them."

"Of course." Angela fidgeted with the fringe of the pillow in her arms.

"Are you sure you don't have any idea who he is?" Mia asked. "Maybe there've been other complaints?"

Angela squirmed on the couch and looked over at the painting hanging behind her desk.

"Ms. Friedman?" Mia asked. "Do you know his name?"

Angela jutted her chin and met Mia's steady gaze. "I can't think of anyone here who would do that." The woman's initial show of grief had shifted to resistance.

Sarah Jane studied the woman's energy. Her aura flickered to dark hazy gray for a second, then back to her normal pale blue. In Sarah Jane's experience, the slight glimmer in color meant concealment. She entertained the idea of casting a compliance spell on the woman but then thought better of it. The last few spells she'd tried had not worked the way they should have, and this was too important.

"What's his name?" Sarah Jane kept her voice even and her gaze steady on Ms. Friedman.

"Like I said, I can't think of anyone here that would do that. Do you have any other questions for me? I really need to get back to work."

"Uh. Yes. Just one more." Sarah Jane forced a smile. "Where did Haley park her car?"

"We all park in the garage on Third street."

"Great. Thank you." Sarah Jane pulled one of her cards from the plastic cardholder she kept in the front pocket of her blazer. "If you could please email me that list of male employees and their phone numbers, I'd really appreciate it."

"Of course. I'll get it for you now." Ms. Friedman rose from the couch and left the office.

Sarah Jane cocked her head.

Mia said, "What's going on in that head of yours?"

"She's hiding something. Maybe covering for someone."

"How do you know that?"

A wry grin spread across Sarah Jane's face. "Let's just call it intuition and leave it at that for now."

Mia nodded. A few moments later, Ms. Friedman returned with a short list.

Sarah Jane looked over the paper with names and phone numbers. "Are any of these folks working today?"

"No. Sorry."

"Okay. I have one other request. We need all the

video footage from your security cameras for Saturday and Sunday."

"Don't you need a warrant for that?"

"I absolutely can get a warrant. But I should probably let you know, if we get a warrant, it may be for more than just security footage. You won't mind if I leave an officer here while I call a judge, will you?"

Ms. Friedman glared at Sarah Jane. "Do I have a choice?"

"Of course you do. You could cooperate." Sarah Jane smiled.

"Okay." Ms. Friedman pursed her lips. "I'm happy to help, especially if it helps you find the person who did this to Haley."

"Thanks. And we're happy to wait while you make a copy for us."

"Right." Ms. Friedman nodded, a bit curtly, Sarah Jane thought and left the office again.

"After this I want to get the street cam footage and any security footage for inside the parking garage," Sarah Jane said.

"Sure. I'm going to step out and call Rodriguez to see if he's gotten Haley's car registration yet. I'll go ahead and have him pull the street cam footage too." Mia dug into her purse for her phone and stood up.

"Great," Sarah Jane said. "Maybe we'll find her car there."

"We can dream right?" Mia gave her a wistful smile and left the office.

Sarah Jane stood up and walked around the office. She stopped in front of an abstract painting. Some art she just didn't get. The bold colors, reds, yellows, and various shades of blue and even black streaked across the canvas in a wide scribble. She glanced over her shoulder and listened for the sound of footsteps. When she was sure she was alone, she moved behind Ms. Friedman's desk and looked over the contents of the shelves hanging on the wall. There were different books on art history and appraisal techniques. A delicate enameled egg rested on a custom stand. And there were several photographs framed in modern clear acrylic. Ms. Friedman and a man Sarah Jane assumed was her boyfriend on some warm tropical beach. Several other frames showcased Ms. Friedman and the same man in different locales. Skiing, Arches National Park, the desert, and in front of the Troll Under a Bridge in Seattle.

Then, as she turned to look away, another photograph caught Sarah Jane's eye. Ms. Friedman and a different man stood on opposite sides of the Harold House auction house sign. They both beamed widely. Sarah Jane removed the frame from the shelf and held her hand over the photograph. Images of Ms. Friedman and the man flashed through her head. The day they took possession of Harold House and the joy and anxiety flooding through Ms. Friedman. The signing of contracts. The day the man met Haley. Sarah Jane focused on him and his feelings of attraction for the young woman.

It bordered on hunger.

"Did you find anything interesting?" Ms. Friedman asked.

Sarah Jane turned around to face the woman. "I was just admiring all your photographs. Looks like you like to travel."

"I do. When I can." Ms. Friedman took a step forward and held out a piece of paper. "All our footage is saved on the cloud, according to my IT guy. You can access it with this login and password."

"Thanks." Sarah Jane took the slip of paper and held up the photo frame. "Who is this man?"

"That's my partner, Ellis Ford. Or, I guess I really should say my investor because he's not part of the day-to-day business."

"Is he on the list you gave me?" Sarah Jane held Ms. Friedman's gaze.

The woman shifted her feet. Red streaked high across her pale cheeks. "No. Like I said, he's not part of the day-to-day."

"Can you please add him?"

Ms. Friedman opened her mouth as if to argue.

Sarah Jane cocked her head. "He had contact with Haley, right?"

"Yes, but—"

"Then I need to talk to him."

"Fine," Ms. Friedman said stiffly. She grabbed a pad of sticky notes from her desk, scribbled down his name and number, then shoved it in Sarah Jane's direction.

"Thank you." Sarah Jane tore off the note and put it in her jacket pocket with her business cards.

"Is there anything else? I really need to get on with my day." Ms. Friedman folded her arms across her chest.

"No, I think that's it for now. Thank you for your time." Sarah Jane laid the photo frame on the desk and made her way out of the building to find Mia.

CHAPTER 14

Sarah Jane sat on Interstate 880 during rush hour traffic, unable to get images of Mrs. Brooks out of her head and the associations that came with them. Notifications of next of kin always brought Dan's death to the surface.

Not just her loss but her guilt. How he died the same morning she caught Jessica King's case. Why had she gone to work that day? Couldn't she have just stayed home, gotten under the covers, and held him?

"It's not your fault, you know," Jessica said from the back seat.

Sarah Jane tapped her brakes, and the car behind her sped around her with his horn blaring.

"Sweet goddess, Jessica! I'm driving here. The least you could do is wait to appear once I'm parked. You could get me killed." Sarah Jane's heart thundered into her throat, and she gripped the steering wheel until her knuckles turned white.

"Not likely."

"What are you doing here, Jessica?"

"Good to see you, too. So, you met Ashlyn."

"Yeah, I also met Haley in a terrifying way. Thanks for that," Sarah Jane said.

"Today must've really sucked."

"Yeah, you could say that. So, any progress on your memory?"

"How many times do I have to tell you, the answer is no?"

"Jessica, what's the trophy room? And don't tell me you don't know because I bet you do."

"It's where he keeps the girls he kills," she said.

"You mean their bodies? I don't understand," Sarah Jane said. She took the exit onto 280 and headed toward home.

"No, I mean souls. He has their souls trapped in his house."

"Are you freaking kidding me?"

"I wish I were."

"Wait. If he's trapping their souls, then why aren't you there? And how is Ashlyn able to get out?"

"You don't remember?" Jessica said, leaning forward. She rested her translucent arms on the two front seats. A grin played on her lips.

"Remember what?"

"My autopsy."

"I'm sorry, Jessica. I didn't attend your autopsy. I looked at the medical examiner's report, but I don't remember anything that stands out. Sorry." Sarah Jane said.

"You don't remember?"

Sarah Jane's jaw dropped, and she shook her head, at a loss for words. "Uh...No."

"I had a pentagram tattooed on the back of my neck for protection. My mom used to call it my devil tattoo. She never got it."

"Protection? Jessica, were you a witch?"

Jessica shrugged. "I guess I was a wannabe more than anything else. I dabbled. It's not like I had a coven or anything, and I wasn't like you for sure. You and your family, you're the real deal."

"Anybody can be the real deal. Sure, I was born into it. But the craft is something you can learn. And dabbling? That just puts you on the path to finding yourself, whether it's witchcraft or Buddhism or whatever." Sarah Jane cocked her head. "Although, I'm surprised a tattoo you got when you were alive is protecting you in death. And that is interesting. I've never heard of that before. But of course that doesn't mean anything." Sarah Jane chuckled. "My Gran always said the path of a witch is paved in shadows, not light because the only way to really progress is to face the shadowy parts of ourselves."

Sarah Jane continued to drive almost on autopilot. "Did Ashlyn have a tattoo?"

"Not sure. You'll have to ask her. But she can come and go as she pleases. He doesn't seem to notice."

"So, you *do* know where he is?" Sarah Jane glared at the spirit in the rearview mirror. "I swear, Jessica. If you've been lying to me."

"I'm not lying. Once I escaped, I...I never went back, and I sure as hell didn't turn around to take a picture. But we're all connected by a spell. That much I do know."

"Wait." Sarah Jane looked in the rearview mirror, so stunned she almost lost control of the car. "Are you telling me he's a witch?"

"Maybe. He has powers. I can't explain it." Jessica leaned back in her seat. "Did I ever tell you I used to leave my body? I used to practice astral projection. Was actually pretty good at it. Turned out to be the only reason I'm not like the rest of them."

"No, you didn't."

"Yeah, every time he'd come in and want to, you know... have sex." Jessica stared pensively out the window. Signs for Sarah Jane's exit loomed in the distance, and before she could gather her thoughts, they were cruising along El Camino Real past the endless strip malls with their big box stores, chain pharmacies, and restaurants of every flavor—from Korean barbeque to Sushi. Mexican to high Chinese Cuisine.

"I would astral project so that it, you know, didn't really happen to me. It happened to my body. But not to me. Does that make any sense?"

"Honey, you didn't have sex with him." Sarah Jane wished she could stop in the middle of the street, face Jessica, and help her understand this wasn't her fault. Instead, she turned onto Scott Boulevard, toward her neighborhood and the streets lined with late 20th and early 21st-century ranch-style homes, drought-tolerant landscaping, and the façade of normalcy that Sarah Jane's job belied.

"Having sex implies consent. He abducted you and bound your arms and legs. There's no way you gave consent. This isn't your fault."

"I know," Jessica whispered. She sniffled and then shook her head and upper body as if the motion might make her bad memories disappear. "By the way. A shit-storm's coming tonight, so buckle up."

Sarah Jane slowed down to stop at a red light. She threw a glance over her shoulder at Jessica, but the spirit was gone.

"You always have to have the last word don't you," Sarah Jane said. The light turned green, and a few minutes later, she turned into her neighborhood.

Her senses tingled, and a heaviness pressed on her chest. Her arms broke into goosebumps when she approached her house and saw Dalton's truck parked behind Amy's Accord and her daughter Selena's Camry on the curb in front of the house. Why were her children at her house on a Thursday night? She pulled into the driveway and hopped out of the car, her defenses on alert before she even walked in the door.

She paused before putting her hand on the doorknob, sensing the energy flowing through the house. Once inside, she put her bag down on the old-fashioned coat tree by the front door, the one Dan had insisted they buy at an old flea market because he loved that it had a seat and a mirror. It'd taken two cleansings before she was satisfied no spirits still clung to it, and all the weird energy around it had dissipated.

Voices came from the kitchen, low whispers, and none of them belonged to her sister. She closed her eyes and visualized her three children sitting around the bar island scheming. She just wasn't sure about what. She carefully closed the door behind her, trying to keep all sound to a minimum.

"Hello to the house."

Her daughter popped around the corner first.

"Hi, Mom." A wide smile crossed Selena's face. Her daughter's eyes went straight to her hip. "You still have your gun on."

"Yeah. I just got here. I haven't had a chance to go to my room yet." She tried not to grit her teeth or give away the fact that she sensed something was off. "What are you doing here, sweetie?"

"I just missed you. Thought I'd come for dinner." Selena leaned in and gave her mother a quick peck on the cheek.

"Okay. Sure."

"Hey, Mom," Dalton said, coming up behind his sister. "How's work?"

"Same old, same old. People die; I investigate." She plopped her purse on the bench near the front door and slipped off her comfortable, black loafers.

"Nice, Mom. Really. Nice." Dalton's lips twisted as if he'd tasted something disgusting.

"So, what's your excuse for being here tonight? Laundry?" Sarah Jane directed her attention to her oldest child.

"No, no. No laundry. Just thought I'd hang with the family tonight, that's all." Dalton's lips stretched into a grin that made Sarah Jane believe he might be lying.

"Right." Sarah Jane narrowed her eyes. She moved into the large space and noticed Larkin in his usual place on the couch with his game controller in hand.

Amy stood in the kitchen with her arms folded. A worried expression on her face. She glared at Dalton for a moment before she took her pink fleece-lined hoodie from a hook by the back door. "I'm going out for a bit. Dinner's in the slow cooker, so you all can eat anytime you're ready."

"It smells great, whatever it is." Sarah Jane's stomach

growled. She gave her sister a grateful smile. The last thing she wanted these days was to come home and cook. Selena and Dalton took a seat on the stools at the kitchen island.

"It's just a ham." Amy shrugged her slim shoulders. "I figured we could have sandwiches. There's potato salad to go with it in the fridge and green beans in the pot on the stove but you may have to warm them up."

"Great. Thank you." Sarah Jane's intuition sang to her. *Something's wrong. Something's wrong.* "Is everything okay?"

"Everything's fine. I'm just going to walk around the block." Amy slipped her arms into her jacket, and cut her eyes at her niece and nephew. "You all be nice to your mother." Amy waggled a finger, her voice full of protective warning. Sarah Jane could count on one hand the times she'd heard her sister scold the kids. Usually, she was the first to defend them.

Sarah Jane watched Amy disappear around the corner to the foyer. After she heard the front door close she turned on her children. "Okay, what the hell is going on? It must be pretty bad if you've chased Aunt Amy out of the house."

"Hi Mom." Larkin left the couch in the adjoining Family room and took a seat next to his brother and sister at the island. "Why does something have to be going on? Can't we just want to hang out with you?"

"No." Sarah Jane shook her head and furrowed her

brow. She eyed them suspiciously. "No. You never want to hang out with me."

"Mom, that's totally not true." Selena picked through the crystals in the hazy selenium charging bowl on the counter before plucking one into her palm. "We just miss you, that's all. We didn't get to spend any time with you the other night."

"Why don't you go put your gun in the safe." Dalton's gaze bounced from Sarah Jane's face to her hip.

"Okay. Go ahead and make yourselves a plate. I'll be back in a minute. Then you're going to tell me the truth." Sarah Jane headed to her bedroom. After she locked her weapon in the gun safe inside her nightstand, she peeled off her black suit and the blue oxford blouse, slipped on a pair of lounge pants and a T-shirt, and headed back to the kitchen.

When she returned, the kids had moved to the dining table but had not helped themselves to any food. They kept exchanging glances among themselves and watched her with cautious expressions while she opened the slow cooker and put a couple of slices of ham, and a scoop of green beans on her plate. She could feel their eyes on her as she opened the fridge and pulled out the container of potato salad and the pitcher of tea. She grabbed a glass from the cabinet next to the fridge and filled it with ice. Sarah Jane had grown up in the south until she was thirteen. She still liked her tea sweet. It was the only little bit of sugar she consumed these days.

She took a sip, eyeing her children over the rim of her glass. "What are you three waiting for? If you want to eat, you'll have to get it yourselves. The days of me making a plate for you are long gone."

Larkin shifted in his chair. Selena shot him a glare. Sarah Jane could feel their silent conversation. She put her plate down at the head of the table along with her tea and took a seat. Mustering her best mom voice, she shifted her gaze from face to face.

"What's going on? Is someone flunking? Is someone pregnant? Is someone fired? I'm not getting a clear picture here other than I know you're covering something up."

This was what Jessica had warned her about, but even with the head's up, somehow, it wasn't enough to erase the unease in her belly.

Dalton protested the loudest. "Geez, Mom." A shadow of frustration and embarrassment passed over his face. "Nobody's fired or pregnant or flunking." He threw a glance toward his little brother. "Right?"

"Nobody's flunking, Dalton." Larkin rolled his eyes, clearly irritated. "I have better grades than you ever did."

"Selena?" Dalton asked.

"Holy goddess, my sex life is none of your freaking business." Selena slapped his arm. "No. I'm not pregnant."

"All right, just cut it out. Selena, tell me the truth. Why are you all here?"

Selena shifted in her chair, pushed her dark hair behind her ears and took a deep breath. "First, we love you. And second, we're worried about you. The anniversary of Dad's death is coming up next month... and...."

Dalton interrupted his sister. "And you still haven't scattered Dad's ashes." He paused and looked at his siblings as if for confirmation of his next move. When it didn't come, he continued. "That's all he talked about at the end. How he wanted to be scattered in the Santa Cruz mountains."

Sarah Jane's face grew hot. "I know what I haven't done for your dad yet. I'm quite aware." The heat spread down her neck to her chest, and she pinched the front of her T-shirt, fanning herself by moving it up and down to get some airflow.

"So, when are you going to do it?" Larkin asked in a quiet voice.

"When I'm ready," she snapped. "And your dad would understand that if he were here."

"Mom. Come on." Dalton shook his head, as if he didn't believe her.

"You know what? You guys can have dinner with Aunt Amy. Because I'm not dealing with this. I've just had a terrible day. I had to tell a woman that her child was murdered. You know what happens on those days when I have to talk to a parent about their dead child?" Her voice grew strident and she wagged her finger at them. "I see your faces. And I imagine how devastating it would be to lose any of you."

Selena's dark eyes widened. Larkin looked as if she had just slapped him. And Dalton made a "yeah, right" face, which made her want to actually slap him. Guilt was the strongest weapon in her mom arsenal, but sometimes it just didn't work on her firstborn.

"I know you're not happy with how slow you think my grief is going. You think I don't hear you whisper among yourselves? 'Oh my gosh, Mom's not getting better.'" She gritted her teeth. "No, I'm not. My husband died. The love of my life. We were supposed to spend the rest of our lives together. We had plans for after you three punks left the house. And now we don't." She swallowed hard, refusing to let one tear fall. "You know what? Just forget it."

"We miss him too, you know." Larkin found his voice. His cheeks burned red, and he glared at her and folded his arms across his chest.

"I don't doubt that you do." She softened her tone but still wasn't ready to apologize. Still wasn't ready to release the anger bubbling close to the surface. She shook her head.

"I'm going out. I need some air."

"Mom," Selena called after her. "Please come back and talk to us."

Sarah Jane rushed to the front door. Anxiety weighed heavy on her chest making it hard to breathe. She slipped on a pair of canvas shoes belonging to her sister, grabbed her bag and keys, then slammed the door behind her.

AFTER AN HOUR OF DRIVING AROUND BLINDLY, SARAH Jane found herself at Alviso County Park. She pulled into the small lot and parked. The sun would set soon. She hopped out of her car and wound her way to the boardwalk over the marsh that led to salt ponds near the end of San Francisco Bay. The evening sea breeze kicked in, rippling across the golden marsh grass. Only a few people wandered about, mostly waiting to watch the sunset, she guessed. She and Dan sometimes did that. They would steal away, leaving the kids with a neighbor just to have a few minutes to be together.

"That's why I love living here," Dan used to say. "It might be hot during the day, but the nights are always cool. And then there's this view." He'd kiss the back of her hand while they watched the sun sink below the horizon. The chilly wind whipped around her, and she rubbed her hands up and down her arms. She wished she'd thought to grab a jacket.

When she got to the salt ponds, she stopped and faced west. The tears that had been threatening to fall since she left the house had nowhere to go except out. She held them in most days, especially around her family.

She expected people at work to want her to get over Dan. To get past this loss that sometimes felt like a dark cave with no sign of light to lead her out.

But she thought maybe her kids at least would give her a break. She knew they were still grieving him. Why couldn't they just let her do the same? Her shoulders shook with the weight of it all, and she couldn't have stopped crying now, even if she wanted.

A couple walked past her on the gravel road around the salt ponds. The woman stopped for a second, and Sarah Jane thought she might ask if she was okay, but the man pulled on the sleeve of her jacket, leading her away. Sarah Jane sank to her knees with her head in her hands and wept. The sounds of the wind and seagull cries penetrated her senses. She cried until her chest ached, and her face felt swollen. Amy would probably scold her later for scrubbing away the tears, especially after healing her eye yesterday.

A warm hand rested on her shoulder and gave it a gentle squeeze. Sarah Jane rounded on the touch.

"What the hell?" She almost choked on the words when she found herself face to face with the woman in red. Bernice, Everett had called her.

"Come on, honey, let me help you up." The woman in red held out a hand. Her compassionate gaze steadied on Sarah Jane's face. A soft smile spread across her full lips.

"Are you real?" Sarah Jane stayed in place, staring

back at her. “Or are you just another spirit haunting me? Why are you everywhere I go? If you are a spirit, you just need to move on. I have enough ghosts in my life.”

“I'm not a ghost, honey. Why don’t we take a walk? We have some things to talk about.” The woman offered her hand again to help Sarah Jane up, but Sarah Jane waved it away and rose to her feet on her own. “I'm Bernice, by the way. I'm your spirit guide. I've been trying to find a way to introduce myself so it wouldn't shock you, but it hasn’t been easy.”

“My spirit guide? Great,” Sarah Jane spat out in disgust. “Just what I need. One more person trying to tell me how to live my life.”

“Oh honey, that’s not my job. I mean, you’ve clearly needed a spirit guide. But you’re right. You really do have too many people trying to get you unstuck. Your coworkers, your kids...It’s like having too many cooks in the kitchen. Somebody’s bound to get burned.”

“I’m not stuck.” Sarah Jane protested, but in her heart, she knew Bernice was right.

“Well, you’re not moving forward either, and in some ways, you’ve even moved backward a little.”

“I like where I am, thank you very much.” Sarah Jane folded her arms across her chest, more for warmth than out of defiance.

Bernice cocked her head. “Do you, though?”

“Fine, maybe I’m a little stuck, but I don’t need you.”

Bernice shrugged. "Well, somebody thinks you do. Otherwise, I wouldn't be here."

Sarah Jane's ears pricked up. "Somebody who?"

"I don't ask questions. I just show up where I'm told."

Sarah Jane huffed at not getting more information. Spirits could be like that. "I don't care. You can go back to wherever you came from because I'm just going to ignore you."

"Hmmm... how's that been working for you so far?"

Sarah Jane gave Bernice a sideways glance while the spirit kept in step with her, despite her two-inch heels.

"Honey, you can barely ignore the ghosts that come in and out of your life," Bernice continued. "I promise, you can't ignore me. Once I'm here, I'm here till the job is done."

"Fine. Consider the job done. You're completely off the hook. You can go now." Sarah Jane hugged her arms tighter around herself.

"Oh, my." Bernice pointed at the sky. Hues of pink and orange surrounded the dark orange orb sinking behind the trees beyond the marshland of the twenty-acre park. "Will you look at that?"

Sarah Jane watched as the sun disappeared a moment later. It always surprised her how fast it moved at this time of day.

"I don't need your help," she insisted. "Did my kids send you?"

Bernice chuckled. "No, but I know where those kids of yours get their stubborn streak." Bernice grew serious. "Don't be so hard on them. They just love you, and they don't want to see you sad."

"Well, I am sad. I'm sorry if that process upsets them. It upsets me that they're not sadder."

Bernice raised her palms, a calming gesture. "Yes. Yes. I can understand that. Just take me at my word. They're sad. Especially Larkin. You should keep an eye on him."

Sarah Jane eyed the woman suspiciously. "What do you mean? What's wrong with Larkin?"

"You'll find out soon enough. I think this park is going to close soon, isn't it? And I'm sure you're freezing out here. Look at those goosebumps." Bernice gestured to Sarah Jane's arms.

A wind blew harder, and the sky began to darken. Sarah Jane shivered again. She couldn't sit here all night even if she wanted to stay mad. Even if she wanted to be sad and alone.

"I'm going home now. But not because you think I should. But because it's late, and I've got an early day tomorrow."

"Right, you've got suspects to find." Bernice's eyes lit up. "You know, I think you're one of the most interesting cases I've ever had."

"That doesn't comfort me, and you're not invited." Sarah Jane made an about-face and headed in the direction of her car. "In fact, I don't really want to see you again. So, whatever you came here to do, you have to do it without me."

"Okay, sugar. I see you like to do things the hard way." Bernice laughed and then disappeared. Another chill skittered down Sarah Jane's spine, but this one wasn't caused by the cold. She gripped her keys tightly in her hands and made her way back to the parking lot.

CHAPTER 15

Mia practically jumped on Sarah Jane the minute she walked into the squad room.

"Lieutenant wants to see us," Mia said.

"What's wrong?" Sarah Jane asked as they walked past the cubicles to her desk.

"Stuckey got a hit on another missing girl. The one you were looking for with the name Ashlyn," Mia said, her dark eyes wide, the heels of their oxfords clicking added to the squad room's white noise of computer printers, ringing phones, and muffled conversations.

"Okay. Did she match the description? What about the MO?"

"It was almost exactly the same except for the dressing and posing of the body. She'd been missing for five days before they found her. By all accounts, she was, you know, a good student, well-liked. Blond, this time, though, which was different. But just as petite as Haley and Jessica."

"Great, so we know for sure the guy's got a type. And Stuckey? Did he let the lieutenant know?" Sarah Jane said.

"He let me know first, and I let the lieutenant know."

Sarah Jane stood at the low wall of her cubicle and nodded for a moment, thinking. "Did she say I was in trouble?" she asked.

"I don't think she would tell me that even if I wanted to know. But I didn't get that feeling. She just asked me how you knew the girl's name."

"What did you tell her?"

Mia shook her head. "I didn't tell her anything. Other than you opened up the search parameters to look for five-day missing's whose bodies had been discovered."

"Great. Let me put my bag away, and I'll talk to her."

"Sure."

But when Sarah Jane leaned down to stick her purse in the bottom drawer of her desk, a printout on her keyboard got her attention, the missing person report for Ashlyn Gehring. She looked at the photo and held her finger up to Mia. "Hang on a sec."

This girl looked exactly like the spirit that came to

her bedroom the other night and begged her not to forget about them. Sarah Jane just wished she knew the rest of their names.

Stuckey stood up at his desk and called to her, interrupting her thoughts. "Hey, Prentice. I got that security footage from the parking garage and the street cams. We can spend some time going through it today if you like."

"That would be great. Thank you. Ready?" Sarah Jane directed her attention to Mia.

"Sure," she answered and the two of them headed to their lieutenant's glass-walled office overlooking the squad room.

Lieutenant Anna Mendoza's office door was always open. And today was no exception. On many days, Sarah Jane swung by after her shift just to catch up. Mendoza had been the only female detective on the squad for years before she decided to jump on the captain's track. She had the best solve rate in the whole department before Sarah Jane came along and ruined it.

Sarah Jane always appreciated Lieutenant Mendoza for never taking Sarah Jane's close rate personally. Instead, she celebrated with her, making her a good leader and someone Sarah Jane trusted. Only a couple of years younger than Sarah Jane, Mendoza had worked hard, and the way things were going, Sarah Jane had no doubt the lieutenant would definitely earn her captain's bars by the time she hit fifty.

The lieutenant often tried to get Sarah Jane interested in moving up beyond Detective Three. But Sarah Jane had no interest in running a squad, much less running a whole division. Right now, her job and her family were all she could manage.

Sarah Jane rapped on the open door and stuck her head into Mendoza's office. "You wanted to see us?"

Lieutenant Mendoza waved them forward into her small office, clean, neat, and modern with black leather and metal chairs perched in front of her desk.

"Come in and close the door behind you, Sarah Jane. Have a seat." She gestured to the open chair and leaned back comfortably in her own.

It was then that Sarah Jane noticed Captain Chris Washington had joined them. Had Mendoza planned to blindside her, or had Washington dropped in on the lieutenant's meeting unannounced? She threw a surreptitious glance at Mia. "You go ahead," Sarah Jane deferred to Mia. "I don't mind standing."

"So, Captain Washington is going to sit in with us to get an update." Captain Chris Washington cut an intimidating figure, mainly because he stood 6'3" and was built like a linebacker. The man had arms thick with ropey muscle and a stare that could make even some of the most hard-ass cops shrink from him. Sarah Jane could almost feel herself shrinking by half. She would've liked to say he didn't scare her because, under most circumstances, when her magic worked the way it should, not many people did, but with her magic on the fritz, her awareness of a man's size, strength, and position put her on guard.

Sarah Jane tightened the muscles in her jaw and waited, alert. This would be about her, no doubt. The screw up at the site with the drone. Maybe even the screw up with the King case.

"Where are we on the Haley Brooks case?" the lieutenant asked.

"We notified her parents, and we talked to her boss yesterday. We also had security footage pulled for her workplace, the garage that she parks in, and the street cams around that area."

Sarah Jane began to rattle off her list, getting into case mode and trying to leave office politics at the door. "Today, we plan to interview the roommate, her coworkers, and the co-owner of the company she works for. If there's time, I'd like to search her bedroom at her parents' home today, and I want to get a warrant for her dorm room to go through things there. Then we'll see where that leads."

"Sure." Sarah Jane noticed the lieutenant exchange an uncomfortable look with the captain.

"That drone footage was unfortunate," the captain said. "Where are we at on getting that taken down?"

"Stuckey's working on it. It should be down today,"

Sarah Jane said. It was on the tip of her tongue to add that it might be a plus because it helped them identify Haley sooner.

"I hear there may be other girls we missed." The captain's voice dropped an octave.

"Why don't you pull up a chair, Sarah Jane," Lieutenant Mendoza said. She gestured toward a folding metal chair leaning next to a bookshelf tucked into one of the corners of the office.

"That's okay." Sarah Jane smiled and folded her arms across her chest. "I assume this won't take long."

"No, I suppose it won't," the captain said. "It's been brought to my attention that there may be more than just the two victims that we found."

"That is a definite possibility," Sarah Jane said. "One that we're exploring at the moment."

"I understand this new victim is outside of our jurisdiction."

"Yes, we still need to run down some leads to verify that it's actually connected to our victims."

"The deputy chief thinks we should get ahead of the media storm that's bound to happen, set up a task force," the captain said. "We need to look like we are trying to be proactive. I will reach out to the other police departments involved. And I've also asked for assistance from the FBI."

"Do you really think that's necessary? I mean, it's a

bit premature. We've only found one other victim, and we haven't even proven she's connected yet." Sarah Jane squeezed her upper arms tightly.

"Yes, I'm sure. The FBI is sending the local behavioral science specialist from the field office in San Francisco."

"Are we giving the case to the feds?" Sarah Jane didn't hide her aggravation. It was early days, but this was her case.

"Of course not, Sarah Jane. He's only going to be here in a consulting capacity," Lieutenant Mendoza said. "Don't get defensive. Honestly, this should have been done months ago."

"Yes, ma'am." Sarah Jane clenched her jaw and stared down at her feet. "I screwed up with Jessica King. I know that, and I'm doing my best to rectify it."

"Sarah Jane, nobody's blaming you. We didn't know exactly what we were searching for when we found the King girl's body. We know what we're looking for now. As horrible as that sounds," the captain said. "You and Mia clean up really well. I want you to be the face of this investigation. Do you understand what I'm saying?"

"Yes, sir." Mia straightened in her chair.

"Yes, sir," Sarah Jane muttered. "Are we calling a press conference today?"

"Yes. I've already set one up for six o'clock today. We'll do it in front of the building. I want both of you standing with the deputy chief when he announces the task force."

"You know they're going to ask if there's a serial killer. We don't even have a possible description of the guy," Sarah Jane said.

"Don't worry. The deputy chief has done plenty of these types of pressers. He can handle the hard questions. You're there to reassure people that the San Jose police force is making this a priority and if you speak, to ask for the public's help. Do you understand? This is as much about optics as it is about information. They're going to be watching us." He pointed a finger at them.

"Yes, sir," Sarah Jane and Mia said in unison.

Sarah Jane shifted her feet. "Is there anything else, sir? We have a long list of things to do today."

"Yes." He directed his comment to Lieutenant Mendoza. "Get a tip line in place."

"Of course. I'll allocate some uniforms to help out with that," Mendoza said.

The captain stood up, forcing Sarah Jane to crane her neck a little to look at him. "Let's find this man, ladies. Before harm comes to any other young women in our city."

"Yes sir," Sarah Jane said. Mia echoed her words.

"Mia, would you excuse us please?" The lieutenant said after the captain left her office.

Mia shot Sarah Jane a concerned look. Sarah Jane

gave Mia a nod, and her partner rose from her chair and left the office, closing the door behind her.

"Why don't you have a seat?"

"Sure." Sarah Jane nodded and finally took the chair closest to the door. No one could accuse her of sitting like a lady. She rested her hands on the tops up her thighs and leaned forward a little, looking her lieutenant in the eye.

"So, how are you doing, Sarah Jane?" Mendoza rested her elbows on her desk and folded her hands together.

"I'm good."

"Really? How are things at home?"

"They're fine. Selena started school at the University of Santa Clara in August. Dalton's got his first job. And Larkin is... well. He's a sixteen-year-old boy. He does what sixteen-year-old boys do. Plays video games and hangs out with his friends."

"That's good. I just wanted to check in on you. It's been, what? A year since you lost your husband?"

"It will be a year on the twelfth of next month." Sarah Jane shifted her gaze away, looking anywhere except at her lieutenant.

"Maybe you should take some time off around then."

"I don't see any reason to do that. Like I said, I'm good."

"Right." The lieutenant stared at her for a moment as if she were unsure that Sarah Jane was telling the truth. "Okay. If you change your mind, let me know."

"I will." Sarah Jane rubbed her hands up and down her thighs. "Is that all you need? I've got a lot of work to do today so..."

"That was it. Just keep me apprised of how the case is going. And please don't bust the balls of whoever the FBI sends."

"I will do my best, ma'am." Sarah Jane left the office as quickly as she could, almost skidding to a stop when she found Bernice sitting at her desk, thumbing through a file folder. Sarah Jane's breath sounded heavy in her ears, and she scanned the squad room to see if anyone else had noticed the woman in the red suit. Bernice waved, giving her a bright smile.

"Morning, Sarah Jane," Bernice called. Sarah Jane's mouth went dry, and she couldn't move her feet. Bernice's smile widened.

"Don't you worry. They can't see or hear me. Only you can. Oh, and course, Everett. He could see me. Because I'm his spirit guide too."

Sarah Jane found it curious that she could see the spirit guide. She could even feel her like a regular mortal. Twice Bernice had touched her. How had she done that? If a ghost tried to touch Sarah Jane, it would go right through her, leaving her cold. Bernice, on the other hand, radiated warmth. Comfort. A part of her liked being around the spirit guide. Liked the way Bernice's energy affected her. It almost felt familiar, as if she'd known her before. Maybe she had. Bernice *was* a spirit guide. A celestial being. For all Sarah Jane knew, Bernice had been there her whole life looking out for her. Of course, she wasn't going to admit any of that to Bernice.

Sarah Jane ignored Bernice. Instead, she headed to Mia's desk. "So, what do we have lined up so far?"

"I've called her roommate, and she's agreed to come down. Stuckey's going through all the footage from the street cams now. And Rodriguez is combing through her social media. So next, I thought I'd start calling her coworkers to get them in here for interviews."

"Great. I can help you with that. I'm going to give Mrs. Brooks a call so we can set up a time to go through Haley's room." Sarah Jane picked up the printout of names, including the sticky note she'd added to it.

"That sounds good. I'll make a photocopy of that, and we can get started."

"Great. I call dibs on this guy." Sarah Jane peeled the sticky note from the paper and held it up for Mia to see.

"Sure, no problem. Why is he so important?"

Sarah Jane leaned over and lowered her voice. "There was a photo of him in Ms. Friedman's office, and I had a vision about him. He was attracted to Haley. Like, very attracted."

Mia's eyes widened, and she pursed her lips. "Then absolutely, let's start with him first."

Sarah Jane gave Mia a sly grin. "I thought that's what you'd say." She glanced at her desk, and Bernice had moved to Stuckey's cubicle. She stood behind him as he watched the street cam video. Sarah Jane thought of scolding her, trying to make her go away but then thought better of it. If Stuckey could keep Bernice entertained, maybe Sarah Jane could actually do some work.

"Let's see what we can get done before lunch."

"Sure thing." Mia nodded.

CHAPTER 16

Sarah Jane tossed the empty container that had held her California turkey club wrap from the food truck parked near the station house every day around lunchtime. She'd spent most of the morning making phone calls. Most people thought detective work was glamorous, but in reality, a lot of it came down to persistence and the ability to make phone calls.

She'd convinced Ellis Ford, the man in Angela Friedman's photo, to come in at 1:00 pm, which hadn't been easy. He'd been evasive, which immediately set off Sarah Jane's suspicions. If he hadn't agreed, she'd have no problem going to his workplace and escorting him down to the squad room. The one thing she wished she had in her arsenal was her magic.

The right compliance spell could go a long way toward helping her solve this case. Or, at least, get to the truth about Ellis Ford and his relationship with Haley. As much as she hated to admit it, her sister Cass was right. She needed her grandmother to diagnose and heal her problem. But that would take the whole coven. For that she needed nine people: her grandmother, all four of her sisters, Selena, Dalton, Susanna's oldest daughter Freja, and of course, herself.

She'd made up with Cass, and Amy was always on her side. But the others could still be upset with her since the birthday blow up. Did she really have a choice? Not if she wanted her magic back. Sarah Jane dug her phone out of her bag, took a deep breath, and jotted off a group text to her sisters.

Sarah Jane: *I know I'm the last person you want to hear from, but I need your help.*

It didn't take long to get a response.

Smiley Eyes Susanna: *You know we're here for you. What's going on?*

Sarah Jane: *I have no doubt that either Amy or Cass has told you all that my magic is, well, let's just say it's on the fritz.*

Rainey to the Rescue: *What does that mean? What happens if you try to cast a spell?*

Sarah Jane: *It fails. It's been happening for a while now, but it's gotten worse in the last few weeks. I tried to subdue a suspect with a simple freezing spell and ended up with a black eye.*

Smiley Eyes Susanna: *OMG SJ! Are you all right?*

Sarah Jane: *I'm fine. Amy took care of me. But I think we*

need to call a coven meeting. And we should probably include the kids—at least Selena, Dalton and Freya. Since they're of age. I'm assuming you'll loop Gran in on this, Rainey.

Rainey to the Rescue: *Of course.*

Sarah Jane: *I have a case that I have to solve, and I'm afraid I can't do it without magic. I haven't confirmed this, but I think I'm dealing with a witch. And he's killing girls, young women, I guess.*

Spitfire Cass: *Holy shit! You didn't say anything about that yesterday when you called me!*

Smiley Eyes Susanna: *This sounds like an emergency. What if we do it tomorrow night? There was a full moon a few days ago. This would actually be a good time.*

Sarah Jane: *What day was the full moon?*

Rainey to the Rescue: *Tuesday. Is that important?*

Sarah Jane: *I don't know. Maybe.*

Amykins: *Why don't we have a potluck?*

Sarah Jane: *Whatever's easiest on you, Amy.*

Smiley Eyes Susanna: *Great I'll make deviled eggs. Why don't we just do sandwiches?*

Rainey to the Rescue: *I can go to Barnes Deli and pick up some ham and turkey, and I'm sure Gran will want to make something. She stopped at one of the orchards the other day and brought home a bushel of apples. SJ, you can't say no to Gran's apple pie.*

Sarah Jane: *She does make the best apple pie.*

Spitfire Cass: *I'll stop at Haines Bakery in Santa Clara. They have the best bread evah!*

Sarah Jane's eyes stung, and she blinked several times, trying to hold back the tears. If there was one thing she could count on in her life, it was her sisters. They always had her back, even when she didn't deserve it.

Sarah Jane: *Thank you*

She wanted to gush how much she appreciated their support. Having her as a sister couldn't have been easy because the truth was, sometimes Sarah Jane wasn't easy to be around. She could be snappish and abrasive, but they knew her like no others. Yet, somehow, they still loved her anyway.

Sarah Jane: *See you tomorrow night.*

Amykins: 5:00 pm.

"You've got a good family there," Bernice said. "A lot of people don't."

Sarah Jane jumped a little at the sound of her voice and hugged her phone to her chest. After a minute, she put her phone to her ear and pretended to be talking to someone. She dropped her voice to a whisper. "I really hate it when people sneak up on me."

"Aw, that's clever." Bernice grinned and sat down on the desk next to Sarah Jane. "And noted. I'll try not to sneak up on you." The spirit guide glanced around. "You know there's enough room in here for an extra chair. Do you think you could get one put in that corner for me? I promise I'll be real quiet."

"No. I can't do that." Sarah Jane shook her head.

"Honestly, I'm not sure exactly what you're doing. But I'd appreciate it if you'd back off. Just go someplace else." Sarah Jane tried to keep her voice civil so her coworkers wouldn't notice.

"Oh, I can't do that, honey. I could just keep sitting here on your desk, I guess." Bernice's gaze swept across the cubicles. "I could even perch myself up on that partition between you and your friend, Mia. That way, I can hear her, too. Just like a fly on the wall." Bernice chuckled, clearly amused with herself.

"Right." Sarah Jane scrubbed her face with her hand. "I have to go because I have an interview in about five minutes." She pretended to press the end icon on her phone and then slipped it back into her purse. When she looked up, Bernice had moved from her desk to the top of the cubicle wall separating Sarah Jane's and Mia's desks. She gave the spirit guide a death glare.

The phone on her desk rang, and she picked it up. "This is Prentice."

"Yes, ma'am, this is Officer Petty in reception. I have Ellis Ford here to see you. He says he has an appointment. "

"Thank you. I'll be right down." Sarah Jane looked past Bernice to Mia. "He's here."

Mia gave her a nod and rose from her desk. "I'll see you in there."

A few minutes later, Sarah Jane escorted Mr. Ford to Interview Room One. Ellis Ford looked his age at thirty-six. She could see why Haley would be attracted to him, with his thick dark hair and broody good looks. He was well-dressed and well-groomed and, based on his background check and credit report, also rich.

"Thank you so much for coming in today, Mr. Ford." Sarah Jane led him into the interview room. She gestured to the single chair at the table across from Mia, and he took a seat.

"Yeah, of course. I'll do anything I can to help you. I still can't believe someone would hurt Haley. She was a good kid."

"So, what can you tell us about your relationship with Haley?" Mia asked.

Bernice piped up from behind Sarah Jane and began to walk around the interview room. "He was having an affair with her." She scowled at Ellis Ford. Almost as if she blamed him.

Sarah Jane did her best to ignore her and focused on Ford's response.

"We didn't really have much of a relationship. I was really interested in art, and she worked at the auction house I own with Ms. Friedman. Occasionally, we ran into each other."

"He's lying through his teeth." Bernice crossed her arms and glared at him.

"Sure. So it was purely professional."

"Yes. Just occasionally ran into each other."

"Right. You said that," Sarah Jane said. "We believe

somebody was stalking her before she was abducted. Had she ever mentioned that to you?"

"No." He didn't look at Sarah Jane when he answered. Instead, he stared down at his hands, resting on the table. "She never mentioned anything like that to me. That's really the first I've heard of it."

"Oh, my stars. This man needs a sign across his chest that says, 'Liar.'" Bernice paced back and forth.

Sarah Jane gritted her teeth and tried to keep her composure. "So, you can't think of anybody who would want to hurt Haley? Maybe one of her other coworkers?" Sarah Jane asked. "Maybe a patron of Harold House who'd taken a specific interest in her? Something like that."

"Nope." Ford opened up his hands and shrugged to show his lack of knowledge. "But again, we didn't spend a lot of time together, so, you know..."

Sarah Jane nodded her head as if she understood. "Right. Of course. Could you tell us where you were on Saturday night around eleven thirty?"

"Yeah, sure. My wife and I are divorced, and it was my weekend with the kids. I took my sons for burgers, and then we went to a movie. Later, we played video games till we went to bed, around eleven, I think," he said.

"Okay, can you tell me what restaurant you went to?" Mia asked.

"I can do better than that. I can show you the

receipts." He dug his wallet out of the inner pocket of his blazer and produced a receipt for a burger joint called Happy Time Burgers. It had a San Francisco address. Along with it he showed them three stubs to the Galleria movie theater. Sarah Jane studied the time-stamps. It all checked out. Not that she expected anything different. But she had hoped he might come clean about his relationship with Haley to at least help them fill out their timeline.

Sarah Jane smiled and handed the receipts back to him. "Thank you. We appreciate you coming in to talk to us."

"Of course. If there's anything else I can do," he said.

"You could be honest for one." Bernice put her hands on her generous hips. "This man was having a relationship with Haley."

"Thanks." Sarah Jane pulled a card from her pocket and slid it across the table. "If you think of anything, please don't hesitate to call me or my partner. Sometimes the smallest detail helps."

"Absolutely." He took the card and tucked it into his wallet along with his receipts. "If there isn't anything else, I really need to get back to the city."

"Of course. I'll have an officer walk you down."

"Thanks."

"I'll take him," Mia said. "I need to stretch my legs a minute and get some water."

"Sure," Sarah Jane said. She waited until they were

out of sight, then put her back to the camera in the corner. "I cannot believe you. I don't need your running diatribe of his failings. He obviously didn't kill Haley."

"Of course, he didn't," Jessica said.

Sarah Jane turned to Mia's empty chair, only it wasn't empty anymore. Jessica sat in it with her feet propped up on the table. She wore a pair of black motorcycle boots, black jeans, and her usual snarky T-shirt, with the iconic Uncle Sam graphic pointing his finger, only instead of saying *I want you*, it read, *I want you to piss off*. "But you already knew that. Interviewing that guy was a waste of time."

"I know he didn't kill her, but he could've brought us a lead. Especially if Haley had told him she was being followed. And since you're not very forthcoming..." Sarah Jane threw her arms in the air. "I'll take any lead I can get at this point."

Jessica folded her arms across her chest and directed her attention to Bernice. "So, I see you introduced yourself. Is that normal for a spirit guide? Aren't you supposed to just be a little voice in someone's head?"

"Honey, maybe you should find a light and walk into it." Bernice folded her arms across her ample bosom and tapped the toe of her red shoes.

"I'm not going anywhere, you overdressed, unwanted do-gooder."

"I have a job to do, and you're just going to get in the

way." Bernice narrowed her eyes. "Don't make me call a reaper on you."

"Reapers haven't been able to catch me so far. And just like you, I have a job to do too."

"All right, that's enough." Sarah Jane held up her hands. "Nobody's calling a reaper. Jessica. Do you have anything new for me?"

"Not at the moment, no. I just came to see how your hellscape was unfolding. I see it's exactly as I thought it would be."

"How exactly do you two know each other?" Sarah Jane's gaze shifted from Jessica to Bernice.

"Everything okay in here, Sarah Jane?"

The sound of the lieutenant's cautious voice made Sarah Jane close her eyes. When she opened them, Bernice and Jessica were gone.

Sarah Jane took a deep breath and turned around. "Everything's fine. Sometimes I just walk myself through an interview before I do it. You know. To practice." She forced a smile.

Mendoza nodded, but Sarah Jane could see it in her eyes. Her lieutenant thought she'd lost her mind. "Right. Rodriguez just brought up the victim's roommate. You better get some Kleenex. She looks like she cried the whole way here."

"Sure. Thanks."

"No problem." The sound of rustling drifted through her senses. The spirits were back. Once Lieutenant

Mendoza was out of earshot, Sarah Jane rounded on them. "If you're going to stay, you both need to keep your mouths shut when I am interviewing someone. I don't need your bickering. It breaks my concentration. This is a very serious investigation. Do you understand me?"

"Are you going to put her in time-out too?" Jessica rolled her eyes.

Sarah blew out a breath through her teeth. "Just get out of here for now. Please."

"Fine, whatever," Jessica said and disappeared.

"What about you?" Sarah Jane directed her attention to Bernice.

"I promise I will be quiet as a mouse." Bernice made a motion across her lips, then turned the lock and pretended to throw away the key.

Sarah Jane had no idea how to get rid of a spirit guide. The rules for Bernice seemed different from those for the spirits of dead humans. She didn't understand exactly how it all worked, and she doubted Bernice would explain it. Bernice was a celestial being, they tended to be very secretive and a bit on the mysterious side. She would ask her grandmother about it when they all got together tomorrow night.

Sarah Jane opened the interview room door and stood outside waiting for Rodriguez. A few minutes later, he rounded the corner from the elevators with a petite young woman with a pointy, mouselike face and unruly, shoulder-length curly hair. A look of terror filled her red eyes, and she wiped her nose with her sleeve, sniffling.

"Here we go, Erin." Rodriguez directed her into the room. "This is Detective Prentice. She'll take care of you from here on out. Is there anything I can get you? Soda, water?"

"No, thank you."

"Thanks, Rob. Why don't we go in here and chat for a little bit." Sarah Jane gave Rodriguez a nod.

Erin nodded and folded her arms across her chest. Sarah Jane gestured to the same chair that Ellis Ford had sat in barely an hour ago.

"I just can't believe it," Erin said. "This is so surreal. I've never known anyone my age who died before."

"I can imagine it's very hard. And I'm so sorry for your loss. Were you and Haley close? "

"She was my best friend at school. Haley and I..." Erin paused to blow her nose on a well-used shard of tissue. "We clicked. Then we just decided that we should room together forever. Sometimes it's a crapshoot with roommates. One summer semester, I stayed in the dorms. The girl they stuck me with cried every night, she was so homesick." Erin fidgeted with her hands. "Summer school's only six weeks long. I have no idea how she would handle a full semester away from home. Haley was the best roommate ever." Erin's face crumpled, and she began to cry again.

Sarah Jane reached across the table and touched the girl's arm to comfort her. "I'm so sorry. I'm just going to step out for a second and get some tissues for you, okay? Are you going to be all right?"

"Yeah, I'll be okay." Erin sniffled.

Sarah Jane gave her arm a squeeze and rushed down the hall to the squad room to grab a box of Kleenex, as well as Mia.

When she returned, she put the box of tissues in front of Erin, and the young woman pulled out three or four and blew her nose. "Thank you," Erin croaked.

"I know this is really difficult, but is there anyone you can think of who was bothering Haley or perhaps had been following her around? Did she mention anybody new that she was seeing?"

"She did just break up with Ellis. He was getting really clingy. I mean, Haley and I are both going to graduate in May." She paused. "I mean were." The tears flowed again hard and fast. "I really can't believe she's gone."

"I know. It's so hard."

"It is. And now I need to plan a vigil. This is just so wrong. Who would do this?"

"That's what we're trying to figure out. Did she mention anyone else besides Ellis?"

Erin pulled two more tissues from the box and wiped her eyes. "There was this one guy she worked with. He kept hitting on her. But she was very serious about her studies and didn't really have any interest in him. Most of the boys at school are... You know, immature." She shrugged. "I think that's why she liked Ellis. I mean, he was actually old enough to be her dad, but that never really bothered her. He was cultured and educated. She liked that a lot."

"But he was married," Bernice chimed in. Sarah Jane folded her hands together and gripped them tightly. It took everything she had not to turn around and scold the spirit guide. "No matter what he said, he wasn't really going to leave his wife."

"Did she tell you the guy's name?"

"No. Just that he was an appraiser. She wanted to be an appraiser too. He said he'd mentor her, but you know how that goes."

"Sure," Sarah Jane said. "What about school? Did she have any guys that took a particular interest in her? Maybe someone she rejected?"

"No. She would've told me if it was somebody at school."

"Okay. We appreciate you coming down. I just want to let you know we're in the process of getting a warrant for Haley's things in your dorm room."

"You're not going to take my stuff, are you? I've got an exam next week." Erin straightened in her chair, alarm on her face.

"Nope. The scope of the warrant is just for her things."

"Oh, good."

"If you don't mind waiting, we should have the warrant soon. Then we'll take you back to school, and you can show us which side is Haley's."

"Sure. I can do that." Erin nodded. "Anything if it'll help you find the guy."

"Thank you, Erin."

CHAPTER 17

He kept watching the news, looking for any bit of information about his work. The video he'd posted on YouTube had been taken down, but surely one of the news agencies should've picked it up and started grilling the police about it by now. A vlogger had sent him a DM, but he'd ignored it. The guy probably couldn't get a real job in the field. What would it take for him to finally get a little recognition?

"Why would anybody give you any recognition?"

His mother's screechy voice grated across his nerves.

"You can't get anything right."

He clicked off the television and stared at her chair, where she used to sit and watch hours of television. Then, after her arthritis became so bad, she couldn't work anymore.

She rocked back and forth. "Please turn the television back on. I get so bored when you're gone. And those girls...all their weeping and knocking." She pressed a ghostly finger to her temple. "It gives me a headache."

"A headache?" He gave her a skeptical look, and his lips curved with disdain. "I somehow doubt that. Since you're dead and all."

"That's how you talk to me?" She practically shrieked at him. "I should've given you up for adoption when I had the chance."

"Just shut up, Mother," he said. "You're the one giving me the headache." The chair rocked harder, and he could see her ghostly form, shadowy, almost see-through. Even in death, he couldn't get rid of her. He reached for the bundle of sage he kept on the end table between the chairs, along with a box of matches and one of her old ashtrays.

"No! Don't make me go away," she protested. "I only criticize you because I love you. It's constructive."

"There's nothing constructive about what you're saying, Mother." He laid the sage across the ashtray.

"You have to be careful with these girls you take. You're too conspicuous. You should be going after girls nobody's going to miss."

"Those kinds of girls are not goddess material, and you know it."

"Oh, honey, anybody can be goddess material once they're dead. What did I always teach you?"

He rolled his eyes begrudgingly. "Everything is intention."

"Exactly. If you want her to be a goddess after she's dead, then she'll be a goddess after she's dead. You just have to do the right ritual. Go get my book."

"I don't have time right now. I need to get ready for work so I can prepare for the next piece."

"Who're you going to choose?" she asked.

"I don't know yet. I don't have a clear vision of her just yet. It could take months to find the right girl."

His mother nodded. "Of course." She sat thinking for a moment. "You know, if you really want to be noticed, you should write the police a letter. Let them know how smart you are. How powerful. I bet they've never had to deal with an artist like you."

"That's insane. Then they would definitely catch me."

"How would they do that, sweetheart?" His mother shrugged. "You wear gloves when you write the note. You seal it with water, not your saliva. I've seen it done a hundred times on those shows I liked to watch."

"How many of those shows did the guy get caught?"

She continued, ignoring his last question. "None of them were a powerful witch like you. With the right spells, they'll never catch you. Not even if they called in the Defenders of Light."

"Geez, Mother," he scoffed. "Don't even put that energy out into the universe. The last thing I need is some nosy magical investigator poking around. The police might be buffoons, but the DOL aren't."

"You're right. I'm sorry. I should've thought twice about the energy I put out." A smile spread across her pale lips. "Now, before you go get ready for work, please do your old mother a favor and shut those girls up."

He sighed. "They're not that bad."

"I know you don't think so, but all their negative energy gets to me while you're gone. Come on. Please?"

"Fine. Is that all?"

"You can turn the television back on so I can keep up with my shows." She grinned at him, but it came off as more of a creepy leer.

"Fine, just don't turn it up too loud, okay? The last thing I need is a noise complaint." He picked up the remote and turned on the television again. Even though his mother was perfectly capable of turning it on and off as she pleased. He thought she just enjoyed making him work for her like she did when he was a kid.

"Of course, honey. Why would I waste my energy on that?"

"Right. Anything else?" He put his hands on his hips, annoyance crossing his face.

"You could try to get rid of the smell of that dead body you have tucked away somewhere."

"I don't have a dead body tucked away anywhere. And you're dead. You can't even smell anything."

"No, but I remember what dead bodies smell like.

Don't forget I used to do hair for Darby's Funeral Home."

"Yeah, like you'd let me forget," he mumbled.

"What did you say?"

"Nothing. There's no dead body here. It's all in your imagination. Just keep the TV volume on low, okay?" She stared at the television as if she didn't hear him.

"I've got to get ready for work now."

"Uh huh."

She waved him off. Some things never changed, even though she was dead.

CHAPTER 18

"You're here early," said Adam Bates, a coworker from the first shift. Bates pulled his timecard from the rack and gave him a curious eye.

He shrugged Bates off. "I believe in punctuality. There's nothing wrong with that. Are you clocking out early?"

Bates grinned and looked down at his timecard. "Nah, man. I'm just getting prepared. It's a Friday afternoon, and I've got a little money in my pocket. I think I'm going to hit up a dispensary and have a mellow weekend. What about you?"

Typical Bates, he thought. No imagination. "I picked up a couple extra shifts this weekend. I need some overtime cash," he said.

"Yeah, I hear you on that."

"So, anything going on that I should know about?" he asked, facing the locker room.

"Oh, yeah. The cops came by earlier."

"Oh?" He tipped his head, his senses tingling. "What did they want?"

"You didn't hear? They found that missing girl." An excited look filled Bates's eyes. He had taken the exam for the police academy three times and failed every single time. He ate up anything to do with the cops. "They came in here and flashed a warrant. Said they needed to look over the girl's room."

"And you just let them?" he asked, angry heat rising under his collar.

"Well, yeah." Bates gave him a confused look. "The cops. It's a warrant. What was I supposed to do?"

"You were supposed to call the Dean of Students. I'm sure they don't want the police just poking around one of the student's dorm rooms."

"Yeah, well, I called the Dean, and she didn't care. She said to cooperate."

"What? Why would she say that?"

"I don't know. I guess because it didn't happen on campus, she doesn't care. I mean, if she doesn't let the police do their jobs, she's going to look like a dick. It's a no-brainer, really."

"Is somebody over there with them at least? I mean somebody from this office should be there. We're campus security, for Christ's sake."

"Yeah, I'm pretty sure they don't care. You know, to them, we're just rent-a-cops. And honestly, they wouldn't be wrong. It's not like the University employs us directly."

"Sure." He tapped his foot impatiently and stared at the time clock. As soon as it flipped over to 2:00 pm, he stepped in front of his coworker and punched in. "I think I might head over there and just check things out. See how they're doing."

"Yeah, sure." Bates gave him a slight sneer. "You do that. I'm outta here."

"Have a good one."

"Yeah, you too."

As soon as Bates was out the door, he clipped a two-way radio to his belt and made his way to Findlay Hall, where Haley Brooks used to live.

AT THE DORM ROOM, ERIN WASTED NO TIME POINTING out to Sarah Jane and Mia the side of the room that belonged to Haley.

"Do I need to stay for this?"

"No," Sarah Jane said, noting the girl's red-rimmed eyes still brimmed with tears. "It's probably better that you don't. We can't have you interfering."

"Sure. Just, if you don't mind, don't touch my stuff," Erin said.

"No problem. The warrant is only for her side of the room and her things. We'd appreciate it if you would show us her side of the closet before you go."

Erin grabbed her backpack from the back of her desk chair and slung it over her shoulder. "Sure." She stopped to give them a tour of Haley's belongings and then with a long look at her friend's side of the room said wistfully, "I hope you find something that helps you. I've got to hit the library."

"Hey, Erin, before you go." Sarah Jane reached into her pocket and pulled out a card. "If you think of anything, even if it seems trivial, give me a call, okay? Sometimes even tiny details can help us figure out leads."

"Sure." Erin took the card and stared at it for a long minute before she shoved it into the front pocket of her backpack and zipped it up.

Sarah Jane and Mia had brought along two uniformed officers to help them go through Haley's room.

"Okay," she said, addressing the team, "so, the warrant says we can only take what belonged to Haley. Billingsley, you go through her closet. Dunbar, check out her bed. Look for any hidey-holes. Anywhere she might've hidden a journal or something like that."

"Yes, ma'am," Dunbar said.

Mia stood in the doorway. "I'm going to canvas the rest of the hall."

"Sure," said Sarah Jane. "I'll go through her desk."

"Okay. I'll see you in a bit."

Sarah Jane got busy unplugging the laptop, rolling up the power cord, and putting them into a cardboard box with the word, *Evidence* stamped across the side.

After Mia left, an abrupt knock on the door drew Sarah Jane's attention. A security guard, a young man who couldn't have been more than twenty-five, stepped into the room. He glanced around the small room until his gaze settled on Sarah Jane. When he hitched up his belt, the flashlight hanging on his hip waggled a little.

"Can I help you?" Sarah Jane immediately moved toward him to block him from coming too far inside the room.

"I need to talk to the officer in charge."

"I'm the officer in charge," Sarah Jane said.

He looked her up and down, and she was clearly unimpressed by his expression.

"I'm afraid you and your officers have to leave." The confidence in his voice almost made Sarah Jane smirk. Who did this kid think he was?

"On whose authority?" Sarah Jane quirked an eyebrow, unable to contain her amusement.

"Campus Security's authority. Anything that happens on campus is supposed to go through us."

Instead of counting to ten, Sarah Jane blew out a slow breath. When her temper cooled, she said, "Listen, kid. This is a police investigation, and if you don't turn around and march yourself out of here right this minute, I will have one of these officers"—she pointed to Dunbar, the brawny six-foot-one officer closest to her —"arrest you for obstruction. We have a warrant. I've already talked to the Dean of Students, and she's not only aware of our presence, but she's also happy we're here. You have no authority here. Now, what's it going to be? Are you going to leave, or are we going to arrest you? Choice is yours."

His nostrils flared, and his eyes narrowed. "What's your name?"

She knew she had definitely pushed his buttons. From the quiver of his thin lips, he did not like to be told what to do.

"Detective Prentice. This Officer Dunbar and this is Officer Billingsley. Down the hall is Detective Johnson. She's questioning the other residents of this hall."

"Okay." He stared at her as if he were memorizing her face. "Do you have a card or something?"

"Sure." Sarah Jane pulled a card from the cardholder in her jacket pocket and handed it over to him. "Don't go too far."

He studied her card. "Yeah. Why is that?"

"Because we have questions for Campus Security. We need to know if Haley had filed any complaints about being followed or bothered by another student."

He shifted gears faster than Sarah Jane expected. "All

right. Why don't I go back to the office and check through the reports? See what I can find."

"That would be very helpful," Sarah Jane said.

"I do not like him." Bernice's voice drifted through Sarah Jane's brain. From the corner of her eye, she saw the spirit guide materialize next to Haley's desk. "There is something off about him."

"We'll be down shortly to your office. In the meantime, if you find anything, please email me the report. My email's on the card."

"Sure, Detective." He held Sarah Jane's gaze just long enough to creep her out. As he turned, he sneered in the direction of Bernice, and for a second, she wondered if he could see her too. She shook off the thought as soon as he left the room and continued to search through Haley's desk.

"You know what," she said to the room. "I want all of it. Just pack it all up. Her clothes, shoes, bags, everything in the drawers. The shelves."

She waved her hand in front of the three utilitarian shelves hanging on the wall above the desk. "Even her bedsheets. I want it all. We can sort through it at the station."

"What about the posters on the wall?"

"Yep. Pack those up too," Sarah Jane said.

Dunbar carefully peeled the poster for an art show from the wall above the dresser. He stopped and stared at the electrical plug. "Um, Detective. I think you should take a look at this."

"What am I looking at?" Sarah Jane stepped up next to him and looked over the items on top of the dresser. A small jewelry box. A photo frame of Haley with her parents in her graduation gown. A photo frame of a gray and white Shih Tzu with a pink kerchief tight around its neck. Dunbar pointed past all of the stuff and tapped his finger on the two-plug outlet with two USB ports.

"Why don't we go out to the hall for a second?"

Sarah Jane gave him a quizzical look but didn't argue with him. She'd done enough searches with him to trust his instincts. "Sure."

He led the way, and after he closed the door behind them, they stood in the hall.

"I think there's a camera in that outlet cover. I've seen them before," he said. "We should get one of the tech guys from forensics down here to check it out."

"Okay. In your experience, do these types of cameras have sound or just video," she asked.

"They can be either one. It depends on the setup."

"That was a really good catch, Dunbar. Have you thought about taking the detective exam? You're pretty good at this kind of stuff."

Dunbar grinned, setting off the square of his jaw. He shrugged his well-built shoulders. "I don't know, maybe someday. Right now, patrol's a lot of fun. Not quite as heavy. You know what I mean?"

Sarah Jane nodded. "Yeah. I do. If you change your mind and need a recommendation, let me know."

"I will." His grin widened. "Thanks, Detective."

"Now, let's get forensics down here. I need to inform the Dean about what's going on. I want to check some other rooms to see if it's just Haley's room or if there are others."

"Good thinking," Dunbar said.

CHAPTER 19

The Dean of Students had no problem with the police checking all of the electrical outlets within Haley's dorm. The police found four more outlets with a spycam, including another one in Haley's room just below the bottom shelf on her wall. Sarah Jane had moved into the hall to speak to the forensic IT tech, just in case their spy was listening in too.

"Yes, so this is what we're looking at." Justin Koebel, one of the youngest forensic IT techs in the department, turned the laptop in his hands so Sarah Jane could see the screen. His dimpled chin always reminded Sarah Jane of Kirk Douglass, which just made her feel old. His blue eyes shone with determination. "I've hacked into the two cameras, and you can see that the one on the dresser shows only part of the room. But this one..." he tapped on his screen.

On the right, it showed the view from the dresser's camera. And on the left, they saw the view from the desk's camera. "It gives almost a panoramic view of the room, including the victim's bed."

"Ugh. This sort of thing makes me want to bleach my eyes," Sarah Jane said, disgusted. "Any chance this footage is stored somewhere?"

"He could have a listening device, too. We'll sweep the room if you want."

She grinned. "You know I do."

"No problem. I'm going to leave one of them active to see if I can trace the Wi-Fi IP, but he could be bouncing it through servers around the world."

"Okay, whatever you need. I'll get the young woman living here moved into another room to keep her safe. I wonder if he's the same guy that sent the drone to my dump scene. We got the video taken down, but you guys couldn't trace it."

"Yeah, I know, I was the one working that. I'm still working on it, by the way. I'm not giving up."

Koebel's youthful energy and confident attitude reminded her of her son Dalton. She'd worked with Koebel on other cases, and when something stumped him, he grabbed onto it and didn't let go until he'd either solved it or was ordered to stop. That drive was something Sarah Jane admired and needed right now.

"I appreciate that." Sarah Jane let out a heavy sigh.

"Okay. I want every single camera we've found shut down. Can you do that?"

"Absolutely." Koebel nodded.

"Any chance you can find out where the cameras came from?"

"Sure, they have a manufacturer's serial number. We should be able to find out who sells them and how many they've sold. I can't promise that we'll narrow it down to the person that these were sold to unless he registered it."

"Which he probably didn't, considering what he used them for."

Koebel made a face. "True."

"All right. Let me know what you find."

"Will do, Detective."

"So, he's a peeper," Mia said. "That has to mean something."

"You don't want to know what I think it means. It's not very politically correct. And probably also not very helpful," Sarah Jane said. "I feel like there are all these layers to him, and we're barely starting to peel them all back."

"I know," Mia agreed. "So, I canvassed every floor. And not everybody knows Haley. Those that did, said she was quiet, kept to herself, very serious. And they had no idea if she was being stalked or not."

"Great." Sarah Jane blew out a frustrated breath. If

only her magic worked, she might get a handle on this guy.

"I want to run by security to see if they have any reports from Haley. Forensics is going to take care of the cameras. Then we need to head over to the Brooks's. I told Mrs. Brooks I'd be there by four, and it's already"—Sarah Jane looked at her watch—"three thirty."

"Don't forget the press conference. We've got that at five." Mia reminded.

Sarah Jane growled a little. "Shoot. I forgot."

"I'll call her and see if we can reschedule for Monday morning," Mia said.

"That would be great. Let's get out of here," Sarah Jane said.

CHAPTER 20

Sarah Jane hated press conferences. Hated all the reporters who'd be staring at her, even though it was unlikely she'd have to answer any questions. Heat crept across the back of her neck and spread to her chest and face as she prepared for the inevitable. Just her luck, she'd get hit by a hot flash when the cameras started rolling. She just hoped she didn't look like a sunburned lobster on the eleven o'clock news.

Times up, she said to herself as she and Mia followed Lieutenant Mendoza out to the front of the building and joined Captain Washington and the deputy chief behind a podium. The reporters stood with their microphones and recording devices ready to go. A captain with Fremont Police Department patches stood next to the deputy chief, along with a tall, silver fox of a man wearing a dark suit that screamed Fed to her. When she took her place next to him, he turned his head, looked her up and down with his almost black eyes, and gave her a nod. She returned the gesture but didn't smile. Instead, she shivered a little, unsure why. No spirits around, at least none she could see.

She focused on the reporters again. She'd given Mendoza all the pertinent information so she could pass it to the deputy chief. Was her suspect watching? Probably. She got the feeling he liked to watch.

"Hey!" Bernice's voice rang out across the crowd. Sarah Jane saw the spirit guide standing in front, dead center. A prime spot the journalists tried to score. Why the reporters left enough space for her puzzled Sarah Jane, but she suspected Bernice had somehow used her spirit guide powers to arrange it. The reporter to Bernice's right loosened his tie, and his face turned red as if he were hot. He kept looking around as if to find a source of the heat. The temperature had gotten up to 75 degrees around 3:00 pm today so it was still warm despite a large tree shading them.

The furnace is standing right next to you.

Bernice waved at her, and Sarah Jane rolled her eyes.

The deputy chief of police and Captain Washington moved closer to the podium, Sarah Jane following behind. Her heart thudded in her throat, and her stomach flip-flopped. Sweat trickled down her back as she stared out into the crowd of press set to grill them about the murder.

Bernice grinned, gave her a thumbs up, and mouthed, “You’re going to do great!” Sarah Jane tried to look anywhere but at Bernice. She was going to banish the spirit tonight no matter what happened.

The deputy chief stepped up to the microphone and put her notes down on the podium.

“Good afternoon, everyone.” The deputy chief put on a smart-looking pair of tortoise shell reading glasses.

“First, I’d like to offer condolences to the family of Haley Brooks. We want you to know we have our finest detectives on this case. And because we’ve uncovered another possible victim, we’re creating a joint task force with the Fremont police.”

As the deputy chief spoke, and then the captain, Sarah Jane’s blouse soaked through with sweat. She felt as if hot coals had been dumped into her chest and legs, burning her from the inside out. She tasted salt on her upper lip and swiped at her brow.

The Fed next to her leaned toward her slightly and whispered, “Are you all right?”

“Fine. Thanks. Just hot.” She turned her attention back to the podium.

“We’re also lucky enough to have the FBI consulting with us as well as an agent trained in the behavioral sciences unit. We are working to resolve this as soon as possible, to keep the good citizens of San Jose safe. I’m going to hand it over to the detective in charge to answer your questions. Detective Prentice?"

The deputy chief held out a hand and gestured for Sarah Jane to come forward. The lieutenant and the captain both looked a little blindsided for a split second but recovered quickly.

"You've got this," the Fed whispered as she walked past him. Who the hell was this guy?

Sarah Jane cleared her throat. She couldn't even think about how the sweat covering her body would look on camera. If she did, she might have taken off running and never come back.

"As the deputy chief said, we're doing our best to find the person responsible for these two murders. If anyone saw anything or has any information about Haley Brooks or Ashlyn Gehring, please don't hesitate to call the tip line. Even the smallest details sometimes help."

A strawberry blond reporter pushed to the front row next to Bernice and blurted, "Is this case relate to the Jessica King murder?" Bernice shot the woman a dirty look.

"At the moment, we're exploring all possibilities and that's as much as I can comment on the details."

Cold air spread across Sarah Jane's shoulders and back. From the corner of one eye, she caught the color red and gazed out on the crowd again. Bernice had disappeared.

"I'm right here. I can be cold if needed." Bernice's

voice echoed through Sarah Jane's head. Then she giggled, clearly amused with herself. The spirit guide radiated cool air all around Sarah Jane, and after a minute or so, the hot flash subsided.

Another reporter asked, "Is the FBI going to take the lead on this case?" Captain Washington gave Sarah Jane a dismissive smile, and she moved back to her place in line.

"No, they're not. They're here as consultants," the captain answered.

Bernice returned to the crowd and milled about, making the reporters visibly uncomfortable with her ability to change the ambient temperature around them. Sarah Jane tried to keep her amusement from reaching her lips. The last thing she wanted to do was smile at a press conference like this one.

"You look better," the Fed whispered.

"Um. Thanks?" Sarah Jane replied in a whisper.

"I'm Kit, by the way. Kit Spencer. The FBI consultant your captain is talking about."

"Sarah Jane Prentice."

"Nice to meet you."

"Sure. Same. We should probably shut up now. There's a reporter watching us."

Kit Spencer nodded and went back to staring at the crowd. Sarah Jane noticed Bernice gazing at her with a strange smile on her face. She gave Sarah Jane a brief wave then disappeared.

Maybe she had been hasty about getting rid of Bernice. Maybe the spirit could be helpful. Wasn't that the whole point of spirit guides? Weren't they the helpers of the universe? At this point, Sarah Jane had to admit, she really could use some help, especially if the body count on this case kept racking up.

CHAPTER 21

Sarah Jane stretched out on the old lounge chair on her back deck to catch the late Saturday afternoon sun. Sometimes she and Dan used to come out in the evenings to sit in their tiny desert-style garden and watch the moon rise. There was too much light pollution to see the stars, but they could always see the moon. And on the rare occasions when they were apart, as corny as it sounded, Sarah Jane knew that they were connected by the moon. He could be standing on a hotel balcony somewhere or in a restaurant parking lot, and they both would be under that same moon. It had brought her comfort. Now, she didn't even bother to keep up with the moon cycles, even though she knew it affected her energy.

The whole family would arrive soon, and she would have to formally apologize to everybody, including her children. Sorry was not her strong suit. She could say "I love you" all day long. But saying "I'm sorry" had always come hard to her.

"You should just say it," Bernice said, suddenly appearing in the empty lounge chair next to her.

"It's not quite that simple with my family," Sarah Jane insisted.

"Well, of course, it is," Bernice answered back just as firmly. "Your family loves you. And they support you, which is even more important than love sometimes. I've seen people do some awful things in the name of love. But it takes a lot for a person to support you. Especially when they're mad."

"Ugh," Jessica said. "Don't tell me you're falling for this pseudo wisdom crap."

The spirit took a seat in one of the nearby wicker chairs and propped her feet up on the ceramic garden seat Sarah Jane used as a coffee table. Jessica had changed her motorcycle boots to black Chuck Taylors. She wore her black jeans and a black Nirvana T-shirt with a gray and white flannel shirt. Sarah Jane had no idea why a spirit needed a flannel shirt; it wasn't as if she could get cold.

Bernice's wardrobe, on the other hand, never wavered from her tailored red suit and matching accessories, which she wore like a boss.

"All right, Jessica," Sarah Jane said, the stress of the

day showing in her thin voice. “I'm really not in the mood for your crap today.”

“No, no, it's all right,” Bernice said. “It’s that negativity that keeps her here, you know.”

“Whatever.” Jessica leaned her head back against the chair and looked up at the brilliant blue sky. She closed her eyes. The warm sun shone down on her, making her shimmer a little. “I do miss sitting in the sun. I wish I could feel it.”

“You could feel the light of a thousand suns if you’d just change your attitude,” Bernice said.

“Yeah, are you going to tell us about the afterlife now?” Sarah Jane only half joked. Some part of her wanted to ask if Bernice had ever seen Dan. If he was okay.

The back door opened, and Jessica disappeared quickly. “Hey, mom,” Selena said. “I thought I'd come by a little early. See how you're doing.”

“I appreciate that, sweetie. You still mad at me?”

“No. I was never mad at you. Are you still mad at me?”

“No. I'm not, and I'm sorry I was mean to you guys the other night.”

Selena shrugged. “You're just frustrated. It's totally understandable. We’re worried about you, though.”

“I know you are, love.” Sarah Jane looked directly at Bernice. “You need to move.”

“I beg your pardon?” Bernice looked offended.

"My daughter needs to sit down, and I really don't want her sitting on you."

"Mom, who are you talking to?" Selena asked, alarm showing in her dark eyes.

"Just a spirit guide that has decided to make me her project," Sarah Jane said.

"I did not decide to make you my project. The universe did that."

"I seriously doubt I'm on the universe's radar," Sarah Jane quipped.

Bernice made an indignant noise and disappeared.

"Okay. The coast is clear. You can sit."

Selena sat down on the lounger with her legs over the side facing Sarah Jane. "So...how long have you had this spirit guide?"

Sarah Jane leaned her head back against the lounger. "At least since Tuesday morning. That's the first time I saw her."

"What's it like? Having a spirit guide? Is she all-seeing, all knowing?"

"Not at all. Or at least, not so far." Sarah Jane grinned. "So...I have a question for you."

"Shoot." Selena leaned forward with her elbows on her knees.

"Did you know a girl named Haley Brooks?"

"She's the girl that went missing, right?" Selena fidgeted with one of the many silver rings she wore.

"So, you knew about her?"

"Sure, everybody on campus knew about her. There are posters up everywhere," Selena said.

"Why didn't you say something to me?" Sarah Jane looked her daughter squarely in the eyes.

"Because I knew what you'd say. You wouldn't make me come home, but you'd make me feel like shit for not coming so..."

Sarah Jane couldn't argue with that. It probably wasn't the healthiest thing to use guilt like a weapon, but sometimes when she felt helpless she fell into old habits, especially with her adult children.

"You're probably right. I probably would have. But only because—"

"Don't say it's because you love me because that's bullshit. You can love me and not make me feel guilty," Selena said.

"You're right about that, too. How did you get so smart?"

"I don't know." Selena grinned.

"Hey," a familiar voice said. Her younger sister Rainey stepped out onto the deck. "I saw you on the news last night. You looked like you were about to have a heatstroke. Are you okay?"

"I'm fine. I just had a case of the nerves and a hot flash." Sarah Jane sat up and curled her legs beneath her. "Come sit down." She patted the empty end of the lounge chair.

Rainey took a seat and folded her legs in a half-lotus

position. Her straight brown hair hung in a long braid over one shoulder. Her perpetual tan from being in the sun almost all the time set off her green eyes, making them glow against her skin. She was shorter than Sarah Jane and a little on the stocky side, but she was all muscle, mainly from running an animal sanctuary for farm animals. She worked from sunup to sundown most days. And she took care of their grandmother.

"What's up?" Rainey asked.

"I'm trying not to make my children feel guilty anymore, but I worry about them a lot," Sarah Jane began. "Especially since I know there's a bad entity out there right now."

"What sort of bad entity?" Rainey and Selena echoed each other.

"I don't want to give away too many details of the case, but I believe we have a witch doing unspeakable things. And I need a way of protecting Selena especially."

"Why me?" Selena asked, concern on her round face.

"Because as much as I hate to admit it, you're his type. Petite, dark hair, dark eyes." Sarah Jane's heart sped up at the thought of something happening to her daughter.

"Have you cast protection over her?" Rainey asked.

"Of course. But that doesn't mean he couldn't still kill her. Or harm her in other ways that are just too horrible to mention."

"Okay, then Selena needs to learn some fight magic."

Selena sat up straight, her attention fully on her aunt. "What's fight magic?"

Rainey looked to her sister as if for permission. Sarah Jane gave her a nod. "Tell her."

"Fight magic is one way a witch can use her energy to control the world around her. Most of the time, we do it with intention and time. You say a spell, for example, light a candle, and you wait for things to happen because you put the intention out into the universe."

Selena nodded her understanding as her aunt explained the spell casting.

"Fight magic uses your physical energy to spell and protect yourself. Especially from another magical entity. Like another witch or a vampire or a demon."

"Although that one is harder," Sarah Jane interjected.

Selena looked from her aunt to her mother and back again. "Are you freaking kidding me? Can you show me?"

"Sure," Rainey said. A grin spread across her lips, and she gave her sister a side-eyed glance. "I'm game if Sarah Jane's game."

"Okay," Sarah Jane said, leaning forward on the lounger. "But you have to go easier on me. These old bones are not used to being thrown around."

"Oh, my goddess, Sarah Jane." Rainey shook her head and looked at her sister with mock scorn. "You're forty-nine, not ninety-nine."

Selena ignored the sisterly ribbing. "How did you learn this fight magic?"

Sarah Jane shrugged. "Gran taught us."

"Gigi? You're kidding me. She's like ninety-two." Selena scoffed.

"Listen, sweet girl. You do not want to mess with Gigi. She may be an old lady, but trust me. She could knock a three-hundred-pound man on his ass with a wave of her hand." Rainey smirked and got to her feet. She held her hand out for Sarah Jane, helping her up.

The two of them walked the three steps down to the yard. Sarah Jane glanced around at the pavers and tiny rocks, the cactus and succulents Dan had so carefully planted.

"This probably isn't the best place to do this," Sarah Jane said.

"Don't worry," Rainy said, taunting. "I'll make sure you have a soft landing."

"Hardy harr harr," Sarah Jane joked with a mocking face. "I'm not worried about me. It's you I'm worried about. I really don't want you to land in the prickly pear."

"Oh, I know how to protect myself just fine, big sister." Rainey squatted into an athletic position and held her hands in front of her chest several inches apart with her fingers splayed. As she moved her hands in a twisting motion, a golden orb of light appeared between them. When she pulled her hands apart the orb glowed brighter and grew larger. Her sister threw the orb into the air and caught it, drawing her hands close together again, making it smaller.

"Show off," Sarah Jane teased. Sarah Jane followed her younger sister's lead and faced her sister. She mimicked Rainey's hand gestures and held her palms facing each other, chest high, her fingers splayed almost like a claw, and she twisted her hands as if she were encircling a ball. A moment later, sparks shot out between her hands, and a golden orb formed.

Her heart pumped harder. Maybe she'd been worrying for nothing. Maybe there was nothing wrong with her magic at all. Maybe she had just been in a slump and was now past it. Her fingers began to burn with little pinpricks that reminded her of when she had been a child and held onto a sparkler. The orb glowed brighter, hotter.

"No. Wait!" she said. She pulled her hands apart, trying to stop the glowing ball of energy in her hand from exploding. Instead, it shot backward, hitting her squarely in the stomach. She flew backward. For a second, all she could think about was the stupid cactus and how she was probably going to end up in the ER getting needles plucked out of her ass this afternoon. She could just hear Rodriguez's voice full of glee, asking, "Why can't you sit down, Sarah Jane?"

She squeezed her eyes shut and braced for the pain, but it never came.

A moment later, she gently landed on the pavers in front of the cactus beds.

"Oh, my God, Sarah Jane. I'm so sorry." Rainey looked stricken as she rushed to Sarah Jane's side. "I totally forgot about your magic not working. I should never have taunted you. I know how you can't resist."

"Mom, are you all right?" Selena darted across the small yard, and she and Rainey helped Sarah Jane to her feet.

"Yeah, I'm fine. I'm just an idiot. You're not the only one who forgot, Rainey. I got caught up in all the trash talk. Thank you for the soft landing."

Selena put her arms around her mother's waist and gave her a hug. Sarah Jane ran her hand down her daughter's long dark hair.

"Anyway, that's sort of what fight magic looks like. Only usually, both people are fighting. It's not something you use unless you're in real trouble. You understand?"

"Sure. It was pretty cool the way you used your energy ball to keep mom from falling into the cactus. It could've been so much worse." Selena held onto her mother, and Sarah Jane didn't protest. Her children rarely hugged her these days.

"Once you understand the principle of calling up that focused energy, you can use it for other things besides fighting," Rainey said.

"Should Aunt Rainey train Dalton and Larkin, too? It's probably a good thing for all of us to know."

"It's an emergency-only type of magic," Rainey said. "I've already taught Dalton some moves. But your mom doesn't want Larkin to learn it yet."

"How come?" Selena asked.

"Because he's sixteen. And at that age, impulse control is pretty poor," Sarah Jane explained. "I trust you'll know when to use it and when not to."

"I promise to be careful and only use it when absolutely necessary. Cross my heart." Selena drew an X over her heart. She cocked her head, a pensive expression on her face. "Have you ever had to use it at work, Mom?"

Sarah Jane hugged her daughter tighter and kissed her temple. "No. Never. And hopefully, I never will."

CHAPTER 22

Susanna set up her massage table in the middle of the family room. Sarah Jane hopped up and dangled her legs over the edge. At Susanna's suggestion, she'd changed into a loose T-shirt and a pair of lounge pants while Gran and Amy finished up the dishes. They'd shared a casual dinner of sandwiches, salad, and chips but decided to wait to cut into Gran's apple pies until after Sarah Jane's healing ritual.

"All that healing will take it out of you, honey," Gran had explained. "I know you're on this no-sugar kick, but trust me, my pie'll help you recover faster."

In her head, Sarah Jane let herself think of it as a reward for doing hard things. She folded her fingers together and rolled her shoulders to loosen them up.

Susanna's gentle touch pressed against her back.

"There's nothing to be nervous about. It's just going to be exploratory at first."

"I know." Sarah Jane nodded. "It just kind of reminds me of Dan's first exam after they told him he had cancer. Has that same feel to it."

Susanna circled her fingers between Sarah Jane's shoulder blades. A sense of calm spread through her chest, and she wondered if her sister had cast a serenity spell on her.

"There's absolutely nothing to worry about," Susanna whispered. "You don't have cancer; you have a magical blockage. Or at least I suspect you do."

"You think this is going to hurt?" Sarah Jane asked.

"Physically? Probably not," Susanna said.

Sarah Jane bit her bottom lip to keep from asking her next question. How badly was it going to hurt emotionally? She suspected there would be tears at the very least, but when she tried to imagine how the ritual would go, she saw it shrouded in shadows.

Selena joined her mother, leaning against the edge of the massage table. Her shoulder pressed against her mom's. Sarah Jane felt a jolt of surprise when Dalton flanked her on the other side.

"You'll be fine, and you'll get your magic back," he said. "Nothing to worry about."

Dalton's version of a pep talk. She'd overheard him use the same tone occasionally with his brother Larkin. Of all her children, Dalton was probably the most like her. Straightforward and no sugar coating of anything. Ever. But it also meant he could be more secretive and hold his cards close to his chest.

"I appreciate you coming today. Both of you. I know you're busy with your own lives now."

"Of course, we'd come." Selena laid her head on her mother's shoulder. "That's what family's for, isn't it? Being there when they need you."

"Wow. You really listen to me." Sarah Jane slipped her arm around Selena's shoulders.

"Kind of hard not to. You tend to go on and on and on"—Dalton exaggerated his voice—"about stuff like that."

Sarah Jane nudged him and chuckled. "Okay, I get it."

Sarah Jane could see over the counter as Amy closed the dishwasher and turned it on, and Gran folded the dish towel and slid it over the handle of the oven door to dry.

"Looks like it's time." Sarah Jane swallowed hard, and her stomach fluttered. Selena and Dalton rose to their feet.

"Okay, sweetie." Susanna lightly tapped her shoulder and helped her lie down on her back on the table. Amy dragged a barstool to the head of the table. Around Sarah Jane, a flurry of handing out black candles ensued. Cass opened the wooden box with two trays of velvet-lined compartments stowed inside.

"These are all freshly charged," Cass said. "I put them out under the full moon just this past week. Where do you want to start, Susanna?"

"First, I need some selenium."

Cass held up the tray of crystals, and Susanna plucked three selenium crystals about two inches long from the box.

"Black tourmaline, of course." Susanna continued to pick up crystals and put them in her palm. "Don't you have a rose quartz heart?"

"That's in my bag. Hang on." Cass dug through the large leather tote bag she took everywhere with her and pulled out a velvet pouch. She untied the drawstring and slid a pale cloudy pink crystal in the shape of a heart into Susanna's hand.

"Perfect," Susanna said. "These may be cold."

"No problem," Sarah Jane said.

Susanna placed a selenium crystal, a black tourmaline crystal, and a clear Herkimer diamond on Sarah Jane's forehead. She placed the same type of crystals along her clavicle, another crystal on her throat, belly button, and on the tops of her feet. She placed the final crystal, the rose quartz, in the center of her sternum.

The sound of a match striking filled Sarah Jane's ears, and the acrid scent of potassium chloride and sulfur stung her nostrils. Her grandmother lit the first candle, the one in Susanna's hands. Susanna touched the flame of her candle to Cass's unburnt wick. And so it went, all the way around the circle of witches surrounding her until every candle burned.

Her Gran took a seat on the barstool at the head of the table. She handed her candle to Susanna and placed her hands gently on Sarah Jane's shoulders without disturbing the crystals.

The elderly woman pulled herself tall and cleared her throat before she spoke as if dispatching any mortal impediments. She closed her eyes for a moment, seeming to slip into a trance, sinking into her trough of wisdom and magic. Centered, she opened her eyes, smiled gently at her granddaughter, and began.

"We come together today united by the craft, so that this child of the universe may be healed and her magic restored."

A warm energy from Gran's fingertips flowed into Sarah Jane's arms and continued even after she took her hands away and retrieved her candle from Susanna.

Susanna handed her candle to Cass and stepped forward next. She held her hands a few inches above Sarah Jane's face. She closed her eyes and took a deep breath, letting it flow naturally from her mouth. Sarah Jane felt a prickling sensation begin beneath the three crystals on her forehead. Susanna progressed down Sarah Jane's body, stopping over each set of crystals until her sister indicated the skin beneath them prickled. Sarah Jane felt the rose quartz over her heart thrumming, sending tiny pulses into her chest.

"I can feel it," Susanna said. She stopped, holding her hands over Sarah Jane's belly. "So much grief. Anger. Even resentment."

"You will never forget him," Bernice said. She saw the spirit guide standing behind her sister, Susanna, and a rush of anger pulsed through her.

What was she doing here? This was a private family ritual. But then Bernice began speaking to her again and drew Sarah Jane's attention.

"He's part of you. But he cannot be the reason you go on. Neither can your children or your work. Life is meant to be lived, Sarah Jane. And you're not living. Not really. You're doing what it takes to get through the day. And it's not enough."

Tears pushed from the corner of Sarah Jane's eyes and streamed down the sides of her face into her ears and hair. Susanna reached the bottom of her feet, and the crystals on her body pulsated with energy almost like a closed-circuit. Sarah Jane squeezed her eyes shut.

Susanna began chanting.

I CALL ON THE ELEMENTS, FIRE, EARTH, WATER, AIR, AND spirit

To restore the flow of Sarah Jane's magic,

from head to heart, from hand to hand and from belly to toe.

Restore her peace, and comfort she receives

from head to heart, from hand to hand, and from belly to toe.

So mote it be, so say we.

A TUGGING SENSATION IN SARAH JANE'S BELLY BUTTON pulled upward and grew stronger with the chant of the spell as the others joined in and repeated the words three times.

"Let it all go, Sarah Jane. Just let it all go."

"I can't," Sarah Jane said. "I can't let him go."

"You're not letting me go." A familiar voice floated through her brain. "You're only letting go of your anger at me. Not your grief. You will always miss me. And I will always love you."

Sarah Jane opened her eyes and glanced around the circle to catch a glimpse of Dan. She expected to see a spirit, like Jessica or Ashlyn. Translucent and shimmering. Instead, she saw Dan's face and a brilliant light glowing around it, radiating so brightly with love, she felt herself recoil from it.

"I'm okay, SJ. And I am always here with you and the kids. Bernice's right. Life is meant to be lived. Please, Sarah Jane. Go live your life. I promise you, we will see each other again. Tell the kids I love them."

Sarah Jane lifted her hand to shield her eyes from the light, and then it disappeared.

Sarah Jane sat up abruptly, and the crystals fell to the

floor.

"Sarah Jane." Susanna touched her arm. "Are you okay? We didn't finish the spell."

"I saw Dan."

Susanna's eyes widened. "Are you sure?"

"Sweetie, I didn't see any spirits," Amy said.

"What do you mean you saw dad?" Dalton asked.

"He just appeared to me. None of you saw him? He was surrounded by a brilliant light as bright as the sun."

"What did he say?" Selena asked.

"He said he was okay, and there was this overwhelming..." Her bottom lip quivered, and she searched for the words to explain. "It was just this overwhelming love. It was so strong I could barely look at it."

Sarah Jane glanced around the crowd looking for Bernice, but there was no sign of her.

"Did he say anything else?" Dalton asked.

"He loved us. And he told me life is meant to be lived."

"He's not wrong," Gran said. "Do you want to try a spell?"

Sarah Jane's shoulders sagged. "Honestly, I don't know that I have the energy to even try. I feel so drained."

"I'm not surprised," Gran said. "Now, aren't you glad we waited to have that apple pie?"

Sarah Jane mustered a weary grin. "Yes, I suppose I am."

CHAPTER 23

Early Monday morning, Sarah Jane and Mia headed to the Brooks's home in the neighborhood of Willow Glen. The pale blue bungalow looked to have been built in the early 1900s. And from all the crown molding, original hardwood floors, and built-ins it appeared the Brooks's took immaculate care of the place.

"Thank you, Mrs. Brooks, for letting us take a look at Haley's room. I hope Mr. Brooks is recovering." Sarah Jane glanced around the small, tidy living room with its mushroom-colored sofa, pale blue occasional chairs, and warm, white-colored walls.

"He's still in the ICU, but hopefully, if all goes well, he'll be moved to the cardiac step-down unit later this week. I don't have a lot of time this morning." Mrs.

Brooks fidgeted with her gold wristwatch. "I need to get to the hospital soon."

"Of course." Sarah Jane nodded. Two abstract paintings hung over the fireplace and drew her eyes with their bold splashes of color and the energy they emanated. Haley's energy.

"These are gorgeous." Sarah Jane pointed to the canvases hanging beyond the couch. She didn't usually like abstract art, but she couldn't stop looking at them. "Did Haley paint them?"

"Yes, she did." Mrs. Brooks cocked her head and gave Sarah Jane a curious look. "How did you know that?"

This question always put Sarah Jane on the spot. *How did you know that, Sarah Jane?* She remembered her mother asking that question after she said, at four years old, that Poppa Prentice was going to get hurt. Two days later, her grandfather slipped and fell on the front steps. He hit his head on the concrete and fractured his skull. It took him almost a week to die. Sarah Jane shook off the memory and smiled.

"It just seems really youthful and fun." Her smile widened, and she could feel Mia looking at her half confused, half *what the hell?*

"Yes, her art was always energetic." Mrs. Brooks shifted her gaze to her daughter's paintings, a look of pride on her face. "She put so much of herself into them."

"Why didn't she study art? She was obviously very good," Sarah Jane asked.

A rueful expression molded Mrs. Brooks's face. "My husband and I were afraid she couldn't make a living as an artist, so we encouraged her to study something else. I guess, in a way, it's our fault she's dead. Maybe if we'd encouraged her dream, she'd have been in a studio, painting, instead of..." Mrs. Brooks's energy shifted, and her regret wafted through the room like a thick fog.

"This isn't your fault. You did the best you could. You wanted a bright future for your daughter. Which is all any parent wants. There's no way you could've known this would happen, and no way you could've stopped it," Sarah Jane said.

Mrs. Brooks covered her mouth with her hand and turned her stricken gaze to Sarah Jane. She sniffled and nodded. "I'm sure you're right. It just doesn't feel that way right now."

"I know. And I can't promise you anything, but we're committed to finding the person who killed your daughter." Sarah Jane patted Mrs. Brooks on the shoulder, and the words, *Angel's Flight*, whispered through her head.

"Do the paintings have a name?"

"Angel's Flight." Mrs. Brooks gave her a somber smile and sniffled. "She's our angel now."

"Yes, she is," Mia said softly. "Do you mind showing us her bedroom now?"

"No, of course not. It's just this way." Mrs. Brooks

led them past the dining room and a modern, remodeled kitchen to a short hallway.

"I closed it up just like you asked." Mrs. Brooks stopped in front of a paneled door on the right side of the hall. Sarah Jane could see the bathroom at the end of the hall and another bedroom door that was ajar.

Sarah Jane's stomach dropped when Mrs. Brooks opened the door. Bernice stood inside, leaning over a dresser with a mirror, looking over photographs stuck into the frame. Bernice turned and grinned.

"Hi! Y'all sure did take your time." Bernice put her hands on her hips.

Sarah Jane ignored her. "Thank you."

"I'll be downstairs if you need me." Mrs. Brooks nodded and left them to pick through her daughter's things.

"I've got the closet," Mia said.

"Okay." Sarah Jane scratched her head. "Um, if you hear me talking to somebody, just ignore it, okay?"

Mia flashed her a frightened look. "Is it a spirit thing?" Her eyes darted around. She circled her hand around as if to prompt Sarah Jane and lowered her voice. "Is there a spirit here?"

"Yeah, but don't worry. It's not like she's going to show herself or anything. I've got this under control. You go ahead and check out the closet."

Bernice smoothed the front of her red suit jacket with obvious pride, then grinned at Sarah Jane as if expecting her to compliment her on her taste in clothes. Sarah Jane just glared at her, so Bernice said, "You know, I work on a vibrational level. That's how this whole spirit guide thing works. You and Everett are the only cases I've had that could see me."

"Great," Sarah Jane muttered.

"What's great?" Mia asked.

"Nothing. It's all good."

Mia disappeared into the walk-in closet, and Sarah Jane donned a pair of gloves, then dropped a couple of plastic evidence bags she'd brought with her on the top of the dresser.

"She sure was a pretty girl," Bernice said.

Sarah Jane pretended not to hear the spirit but couldn't disagree. She leaned in closer to get a better look at the photos lining the mirror. "And she had a lot of friends." Bernice gazed over Sarah Jane's shoulder at Haley's image. "You know what?"

Sarah Jane scowled in Bernice's direction. "I have no idea, but I'm sure you're going to tell me." She opened the top drawer and began to dig through it.

"Here's the lying liar." Bernice pointed to a photo tucked in the mirror's frame behind another photo. The spirit guide's generous, warm energy brushed against Sarah Jane's arm. She glared at the spirit.

"Do you mind? I'm trying to work here."

"Sorry. I'm just trying to help."

Sarah Jane's jaw tightened. "I don't really need your help."

"I think you do. Just take a look." Bernice continued to point at the photo.

Sarah Jane scowled but looked at the photos. She leaned in close. The first was a picture of Haley standing in front of her two paintings, holding a blue ribbon in her hand, beaming. Ellis Ford stood next to her with a certificate. Haley appeared younger in the picture. She plucked the photo from the mirror's frame, and an image of a banner flashed through Sarah Jane's mind. *Santa Clara County High School Art Competition.* Another more recent photo of Haley sent a sharp pang of suspicion through Sarah Jane's chest. Haley sat on Ellis Ford's lap with her arms wrapped around his neck and a drunk smile plastered across her face. Ford had one arm wrapped around Haley's waist and another on her thigh beneath the short skirt she wore. Sarah Jane grabbed the photo and studied it.

"See?" Bernice said. "It's the one you interviewed earlier."

"Yeah, I see that. We know he had a relationship with her, and while it's kind of gross that he obviously met Haley when she was still in high school, he's not the one who murdered her. If you really want to be helpful, you'll tell me the killer's name. You are the spirit guide here."

"I'm your spirit guide, not his. I don't know his

name," Bernice said. "I still don't like that guy," she said, nodding at the photo. "You should take that with you. Maybe he has a thing for young girls."

"That's not my case." Sarah Jane growled. "But I'm taking all the pictures with me."

Sarah Jane removed all the photos from the mirror's frame and dropped them into an evidence bag. She took a pen from inside her jacket pocket and wrote down the date on the bag and the location where she'd collected them.

"Oh my goodness," Bernice said. "That looks more like butt floss than underwear." She pointed to a pair of black thong panties that caught on the dresser's knob when Sarah Jane had searched through the drawer.

"Thanks, but can you keep your commentary to yourself?" Sarah Jane quickly untangled the thong and shoved it back into the drawer.

Bernice glanced around, unruffled. "You know, I bet Haley was the kind of girl who kept a diary."

"Yeah?" Sarah Jane glared at Bernice. "Were you her spirit guide, too?"

"You have a smart mouth," Bernice said.

"You have no idea."

Sarah Jane eyed the nightstand next to Haley's bed. She opened the drawer and found some acne cream, a small sketchbook along with a package of colored pencils, and a sharpener. And the book, *How to Win Friends and Influence People*.

"She must've been shy." Bernice grinned. "People who read that are generally shy or awkward."

"Is that from your vast experience as a spirit guide? There's no diary here." Sarah Jane put the book back. She thumbed through the sketchbook, perusing Haley's studies of mostly ordinary-looking flowers. Nothing like the beautiful abstracts hanging in the living room. It reminded her of her son Larkin. He always had a sketchbook with him to capture ideas and spirits that bothered him.

"Right. If I were a young woman, where would I hide my diary?" Bernice tapped her lips with her finger.

"If she were my kid, she'd probably stick it somewhere no one ever cleaned." Sarah Jane got down on all fours and looked under the bed. A piece of ripped black mesh hung down from the bottom of the box spring. She stretched out on her back and maneuvered herself under the bed for a better look. A black leather notebook shoved into a hole in the fabric caught her attention.

"Bingo." Sarah Jane reached through the slats and retrieved the notebook, then slid out from under the bed.

"I was right!" Bernice beamed.

Sarah Jane propped her back against the bed, ignoring Bernice's self-adulation. Her mother's instinct had led to Haley's secret hidey-hole, but she didn't need to shout it out. Sarah Jane slipped off the elastic around the book and opened it. She flipped to the back of the book and read through the last entry from just a month ago.

A warm sensation pressed against her arm. Sarah Jane turned her head and found Bernice sitting next to her, trying to get a look at the diary pages.

"Do you mind? You're giving me hot flashes." Sarah Jane huffed and leaned away from the spirit's hot energy.

"Oh, I'm sorry." Bernice sat up straight. "I forget my energy is a little on the warm side."

"Yeah. You can say that again." Sarah Jane went back to reading.

July 29th

E's wife found out about us. I asked him point blank if he was going to finally leave her like he promised and he wouldn't give me a straight answer. Just kept trying to bullshit me. I told him never to text me or contact me again. He begged me not to end things this way. Said it could damage my position at HH but I told him if he did anything to hurt my career before it's even begun I'd make sure every one of my Insta followers knew his name and face. He backed off but I'm still not sure I trust him to leave me alone. How could I have ever believed him? I feel like the biggest idiot and my heart literally aches. All the time. I think I'm going to tell Angela. It may totally screw up my job, but I can't tell my parents, and none of my friends understand about E. I have to talk to someone. This whole thing is killing me.

"HOW'S IT GOING OUT HERE?" MIA STEPPED OUT OF the closet with a couple of leather bags in her hand.

"Ellis Ford is evidently a lying liar. First off, he's not divorced." Sarah Jane glanced up and held the diary so Mia could see it.

"Told you." Bernice chimed in.

"And Haley's life was not as uncomplicated as we thought." Sarah Jane took another evidence bag and slipped the diary inside. "What are those?"

"Some very expensive purses. What've you got?"

"A diary, an illicit affair, and a photo of Ford with his hand up Haley's skirt."

"Nice." Mia's lips turned down with disapproval. "Is Jessica still here?"

"It's not Jessica. It's a different spirit," Sarah Jane said with a touch of annoyance. "What are the bags?"

"One is Givenchy, and the other is Burberry. They're worth at least a grand each."

Sarah Jane let out a whistle. "Wow. I guess Ellis Ford is really a sugar daddy. We should press him a little harder."

"Have you changed your mind about him being our perp?" Mia asked.

"Nothing's off the table yet. Although Jessica and my

other spirit have flat out said it's not him. But he knows something, and now we have leverage."

"Yes, we do." Mia smiled. "Let's get this stuff bagged up." She pulled her phone from her jacket pocket. "We have a lot more interviews today, and I told Xavier I'd be home at a decent hour tonight."

"Yeah, I hear you. I thought I'd bring home a pizza and spend some time with Larkin tonight if he doesn't have too much homework. Word on the street is he's having a hard time. I want to see if I can get him to talk to me. Then maybe I'll take a bubble bath."

"So you do listen to me." Bernice grinned. "Pizza sounds delicious. I'll see you back at your desk."

Sarah Jane opened her mouth to argue, but Bernice vanished before she could tell her not to bother.

"A bubble bath sounds like heaven to me," Mia said. She packed the purses into evidence bags. "We should get this stuff back to the squad room."

"Agreed," Sarah Jane said.

CHAPTER 24

Lieutenant Mendoza texted Sarah Jane as she rode to the station house, Mia driving and their evidence from Haley's bedroom carefully tagged and bagged. Her stomach dropped when she read the message.

Mendoza: *When you and Johnson get back, come see me.*

Those were never good words.

"What is it?" Mia turned on the blinker and made a left turn.

"Nothing. Lieutenant wants to see us when we get back, that's all."

"She probably wants to introduce us to that FBI guy. He's supposed to arrive this afternoon."

"How do you know?" Sarah Jane shot Mia a look, her friend and colleague checking the light traffic on 280.

"How do you think?" Mia chuckled. "Rodriguez. He

stopped me in the break room this morning before we left for the Brooks's and let me know the guy was probably going to set up in Foley's old cubicle."

Sarah Jane rolled her eyes, then looked out the window. Just her luck to catch the exact same Prius Dan used to drive, passing in the next lane. She forced her attention on the by-the-book jackass who'd come to take over the case. Better a rush of anger at the captain's decision to call in the FBI than her constant well of sadness.

"Why does he even care who's using Foley's old desk?" she said to Mia's profile. In the next moment, she knew she wasn't being fair to the agent. He was just doing his job. But still, the captain's decision rankled.

"I don't think he really does." Mia mused. "I think he just enjoys gossiping. I swear, he's like my grandmother's friends. If they didn't talk about other people, they wouldn't have anything to talk about."

"I sort of met him on Friday at the press conference. He seemed nice enough. Friendlier than most of the feds I've met, I guess."

She'd give him that, but then Sarah Jane's phone chimed again before she could go any deeper about her feelings for the agent whatshisname. Kit. Right. She surprised herself by remembering.

She turned her phone over in her hand and read the text, halfway expecting it to be from the lieutenant. But it was from Erin, Haley's roommate.

Erin: *Hi Detective it's Erin. Haley Brooks's roommate. I just wanted to let you know we're having a vigil for her tonight in front of the old mission on campus. Starts at 7:00 pm. You're welcome to come.*

Sarah Jane looked up through the windshield. "Erin just texted. She said they're having a vigil for Haley tonight. Are you interested?"

"What about your plans with Larkin?"

She grimaced, thinking, then shook her head. "I should probably wait until Friday. It *is* a school night. And he always has a ton of homework."

Mia changed lanes and exited the freeway, then said, "That makes sense. You think you can handle it on your own?"

"Yeah, of course," Sarah Jane said.

"I'll go with you," Jessica said from the back seat.

Sarah Jane clenched her jaw and turned to see the spirit with her foot propped up on the back of Mia's seat. She wore her usual black jeans and a gray T-shirt with the phrase, *Please don't interrupt me while I'm ignoring you.* Sarah Jane shook her head, not in the mood for the spirit's snarky attitude.

"Get your foot off her seat." Sarah Jane scolded. "Have some respect."

"I see what kind of mood you're in today." Jessica cocked her head. But she slipped her foot off the back of Mia's seat and sat up straight.

"Who are you talking to?" Mia gave Sarah Jane a side-eyed glance, her eyes wide and fearful.

"It's just Jessica," Sarah Jane said, casting a look over her shoulder. "Don't worry. And, no, thank you. I can handle the vigil all on my own."

"Fine. But you can't stop me from going." The spirit crossed her arms and shifted her gaze to look out the window at tree-lined streets blurring by as they drove downtown.

Sarah Jane shook her head and turned to face forward. She had no patience this morning to argue with the spirit.

Twenty minutes later, they arrived and parked in the police department's garage. The dread in Sarah Jane's gut twisted tighter and tighter with every step toward their squad room. She wondered if the Lieutenant would dress her down for her performance on camera Friday afternoon. Although, in her defense, she knew it wasn't like she could have stopped the hot flashes from happening, and she always sweated heavily when she was nervous. The two together were a terrible combination. They dropped the evidence bags on her desk and headed to Mendoza's office.

Sarah Jane knocked on the open door. "You wanted to see us?"

Mendoza held her hand up and waved them in. "Yes. How'd the search go?"

"We found a few things that may implicate the

owner of the auction house where Haley worked. He may have been having an affair with her. So, basically, he lied to us."

Mendoza nodded. "You should call him in again. Maybe let our FBI consultant here"—the Lieutenant gestured to one of the chairs in front of her desk, where Special Agent Kit Spencer sat—"take a run at him. That's why I called you in. This is Special Agent Kit Spencer. He'll be helping us get into the mind of our—"

He turned and met Sarah Jane's eyes and gave her a slight smile. "Unsub. Or unknown subject," Spencer interjected. His steady gaze remained on Sarah Jane, and she tried to look anywhere except at him but found herself unable. He seemed to be studying her, so she pretended to cough and folded her arms across her chest. She couldn't deny he was very debonair in a Hollywood sort of way. But his intense dark eyes made her feel as if he could see right through to her soul. The lack of wrinkles on his face didn't match his silver hair, and she wondered how old he really was.

Mendoza nodded. "Unsub."

"Right." Sarah Jane said. "Well, we're set up in a conference room. We'd be happy to show you the files and our murder board."

"That'd be great." His silky voice slid across her senses.

She shook off the strange feeling of attraction. No way was she ready for that. She'd just learned her husband's soul appeared to be okay in the afterlife. And even though he'd told her to live her life, she needed to start with baby steps. Teeny, tiny, baby steps. She broke her stare and gestured to the door. "Right this way."

Mia grabbed the evidence bags off Sarah Jane's desk, and the three of them headed to the conference room.

CHAPTER 25

Sarah Jane stood back while Agent Spencer looked over the murder board. He studied it closely, scratching his clean-shaven chin.

"There's more in the file," Mia said. "We really haven't had a lot of leads so far." She held the file folders in her hand.

"What about this Ford character?" He turned his attention to Sarah Jane. "You mentioned in the lieutenant's office that he lied to you in his first interview."

"Yes, but I don't think he killed her. I do think he might know where she was the night she disappeared. I definitely want to reinterview him. I'll call him this afternoon and see if he can come back in."

"So, who do you think did kill her?" His gaze shifted from Sarah Jane to Mia and back to Sarah Jane. "Let's talk about what we know." Agent Spencer proposed.

Sarah Jane took the lead. "We know Jessica King and Haley have very similar body types. Ashlyn is also about the same size. The big difference is she had blond hair. So he seems to have a type.

"Any chance she dyed her hair?"

"Anything's possible, I suppose. I'm still waiting on the file from Fremont police to learn more information about her."

"If you need me to make a call to grease the wheels, I'm happy to do that," he said.

"It's only been since Friday, so I don't think that's necessary at this point. Those sorts of things just take time. And really, I just need a password so I can pull the files from a cloud server, so... I just need to make a call to the captain in charge of homicide."

"Of course. So let's continue," he said.

"You don't want to look at the files?" Mia asked.

"Of course, I do. But I like to talk things through with the investigation team first."

"Sure. I can understand that," Sarah Jane said.

A knock on the conference room door interrupted Sarah Jane's thoughts. She held her hand up. "Sorry, just a second."

Stuckey entered the room full of frantic energy. The kind he usually got when he made a big discovery. He took the laptop in his hands and plopped it down on the table.

"I found something on the video."

Sarah Jane did a quick introduction. "Agent Spencer, this is Detective David Stuckey. He's our resident expert on all things technical and usually goes through video for us."

"Nice to meet you," Stuckey said and briefly shook the FBI agent's hand. "We work as a team. We all have our specialties."

"Good system," Spencer said. "What do you have on video?"

Stuckey turned the screen so Sarah Jane, Mia, and the agent could see it better. He pressed the Start button, and the video began to play.

"Okay, so this is the parking garage a few blocks from where she works. That little Civic right there is Haley's. You can see the license plate. She's parked close to the elevator, and the door in the upper right-hand corner opens, and she steps out."

Stuckey continued the play-by-play, gesturing with his finger to make sure they followed the action.

"She's on her cell phone. And..."

The grainy back and white video showed a man dressed all in black with a hoodie and a ski mask over his face stepping around the SUV parked next to her. He quickly grabbed her from behind and pressed something over her face. She struggled for just a moment before completely going limp in his arms. He opened the back door of her car and lifted her into the back seat. During the struggle, she dropped her cell phone and her keys, and he scooped them up, got into the driver's seat, and drove away.

"Holy shit," Sarah Jane muttered. "Do we have any more footage of her car? Any traffic cams catch it at any intersections?"

Stuckey did some finagling on his keyboard and pulled up a photo. "We do, but it's not really helpful. He didn't take the ski mask off right away. This was the best one of his eyes. Not that it helps us much."

"I wouldn't say that," Spencer said. "Can you roll it back to where he comes up behind Haley and freeze it?"

"Sure." Stuckey nodded and rewound the video. "Here you go."

"How tall is Haley?" Spencer asked.

"She's five two," Sarah Jane said. "So were Jessica King and Ashlyn Gehring."

"He's not much taller than her, maybe half a foot at the most. Look where his head falls against hers."

Sarah Jane leaned in closer for a better look. "You're right. He has a very slight build. He's probably not any taller than five foot eight."

"See? That's something. We know we're dealing with a smaller guy."

"And he chooses smaller women because they're easier to control," Sarah Jane said.

"Probably," Agent Spencer said.

"It's kinda weird, though," Stuckey said.

"What is?" Mia asked.

“There's this weird kind of foggy shadow on the video anytime he's on screen.” Stuckey pointed to the video screen in the area right behind their unsub.

“Holy shit. That's his mother.” Jessica's voice grated across Sarah Jane's nerves. “Are you telling me we can show up on video?”

Sarah Jane turned to glare at the spirit. Jessica stood with her eyes wide open, full of terror, her mouth ajar, staring at Special Agent Spencer. Jessica made a strange high-pitched noise in the back of her throat and disappeared.

Sarah Jane looked to Agent Spencer, trying to figure out what about him had frightened the spirit. He gave her a serene smile and nodded. She cleared her throat and put her attention on the video again.

“It's probably just poor quality cameras,” Agent Spencer said.

Stuckey ran his hands through his thinning gray hair. He frowned, causing the wrinkles in his cheeks and around his mouth to deepen.

“Yeah, you're probably right. It's just weird it shows up on every camera that caught this guy.”

Sarah Jane patted Stuckey on the shoulder. “It's probably just a glitch. Glitches are a thing, right?” she teased.

“They certainly are.” Stuckey nodded. “Anyway, I thought you'd want to know.”

“I appreciate it,” Sarah Jane said. “Thank you for

going through all that footage. Can you email me the timestamp of when she was kidnapped?"

Stuckey folded the laptop closed. "You got it. I'll let you get back to it."

"Thanks."

CHAPTER 26

The lights in front of the two-hundred-forty-year-old mission on the University of Santa Clara's campus glowed brightly even though the sun wouldn't set for another half hour. A hundred or so students, mostly women, gathered in small groups chatting, waiting for the vigil to begin. Haley's roommate Erin, along with two other girls, handed out white candles with a paper drip-catcher attached.

The temperatures had already dropped into the low sixties, even though the sun hadn't completely disappeared below the horizon. Sarah Jane dressed down for the occasion wearing jeans, running shoes, and a long-sleeved, navy blue T-shirt with the ubiquitous Stanford logo. And, of course, she brought her business cards too, tucking them into the back pocket of the leather cross-over bag she always wore. She even French braided her hair.

Someone came up behind her and tugged gently on her braid. Sarah Jane turned to find her smiling daughter, Selena.

"I didn't expect to see you here," Sarah Jane said, giving her a spontaneous hug. "I thought you had an exam to study for."

"I do. But I wanted to drop by the vigil." Selena's gaze panned across the crowd. "It's not as big of a turnout as I had hoped."

"College crowd. They probably have exams, too, sweetie," Sarah Jane said.

"Sure. You're probably right. You remember my roommate, Aisha?" Selena jerked her thumb at the young woman who stepped up to join them. Aisha gave Sarah Jane a bright smile and a wave of her beringed hand.

"Hi, Mrs. Prentice."

"Hi, Aisha." Sarah Jane had not seen the young woman since the day she first moved Selena into the dorm. "How are things going?"

"Pretty good."

"How are your studies?" Sarah Jane never felt more like a mom than when she was grilling one of her kids' friends. She hadn't spent much time with Selena's new friend and had no idea of her interests.

"Pretty good. I really like my communications teacher. She's halfway convinced me to change majors."

"Well, it's your first year. You don't have to make any rash decisions just yet. Plenty of time for that," Sarah Jane said.

Aisha chuckled. "That's exactly what my dad said. To slow down and just get my core classes done first."

Sarah Jane couldn't help but smile. "Your dad sounds like a wise man."

"Prentice," someone called from the crowd.

Sarah Jane glanced around, trying to find the voice, then she spotted Agent Kit Spencer. She thought about rolling her eyes but instead found her hand in the air, waving at him. What the hell was she doing?

"You're living your life." Bernice stepped up beside her, and Sarah Jane could see her tugging on her red suit jacket from the corner of her eye. "Although I don't know that you should live your life with the likes of him. He's a little more complicated than you need right now."

Sarah Jane pursed her lips. What the hell was that supposed to mean? She glared at the spirit guide. Bernice knew she couldn't talk to her in the middle of a crowd. Especially not with Selena and her roommate standing with her. She tried to ignore the spirit.

"I will say this. He *is* mighty fine looking," Bernice said.

But someone else caught Kit's attention before he joined her. Then Sarah Jane heard her name, and she turned to see Haley's roommate approaching. Sarah Jane breathed a sigh of relief at the interruption and turned away from Bernice.

"Detective." Erin beamed, relieved, Sarah Jane guessed, to see a friendly face. "You came."

"Yes, I did." She stammered for a moment. She didn't like having her family meet witnesses in a case, but she had no choice. "Erin, this is my daughter Selena and her friend Aisha. They go here, too. Selena, this is Erin. She helped plan the vigil for Haley."

The three young women exchanged subdued hellos, and Selena said, "I'm so sorry about your friend. Mom didn't give me much details, but then I heard about the vigil, and Aisha and I wanted to show our support. It's just so awful."

Tears brimmed in Erin's eyes. "Thank you so much for coming. It means so much." She couldn't say more over the grief clogging her throat, so she handed Sarah Jane a candle and then gave one to Selena and Aisha.

She cleared her throat, which helped her regain her composure. "I wasn't sure what we would get. Haley pretty much kept to herself, so not a lot of people knew her. I'm happy this many people came. Anyway, I appreciate you coming, and I'm sure Haley would have too. I've got to finish handing out candles. We'll get started in a few minutes."

Sarah Jane smiled sadly. "Sure thing," she said and

watched Erin move on to the next group to hand out candles.

She scanned the crowd as they waited for the speakers to begin. A few students biking by stopped and joined the little group, unaware it seemed of the vigil, though they accepted Erin's candles and hung around.

Her mind was on many things at the moment—the presence of Kit, the to-do list she'd worked out with Mia, her healing session with her family—when suddenly she spotted the security guard, that obnoxious guy from the day she and the team searched Haley's dorm. He was standing on the sidelines, watching the crowd. Did he expect things to get out of hand?

And then, as if she needed something else to throw her just a little more off-kilter, she heard Agent Spencer arrive behind her. "Hi, Prentice."

Sarah Jane mustered her most professional voice. "Agent Spencer. I saw you earlier but frankly, I wasn't expecting to see you here."

He'd also dressed down for the occasion wearing a pair of khaki slacks, loafers, and a blue button-down beneath an argyle v-neck sweater. He looked ready for golfing, not a vigil at a college campus. "I thought it couldn't hurt to take a look. Sometimes an unsub will show up to an event like this."

"Sure." Sarah Jane's voice rose half an octave. "Agent Spencer, this is my daughter Selena and her roommate Aisha. They attend school here."

"Oh. Um..." A look of surprise molded his handsome features. "It's nice to meet you."

"Nice to meet you too," Selena said. "You work with my mom?"

"For the time being, yes. I'm helping her on a case."

"Awesome. Mom you didn't mention that you're working with the FBI," Selena said.

"No, I didn't. And for very good reasons."

Selena gave her a knowing look. "We're going to move closer to the front. See you later?"

"I'll see you later, sweetie. Be safe."

"I will." Selena and her friend moved through the crowd and found a spot on the front steps of the mission.

"Sorry about that," Spencer said. "I didn't realize your daughter went to school here."

"She started this semester, actually. Do you have kids?"

"No. I don't."

"Married to your career, huh?"

"Something like that." He gave her a smile that sent a shiver through her. She tried to shrug it off. "Listen, I'm going to mill around. See if anything stands out."

"Sure," Sarah Jane said, trying to get her bearings. "Why don't I take the left side, and you take the right, then we can meet in the middle and compare notes."

"All right. That sounds good."

Sarah Jane watched him walk away for a moment. He

moved through the crowd with ease, but his stance was alert. Almost as if he expected to find something. Or someone. She pivoted and headed in the opposite direction, scanning faces, unsure exactly what she was looking for. But hoping she would find it anyway.

HE WALKED AROUND THE PERIMETER OF THE CROWD, buzzing on the energy. So many young women. What was that saying? Like being locked in a candy store. He scanned each face, searching for the right eyes, the shape of the brow. Could she be the next masterpiece? Not that one, too tall. Not that one, too wide-eyed.

Even though he wasn't finding his goddess, he was still thrilled at the elimination process, looking, checking, breathing in the scent of the girls. Their closeness. Their potential. His mind swarmed with ideas. Some of these beauties might work in the future, but for now, he had to focus. Tonight he must find the perfect female for his work in progress.

How clever he was to choose this job, this uniform. The ideal cover. No one would suspect his true purpose as he moved through the bodies huddled together, seeking comfort for their lost friend. No one paid any attention to him eyeing the crowd. If they did, of course, they'd just dismiss him as a security guard doing his job.

He perched on the top step to get a better look at

the people attending the vigil, their pitiful candles flickering in the growing dark. If they only knew the glory of their departed sister, how he'd... But wait. Was that?

Squinting for a better look, he was sure. Yes, he'd spotted that detective who'd shown up at the dorm and threatened to arrest him.

Bitch.

If he'd had his way, she'd be the one thrown off campus. She'd found all his cameras in the dorm. All that work, wasted. After that, he'd had to figure out another way to find the right girl, to watch her, and see if she was worthy.

A sour taste rose in his mouth every time he thought of that woman, her disdain for him, as if he was just a mere rent-a-cop. A rage began to build in his chest the way it sometimes did when his mother ranted on him, but then something pulled the plug on those foul thoughts.

Abruptly, his mood changed, and he watched transfixed as two girls approached the detective. Quickly, he left the steps and wound his way around the crowd, trying not to be noticed by the detective. He pushed through the crowd to get closer. Candlelight vigils had become commonplace, and unlike so many others, this one was rather sparsely attended given the size of the school

His thrill intensified as he was able to get a better look at the girl. She was perfect, and the tingle he felt in the presence of true goddess material spread from his chest into his extremities. His fingers twitched with energy. The pale golden halo glowed around the dark-haired girl with green eyes. Could it have been this easy? It had taken a couple of months for him to spot his last goddess, Artemis.

"...this is my daughter Selena..."

He held his breath and listened to her voice, like liquid gold, as she said hello to the man that had joined their crowd. Wait. So, this was not an acquaintance of the bitch. This was her daughter! He almost laughed out loud. How perfect. He shivered, reveling in the twist fate had delivered to him. She was not only his perfect model but also the agent of his revenge. He turned his attention to find Selena. Her mother called her Selena. But he was about to change that.

This one would be his Hecate. Goddess of magic. He could feel it in his bones. She would be the one to transform them all. Her halo pulsed in a way none of the others had. He didn't dare draw closer to her with her mother here. But there was something about her. Something almost magical. Could she be a witch? Was that the energy he sensed? He hadn't sensed much magic from her mother, but might have been a craft she learned on her own.

But that was to think about later. For now, he couldn't wait to get her alone. To touch her, to breathe her in. For the next two hours, he stayed close to the crowd, listening to them drone on about Haley Brooks, her life, the tragedy of having it cut short so soon. They had no idea what she had become.

When the crowd began to disperse, he hung back until the detective left the area. Then he followed his goddess to her dorm. He made sure no one noticed him as he slinked through the halls, sticking to the shadows, keeping just close enough so he wouldn't arouse suspicion.

He held back, staring longingly at her when she and her roommate paused at their door. Sharing a joke, laughing. She put her key into the door and gave her dark hair a toss as they slipped inside. When her door closed, he continued past, stopping briefly to read the number.

333.

His heart lurched in his chest, and a smile spread across his face. It was a sign. She was destined to be a goddess. He quickly made his way out of the building. He had plans to prepare. Everything had to be perfect.

CHAPTER 27

Sarah Jane poured herself her third cup of coffee and dosed it with sweetener and half-and-half. She and Mia had slogged through more interviews with employees from Harold House, but they yielded nothing significant. She still had a few more calls to make to check alibis, but none of them made her witchy senses go off. If only she could get Jessica to talk. But the spirit had made herself scarce ever since her encounter with Agent Spencer. Bernice, on the other hand, still showed up every day, mostly to give her unwanted advice.

Sarah Jane grabbed her yogurt out of the fridge, along with a plastic spoon from the utility drawer and headed back to her desk.

She found Bernice pacing back and forth in front of her cubicle, a frantic look on her face. What on earth could be bothering her now? As soon as Bernice saw Sarah Jane, she darted toward her.

"I have got to talk to you. Right this minute."

Sarah Jane moved past her into her cubicle and sat down. She retrieved her phone from her bag and acted like she was punching in a number to cover up their conversation, then put the device to her ear.

"Hi. What's going on?"

"We have a major problem."

"I really don't have a lot of time for this today. Can we reschedule?" Sarah Jane glared at the spirit.

"You don't understand. There's been a shift." Bernice stared at her with a strange intensity that sent a chill down Sarah Jane's spine.

"I'm sorry, I don't know what that means." Sarah Jane massaged her forehead.

"Vibrationally. There has been a shift. The last time I felt it..." The spirit stopped and swallowed hard. As if she were thinking about how to proceed. "Last time I felt it, Dan died."

"What are you talking about?" Sarah Jane's voice dropped. Every hair on her arms stood at attention, and she stared into the spirit's face.

"Something's wrong. I don't know what yet. I don't have details. I just feel a shift."

"And exactly how does that affect me?" Sarah Jane asked.

"Well, honey, I'm only attuned to human beings at

the moment. And I know, whatever it is, it has to be something to do with your life."

Jessica appeared behind the spirit guide. She looked paler, if that was possible.

"She's not wrong." Jessica's voice shook as she spoke the words, her snarky tone gone. She pushed past the spirit guide into Sarah Jane's cubicle and took a seat on the desktop. She reached out and placed a cold hand on Sarah Jane's shoulder. A shiver traveled through Sarah Jane from head to toe, but it wasn't from the spirit's touch.

"He's taken a new girl."

"You better be joking," Sarah Jane muttered into the phone. She ran her other hand through her hair.

"I wish I were," Jessica said.

"No. Don't tell her here," Bernice said. Then to Sarah Jane, "The ghost will be able to explain it."

Sarah Jane pinched the bridge of her nose. "You two are making me dizzy with all your arguing amongst yourselves."

Jessica pushed her face into the spirit guide, challenging her.

"*You* have to tell her. We're wasting precious time. They need to start searching now."

Bernice put her hands on her generous hips. "And how the hell is she supposed to do that if you can't even tell her where they are."

"Please just shut up," Sarah Jane said, squeezing her

eyes shut. She didn't know how much more she could take of these two.

"I... Holy..." Jessica's eyes widened.

"Hello, Prentice." Agent Spencer stopped at her cubicle. "You look like you had a day, and it's barely lunchtime."

Sarah Jane looked up and noticed him staring past her. She followed his gaze, and it appeared to land on Jessica.

"I can't do this," Jessica muttered and disappeared.

Bernice faced Agent Spencer. She looked him up and down. "I can't put my finger on it, but there's something wrong with him. I thought he might be a good match, but I'm not so sure now. You keep an eye on him. I'm going to see if I can find out more information."

"You do that," Sarah Jane said and pretended to end the call. She looked up at Agent Spencer and smiled. "How are you doing this morning? Any insights on the interviews you watched?"

"Nothing helpful, I'm afraid. They all seem like dead ends," he said.

"Couldn't agree more," she said sourly. "We need to make a few more phone calls just to verify alibis, but it definitely feels like we are slogging through mud for sure."

Agent Spencer looked at his watch. "Would you care to get some lunch?"

"It's only eleven thirty," Sarah Jane said. "And we've got Ellis Ford coming back in around one."

"I promise we'll be back long before one o'clock," he said.

Sarah Jane's stomach fluttered. Why the hell was she so nervous? It wasn't as if he asked her on a date. It was just lunch with a colleague.

"Okay. What are you in the mood for?" she asked.

"Ladies choice," he said.

Her phone chimed, and she picked it up but before checking it said, "You know my husband used to pull that crap just so he didn't have to make a decision."

"Your husband sounds like a smart man," Spencer said.

Sarah Jane turned her phone over to read the text. "Sorry, it's my son. I have to take this." She opened the text, and her stomach dropped like an icy rock.

Dalton: *911*

Sarah Jane immediately dialed her son's number. He picked up on the first ring.

"Dalton, what's wrong? Are you okay?"

"When was the last time you talked to Selena?" he asked.

"Last night at the vigil at her school for a student who'd been murdered. Why?"

"She texted me last night around eleven thirty. I kind of ignored it until just a few minutes ago. I was busy."

"Okay." Sarah Jane's stomach flip-flopped. "Don't drag this out, honey. You're freaking me out."

"She sent me a skull emoji."

Sarah Jane shook her head. "I don't know what that means."

"Remember when I was in high school, and you told me that I could text you or dad no matter what with a random emoji, and you'd come pick me up if I were in a bad situation, no questions asked?" Dalton said.

"Yes, of course. Larkin has the same code. Why?"

"Well, when Selena went to school, I told her that she could text me. Only we made a code with our emojis."

"What kind of code?" Sarah Jane said.

"You know, the beer stein emoji for I'm drunk and I don't want to drive, or I don't have money for an uber? That kind of thing."

"Yeah, I think so. What does a skull mean?" Sarah Jane asked, but she wasn't sure she wanted to know the answer.

"It means I'm in danger. Come get me immediately."

"And this came in last night?" Sarah Jane's cheeks filled with heat. "And you just ignored it? What is the point of having a code with your sister if you're not going to pay attention to it, Dalton?"

"You're right. I know, and I'm sorry," Dalton said. "It was a dick move, okay? I was in bed, and I was thinking that I was going to have an early day, so I ignored it."

"Did you try calling her? Is she okay?" Sarah Jane asked.

"I called, but there's no answer. It just goes to voicemail." Dalton's voice dropped to almost a whisper.

"Well, that's just great," Sarah Jane said. "You're twenty-three years old. I shouldn't have to lecture you about being responsible."

"I know, Mom. Geez, I said I'm sorry. What do you want? A pint of my blood? My firstborn?"

"No, I want you to help me find your sister."

"Okay. I'll take the rest of the afternoon off. I'll go door-to-door if you want me to."

"First, we'll go home and make a plan," she said. "Meet me there in thirty minutes."

"Fine. Thirty minutes."

Sarah Jane ended the call. She covered her mouth with her hand and stared at her phone.

"Is everything all right, Detective Prentice?" Spencer asked.

"I don't know. My daughter's not answering her phone, and she sent my son a text basically saying that she was in danger last night, and he ignored it."

"What can I do?" he asked. She noted the concern on his face, and instead of comforting her, it added to her worry.

"I don't know if there's anything you can do." She squeezed her eyes shut. What if she's the girl Jessica mentioned? The insidious thought slithered through her brain, taunting her. It had been the thing she was terrified of once she realized the psycho had a type and that her daughter fit it. She'd done the presser. He could've easily figured out who she was and who her daughter was. Her heartbeat bounced against her rib cage like a hard rubber ball.

"Is your daughter on your phone plan?" Spencer asked.

"Sure, why?" Her mind filled with thick fog, and she could barely think through things.

"Maybe you have one of those find your phone things available to you then."

"Oh, my God, you're right. I actually do have that app. I installed it on their phones when they were in high school, so I could track them down. Thank you."

Sarah Jane quickly thumbed through the apps on her phone until she found what she was looking for. She opened it and selected Selena's phone. It took several minutes for it to triangulate. A blue dot pulsed on the screen showing the location of her phone.

"What does it say?"

"This can't be right."

"May I?" Agent Spencer held his hand out, and Sarah Jane gave him the phone.

"It says she's still at school."

"All right. Let's talk to Lieutenant Mendoza and see what we should do next. Perhaps it's just a misunderstanding."

"Yeah, perhaps you're right." Sarah Jane nodded. Her phone chimed again with a text, and she quickly opened her messaging app, praying it was Selena.

She didn't recognize the number, but when she opened the message, she fought back the urge to vomit.

A photo of Selena bound and gagged appeared on the screen with the caption, *Thank you, detective. I've found my Hecate.*

Sarah Jane dropped the phone and screamed from the bottom of her soul.

CHAPTER 28

The entire squad gathered in Lieutenant Mendoza's office. Most of them stood in a semi-circle around Mendoza's desk. Except Sarah Jane and Mia. Sarah Jane sat in one of the two chairs in front of the lieutenant's desk. Mia Johnson sat next to her, her dark eyes never leaving Sarah Jane's face. Mia's wary energy spilled onto Sarah Jane. She knew her partner wanted to take her hand and comfort her. But they'd worked together a long time now, and Mia knew what Sarah Jane needed. Space.

Space to process. To figure things out. Space would help Sarah Jane right now more than comfort.

"Mia," Lieutenant Mendoza said, drawing Mia's attention. "I need you to take point on this case now. Are you comfortable with that?"

"Of course," Mia said.

"Wait a minute." Sarah Jane looked up from her phone, from the photo he'd sent of her daughter. "I'm still point."

"No, Sarah Jane, you're not. And you're not thinking clearly. He just made this personal. I can't let you continue as point on the case. You know that as well as I do. You can't be clear and objective right now, right?"

Sarah Jane seethed, rage at the monster who took her daughter as palpable as a fifth limb. She glowered at Mendoza. Did she really expect an answer?

Mendoza said, her tone lowering to a gentle cadence that belied her steely resolve, "Please, Sarah Jane. You know it's not personal. It's the way we have to do it to find Selena. In fact, I think you should take some time off."

And then Agent Spencer added his two cents, fuel to the fire. "I know this probably really isn't my place, but I agree with your lieutenant."

Sarah Jane glared at him. Who had let him in? She wanted to spit out, who asked you, but had enough sense to know that wouldn't help her case. She said in forced, even tones, "Listen, Agent. I know you have a job to do, but this really isn't your call." Then she turned back to her lieutenant. "Please, Lieutenant. I need to work this."

"No. I'm sorry." Gone was the gentle advice. Mendoza was back in boss mode. Kind but firm. "You're too close to it."

"Fine," Sarah Jane said, clipped and brittle. "I'll work

the tip line." She nodded to Mia. "We can do a press conference again, release Selena's picture. Maybe someone saw something."

Mendoza nodded in agreement. "And we'll do all of that. I'll even have you speak to the press."

Agent Spencer cleared his throat but avoided looking at Sarah Jane. "You may want to hold off on that for the moment," Agent Spencer said. "He's clearly trying to get a response out of you, Detective Prentice. Your team should continue the investigation before you go public."

"I should be here," Sarah Jane protested. "What if—"

"No." The lieutenant held up a hand and shook her head. "Your role in this is as a parent. Not a cop."

"But—"

"I'm not sure if you know this," he said, "but I'm a trained psychologist. Detective, your very presence here could jeopardize your daughter's safety. People under this much stress can act rashly. It may be better if you take some leave. Your family needs you now. Go be with them."

Sarah Jane gritted her teeth, trying not to say the ugly things floating through her head.

"I hate to say this, but I agree with Agent Spencer," the lieutenant said.

"For the record, I hate this. Every single one of you would want to be here if you were in my shoes," Sarah Jane said bitterly.

"She's not wrong," Rodriguez piped up.

"We'll make sure to keep you in the loop, Sarah Jane." Stuckey patted her on the shoulder.

Sarah Jane met her lieutenant's gaze. Tears blurred her vision. "You have to find my daughter."

"We will, SJ. I promise you," Stuckey said before Mendoza could respond. Rodriguez nudged him in the ribs. "What?"

Rodriguez lowered his voice. "What's the rule, Stuckey? We don't make promises we can't keep."

"I know, but this isn't just anybody. It's SJ." Stuckey threw his hands in the air to show his frustration. "I don't know about you, but I'm going to bust my ass to find her daughter."

"Thank you, Stuckey," Sarah Jane whispered.

"I already sent some uniforms out to find her phone. I'm expecting a call any second now," Stuckey said. "I'll start working on a warrant for her phone records as soon as we're done here. Just in case we need them."

"That's great. As soon as you get the location Stuckey, you and Mia head out there," Lieutenant Mendoza said.

"Yes ma'am," Stuckey said.

"Sarah Jane, as of this minute, I'm putting you on leave," Lieutenant said. "Why don't you go home. Tell your family. You have some support there, right?"

"Yeah. I do, it's just..." Sarah Jane squeezed her eyes shut, and the tears spilled onto her cheeks. "I just don't know how I'm going to tell them."

"You'll find a way." Mia finally broke down and took Sarah Jane's hand. "I can go with you if you want."

"No. I want you working on the case." Sarah Jane patted the top of Mia's hand, grateful for her partner's offer. "I can handle it."

"All right, then. Everybody know what they're doing?" Lieutenant straightened in her chair.

A chorus of, "Yes, ma'ams" went through the office.

"Great. Let's get to it. Sarah Jane, could you stay just a moment, please?"

Sarah Jane nodded. Mia let go of her hand and followed everyone out of the room, closing the door behind her.

The lieutenant leaned forward with her elbows resting on her desk, folding her hands together. "SJ, I know this is hard. And I know you don't really agree with my thinking here. I just don't want you to do anything stupid. I've seen cops get too emotional on a case and ruin their careers."

"I understand," Sarah Jane said.

"Good. Just so we're clear. You are not to come near this case. You go home, take care of your family. And wait."

"Of course." Sarah Jane scrubbed the tears away from her cheeks and sniffled. "But you will call me as soon as you find her or..." Sarah Jane's lips quivered, and she couldn't bring herself to finish her thought because it meant facing the unthinkable.

"We're going to do everything in our power. Now go home."

Sarah Jane rose from her chair and left the lieutenant's office. Every step she took through the squad room felt as if she were moving in slow motion. How could this be happening? How did he even know Selena was her daughter? Or where to find her? She stopped briefly at her desk, ignoring Bernice sitting in her office chair.

"Oh, honey," Bernice began, her huge dark eyes ringed with sorrow. Sarah Jane held up her hand to silence the spirit guide, and for once, Bernice shut up. She glanced around the squad room. The office buzzed with phone calls and voices, her team moving in double-time. She hoped to see Jessica. But there was no sign of the spirit. Her shoulders sagged, and she grabbed her purse from the desk drawer, defeated, and headed to the parking garage.

CHAPTER 29

By the time Sarah Jane arrived home, her family's cars had clogged her driveway and the curb in front of her house. Everyone's except Selena's.

Stuckey had called her on her way home to tell her they'd been unable to find Selena's car in the campus parking lot. But they did find her phone chucked in a trashcan near the parking lot exit.

"Thanks for calling, David," Sarah Jane said. "Make sure the lieutenant doesn't get wind of this, okay? I don't want you to get into trouble."

"Don't you worry about me. You take care of yourself, okay?" Stuckey said.

She knew he had a daughter Selena's age and probably pictured his girl in Selena's place, saw himself going raving mad too, feeling as helpless and angry as she was that he was forbidden from working the case. That's exactly what she would've done.

"I will. Thanks again."

She parked behind Amy's Accord but couldn't find the strength to get out of the car.

She closed her eyes and sank into a semi-trance. "Jessica, if you can hear me, I need to talk to you. Please. I know you know where he's keeping my daughter. Please."

Bernice appeared in the passenger seat. "I think she's in hiding." Sarah Jane peered at her spirit guide next to her. Her pert red hat was slightly askew over her loose black curls as if the strain of the case was taking its toll on Bernice's usual impeccable appearance.

"Of course, Jessica's hiding out. Just when I really need to see her." Sarah Jane shook her head. "I don't suppose you have any insight?"

"I'm sorry, honey, but I don't. My job here is to look after you and help you through your crises however I can." Bernice put her hand on Sarah Jane's shoulder. The spirit guide's warm energy flowed through her, giving her comfort.

"I can't lose Selena, too. I don't think I could survive that." Sarah Jane's voice shook, despite her efforts to remain strong. "Even though I didn't want to lose Dan, I expected it because of the cancer. I was able to prepare for it. But this... No parent is ever prepared for this."

"You're going to find her." Bernice sounded so confident that Sarah Jane sat up and turned to look her in the eye.

"How do you know?"

"I just feel it." Bernice gave her shoulder a gentle squeeze. "You're a witch. You know what you have to do." Bernice didn't slow down long enough for Sarah Jane to protest.

"Everything is intention, sugar. Focus your energy on finding her alive."

Sarah Jane let out a discouraged sigh. "What good will that do? I'm not allowed to work this case."

Bernice drew her lips into a scowl. "Have you forgotten everything you've learned? You don't have to work the case to focus your energy on it. And no, you can't work it officially as a detective. But you're more than just a detective, aren't you? You always used your abilities to aid you in your work before this happened. Your magic is coming back. Use it to help find your daughter."

Sarah Jane shook her head. "I don't know. I can't think about that right now." She glanced out the window at the overgrown irises. Yard work was Larkin's responsibility, but she couldn't muster the energy to be angry with him. If the neighbors complained, she'd deal with it.

"Of course." Bernice nodded in understanding. "I'll give you some space to talk to your family."

Sarah Jane slumped in her seat. "If I call you, will you

come?" she asked. She met the spirit guide's eyes. A smile tugged at the corners of Bernice's mouth despite her obvious attempt to suppress it.

"Absolutely. You don't even have to say it aloud. All you have to do is think of my name, and I will come to you."

"Thank you, Bernice," Sarah Jane said. "I know it was you that somehow arranged for Dan and me to see each other again." It was that act more than anything that softened Sarah Jane's feelings about Bernice. Not that she couldn't still be a thorn in her side with her sharp tongue and pointed opinions. But that was for another time. Right now, she felt a rush of gratitude for her presence in her life

Bernice returned a kind smile. "Honey, he was as eager to see you as you were to see him. It seemed like the right thing to do. To let the veil thin just a little bit."

"I appreciate it more than you'll ever know. It gave me great comfort."

"I'm so glad, honey."

Sarah Jane glanced at the front door of her little ranch house. The dark shadow that had hung over it for the last year had lightened. Even with Dan gone, love radiated from inside. Although until Selena came home, it was incomplete.

"I guess I need to go inside and see my family."

"Yes. They've been waiting for a while now."

Sarah Jane removed the key from the ignition, tossed it into her bag, and went inside.

CHAPTER 30

"Come on. Ring," Sarah Jane muttered to the walls of her family room. She dug her fingernails into her scalp and stared down at the phone in her hand, oblivious to the endless cups of tea Amy kept making for her, all grown cold, but still, no news. It had been almost twenty four hellish, sleepless hours since Selena went missing. She didn't know how much more of this she could take.

It took everything she had to fight her instinct to strike out on her own and find her daughter. She played with one thought like a pulled thread on a sweater. What if she got her family to help her? She'd had glimmers of hope that her magic was returning since the healing on Saturday. Susanna and Gran both agreed it would take multiple healings before her powers came back full strength. But at this point, a quarter of her magic was better than none. And at least, it didn't seem to backfire on her anymore.

The doorbell rang, the sound breaking into her thoughts. She ran for the door, heart pounding and every nerve on alert, hope alive again. She opened the door, and disappointment hit her when she came face-to-face with Special Agent Kit Spencer.

"What are you doing here? Shouldn't you be at the squad room helping them figure out where the hell my daughter is? You obviously don't need me."

"That's a fair response." His measured answer and calm demeanor both pissed her off and strangely comforted her at the same time. "I wanted to talk to you about something important. Can we go someplace private?"

Sarah Jane glanced over her shoulder and listened to the sounds of her family all gathered around her kitchen table, sitting on the couch, chatting, theorizing about spells they could use to help find Selena. They had dropped everything for Sarah Jane, had canceled appointments, and rearranged schedules. Rainey's employees agreed to step up and take over her regular duties for the duration. There'd been no reason for her family to show up for her, but still, they did. Just like they had when Dan died.

"Let me tell my family where I'm going."

"Yes, that's probably prudent." His smile warmed her, and instantly, she hated that she found him attractive. What kind of mother was she, thinking about a man when some psycho had her daughter? *What's wrong with me*, she worried as she turned to get her jacket.

Sarah Jane rounded the corner from the foyer and ran into Susanna as she was putting her keys in her pocket.

"You okay, SJ?" Susanna asked. "Who's at the door?"

"It's just somebody from work." Could her sister see the flush rising on her cheeks?

She looked into the family room and saw each of her family members sit up and give her their undivided attention. She didn't need psychic powers to know what was on their minds.

"There's no news. I'm sorry. It's just the FBI consultant with some more questions, so I'm going to answer them. We're going for a walk for a little privacy."

"You could go into Dad's study Mom," Dalton said.

A cold pang pressed on Sarah Jane's chest. She shook her head. "A walk is better. But it's a good idea, sweetie. We should start using that room more. I'll be back soon. I've got my cell, so just call me if you need me."

Sarah Jane slipped on Amy's canvas shoes, tucked her cell phone in her back pocket, and shut the door behind her.

THE LEAVES HAD BARELY STARTED TO TURN IN THE early autumn weeks of September. Mabon was coming, but no one in Sarah Jane's family was thinking about it right now. Just like her birthday, the high holidays held no interest for her. Not with Selena gone. The wind blew through what few trees grew along her street, and their leaves rustled. Sarah Jane folded her arms and focused on the clicking of Kit's highly polished oxfords against the sidewalk.

"What did you want to talk about?"

"I wanted to explain my recommendation."

"There's nothing to explain. You're the one with the doctorate in psychology, right? I bet the Bureau just ate that up. I'm surprised they didn't keep you in Washington."

"Technically, that would be Virginia. That's where the FBI headquarters are."

"Right," Sarah Jane said.

"I didn't recommend that you leave the task force because of your mental state. Your superiors would've done that anyway. You were too close to the case to begin with, and your daughter's involvement, well it was, as they say, a no-brainer."

"Right, but you went out of your way to—"

"I did it because I wanted you out of the office."

Sarah Jane stopped in her tracks and glared at him. On top of everything else, this guy was deliberately sabotaging her? This was too much. "You know, I'm not really fond of you either, but I at least expected you to be professional."

"Sarah Jane, I want to work with you. And since I knew they would take you off the task force and probably put you on leave, I chimed in to make it easier for them to do so."

She looked down at her street, at the sheltering trees, the familiar gardens, her neighbor's window dressings, autumn wreaths, their kid's school logos, the lone political sign. Evidence of her community, but today she felt like a stranger. None of it offered her comfort. And now, this man seemed to have betrayed her at the one anchor she had left. Her job.

"I'm not following you. You wanted to work with me, but you wanted me on leave? That makes no sense. I know rogue cops are a thing on TV and movies, but if I do something stupid, like continue to investigate this case, which my superiors strictly forbade me to do, I could lose my job. My pension."

"I understand. Truly I do. But I need your help."

"You have plenty of help. Mia Johnson is a great detective. And as much as Rodriguez is a pain in my ass sometimes, he's a good detective. Actually, my whole team is great. You're in good hands."

"Yes, but none of them are witches."

Sarah Jane took a step back and stared at him, her mouth ajar. "I'm not a—"

"Yes, you are." He cut her off. "It's okay."

"Wait a minute, are you really FBI? Or... are you something else?" She looked at him closely for signs he was a fraud, that he was pulling something over on her or the department.

"No, I'm FBI, but I'm also something else."

"I feel like I've just stepped into one of my son's D&D games, and I'm at a bridge talking to a sphinx that's talking in riddles." Sarah Jane put her fingers through her hair and tugged on it. She squeezed her eyes shut and clenched her jaw before she glared at him.

"Fine. I'll bite. What kind of something else are you? You don't strike me as a vampire or a demon, but it's been a while since I've encountered either. Are you a witch?"

"No. I'm not." He cleared his throat and shifted his feet. "I don't usually reveal this, and it's a little difficult to say because it usually frightens people."

"There's not much you could say to frighten me." Sarah Jane jutted her chin. "So spill it."

"I'm a reaper."

Sarah Jane snorted. "Yeah, right."

"You don't believe me?" He looked puzzled.

"Of course, I don't believe you. Everyone knows you can't see reapers." Her hands fluttered, showing her disbelief. She stopped as a thought formed, and her arms floated to her sides. "Unless... you call one. And I sure as hell didn't call one."

"I would never reveal my true form to you on

purpose. And for the record, reapers can be seen without being called."

"All right." Sarah Jane took two deep breaths and blew them out slowly, one after the other before she had formed her next thoughts. "Let's just say I believe you. How is it that you look like that? I mean, do you peel that skin off like a snake at night or..."

"It's a glamour," he said softly.

"Magic. Figures." She stared at a crack in the sidewalk. Her mind reeled from this information. "Why are you really here? It's not to help me or my daughter. Reapers are notoriously mission-minded." She shifted her gaze and steadied it on his face.

"Your unsub has something of mine. Or, to be more accurate, something I'm responsible for, and I need to get it back."

"What could he possibly have that you want?" Sarah Jane asked.

"The young women he kills? He's keeping their souls. Collecting them. Like trophies. But you already knew that, didn't you? That spirit that follows you around, she's told you it, right?"

"Jessica? No, Jessica's still too traumatized to tell me any real details. She just likes to hang out and be snarky. How is it you know this?"

"They're all in my book."

"Your book? What? The book of the dead?" She only half joked.

"Something like that, yes." He nodded. "It's a list of the souls I'm to ferry to their afterlife. They weren't supposed to die so soon. Their dates changed because they were murdered. Changes like that sometimes make it difficult to find a spirit and carry out my duty. If Jessica didn't tell you about them, who did?"

"Another girl. Ashlyn. She begged me not to forget them."

Sarah Jane pressed her fingers against her lips to stop them from quivering. A burning tornado of emotion spun through her chest. All she could picture was Selena, her beautiful, vibrant daughter, made into a trophy and kept in some dark place that Sarah Jane would never find. Her eyes blurred with tears. She didn't want to ask, but she had to know. The words came out as barely a whisper. "What's he doing with their souls?"

"I'm not sure. Human souls are incredibly powerful, and there are many uses for them. I know creatures who will kill for possession of just one. He has nine," he said, and his calm silky voice wrapped around her senses. "My goal is to find where he's keeping these souls and to ferry them where they belong. But it's also to ensure that your daughter doesn't become number ten."

Sarah Jane nodded and brushed away the tears falling on her cheeks. She sniffled and squared her body to his. "I'll make you a deal. You help me find my daughter, and I'll make sure every single one of those souls is delivered to you."

"What about your whole rogue cop speech? How you're not willing to risk your job."

"I'm not willing to continue investigating as a cop. But I am willing to investigate as a witch. That will take some help from my family. When we do find him, you're the one who's going to have to finagle calling in the police. I can't have even a trace of my involvement, I can't lose my job. I have my kids. And not to mention a mortgage and college to pay for."

"I completely understand. And I will do everything I can to shield you."

Sarah Jane put her hand out and it shook a little. "Why do I feel like I'm making a deal with the devil?"

Kit took her hand in his. It surprised her how firm and warm it was. How human it felt.

"Come on, Sarah Jane. You know there's no real devil." He smiled, his dark eyes glistening.

"I guess if we're going to be working together you should call me SJ. That's what everyone else calls me."

"And you should call me Kit."

"All right, let's go enlist my family." She let go of his hand. "We're going to need a necromancer."

"Do you know one?"

"Yes, I do. Very, very well, actually."

CHAPTER 31

"Hey," Sarah Jane said to the house when she returned from her walk with Kit Spencer. She showed him into her family room and everyone looked. Except Larkin, who was in school.

They'd argued about it that morning.

"Why can't I stay with the family? I need to be with you all. Maybe I can help," Larkin protested.

But she'd ignored his puppy-dog eyes, his pout when he resorted to truculence. She had enough on her hands, and she put her foot down. "Things need to stay as normal as possible for you, Larkin. Just trust me on this, honey. It's how you can help. By keeping the energy positive and, well, normal."

He relented, and she thanked him for not resisting anymore, even though she loved having everyone in the family around her. Except for the times she needed to be alone.

Holy mother goddess, this was so hard.

She addressed everyone's questioning face as they studied Kit. "I need to talk to you all about something," she began.

"Who's your friend?" Susanna asked.

"Hello," Kit said. He raised his hand in a slight wave. "I'm Kit Spencer. I work with Sarah Jane."

"He's an agent with the FBI. He's consulting on the case I was working on when Selena disappeared." Sarah Jane exchanged an anxious glance with Kit, and he gave her a supportive nod.

"But as it turns out, he is more than just an FBI agent. I need you all to brace yourselves."

Curiosity showed in the eyes of each of her family members. Sarah Jane took a deep breath and just said it.

"Agent Spencer...Kit... is actually a reaper."

Susanna and Amy both let out gasps.

"No way," Cass said.

"Seriously?" Rainey was the only one who seemed brave enough to step forward for a closer look. "You look like a real boy, Pinocchio."

Kit chuckled. "I am a real boy as long as I wear this glamour."

"What do you want with us?" Susanna asked.

"I want to help you find Selena," he said with an earnest look on his handsome face.

"But the man who has taken her is also keeping captive the souls of the other women he has killed. I am the reaper responsible for ensuring they get to their afterlife. And I assure you, I am very serious about my job."

Sarah Jane interrupted him. "So, Kit and I, we've just made a deal. He'll help us find Selena alive, and we, all of us, our family that is, will help him find the captive souls so he can release them to their destination."

Susanna looked skeptical. "What if we find Selena and we don't find the souls? What happens with your deal?"

"Yes. Theoretically, that could happen. And I have an idea about that." Sarah Jane took a deep breath. "Amy. Do you think you could summon a spirit for us? I'm talking about Jessica. I've told you about her. She's a bit on the difficult side, so you may have to use a little force."

"Me?" Surprise lined Amy's delicate face.

"Well, you are the best necromancer I've ever met," Sarah Jane said.

"That's not true," Amy said. "Mama was a better necromancer."

"You're right," Sarah Jane said. "I forgot. But she's not here, and you are. So will you do it?"

"Here?"

"Yeah."

"I just recently cleansed this whole house. Who knows what else will come in if I open the door?"

"Amy, we'll help you cleanse it after," Susanna said. "If it will help us find Selena, don't you want to do whatever it takes?"

"Of course, I do. Of course. Actually, we should probably do it outside in the backyard. The spell would be more powerful, and we'd be surrounded by one of the elemental forces like the earth."

"All right. What do we need?" Sarah Jane asked.

"We need to gather some supplies," Amy said. "Cass, did you bring your crystals, by any chance?"

"You know I did," Cass said.

"Great. Go get them," Amy said.

CHAPTER 32

Kit Spencer gathered with the small crowd of witches in Sarah Jane's backyard.

"Let's form a circle," Amy said.

Each of the family members held a white candle, and then Amy set up a second circle within the outer circle with four colored candles—gray, purple, white, and blue—representing the four Cardinal points. North, South, East, and West.

Inside the Cardinal points, she placed five crystals representing the elements of fire, water, earth, air, and spirit. Sarah Jane had instructed her to create the inner circle large enough to hold the spirit of Jessica King.

"All right," Amy took a box of matches from the front pocket of her jeans and struck a match. She touched the flame to her grandmother's candle first.

Each person lit the candle of the person standing next to them until all the candles burned with a bright flame.

"Put your candle and its holder down on the ground in front of you," Amy instructed. "Make sure it stays upright, though. Then everybody join hands."

Necromancy, or the controlling of spirits, was serious and sometimes scary business. Sarah Jane had only seen Amy do this twice, and on both occasions, the spirit had been angry and uncooperative even under Amy's gentle coaxing. If the spirit appeared and was too angry to comply, Sarah Jane hoped her sister's gifts could calm Jessica and put her at ease.

Every circle Amy created with crystals, candles, and even the presence of the witches themselves was a layer of protection from malevolent energy. An angry spirit could be destructive and even vindictive. The last thing Sarah Jane wanted was for Jessica King to take her wrath out on her family.

Sarah Jane leaned into Kit and whispered, "Are you sure you want to be here?"

He stood next to her in the circle, holding her hand. "Of course. I'll make sure she knows I'm not here to reap her at this point. I think she must recognize me, which is why she's disappeared every time I've been around."

"I don't think she's going to be very receptive to this cognitive interview you want to do with her."

"Perhaps. You may have to take the lead on this one."

"I only took one seminar on it through the Bureau. It's not like I studied it in-depth the way you have," she said.

"You'll do fine, Sarah Jane," he said. "Have a little faith in yourself."

"If everyone's ready," Amy said. She gave Sarah Jane a pointed look.

Sarah Jane nodded and pressed her lips together to indicate no more words. Amy held tight to Gran's and Rainey's hands. She breathed in deeply through her nose and out through her mouth, relaxed her shoulders, and began to speak.

To the universe that surrounds us we give you thanks.

Spirits to the North, South, East, and West, we call on you to aid in our quest.

Elements of water, earth, air, and fire, bring forth the spirit that I desire

Jessica King, you may no longer hide.

I command you to come forth beyond the veil from the other side.

THE FAMILY FOLLOWED AMY'S LEAD, REPEATING THE spell with her two more times. The colored candles began to flicker as if a breeze had just blown through. The spirit of Jessica King appeared in the inner circle. She materialized at first, pale as a gossamer cloud. Her eyes searched the crowd around her, and she turned in a circle. Finally, her gaze locked on Sarah Jane.

"What the hell, Sarah Jane?" She wore ripped black jeans and red cowboy boots with a black T-shirt that read, *Wait. Did I just say that out loud?* The spirit tried to move but was constrained by the confines of the circle.

"I'm sorry it had to be this way, Jessica," Sarah Jane said.

Jessica folded her arms. "He needs to leave."

"Does she mean me?" Dalton asked.

"No, sweetie. She means Agent Spencer." Sarah Jane sighed. "Don't you? You know what he is?"

"Of course, I know what he is. Can't you see?"

"You can see his true form?" Sarah Jane asked.

"Yeah, he's goddamn terrifying."

"I can't see that. I see the glamour he's wearing."

"Lucky you." Jessica rolled her eyes. "Now, let me go."

"I can't do that, honey. I'm sorry, but it's time to do the thing that you don't want to do. You need to help me find my daughter. You're the only one here who knows where he's holding her."

"No." Jessica shook her head. "I don't know how to get there. Like I said, I've never been back since he took me."

"Jessica," Kit said. His deep voice rang out, commanding the attention of everyone in the circle. "I realize you're frightened of me. But I promise you, I'm not going to hurt you."

Jessica planted her feet and took a stubborn stance as she faced him. "I don't believe you. What about that scythe hovering near you?"

"My scythe? You can see it?"

"Yeah," Jessica said, averting her eyes. She squirmed.

"I apologize," Kit said, his voice so silky and smooth, it put Sarah Jane at ease just listening to it. "Better?"

Jessica stole a glance at him and nodded. "Thanks. I swear to God, I don't know how to help you. I didn't..."

"You didn't what, honey?" Sarah Jane asked.

"I don't want to talk about it."

"Jessica, you are my daughter's only hope. Please."

Pain streaked the spirit's nearly translucent face. "What do you want me to do?" she asked, her tone reluctant.

"I'd like you to agree to an abbreviated cognitive interview with me."

"Well, that doesn't sound fun," Jessica sneered.

"It won't take long," Kit said. "I'll work with Sarah Jane to help you remember what happened to you," Kit said. "If you let me."

"No way. Sarah Jane can ask me questions but not you. I don't know you."

"Okay," Sarah Jane said quickly before Jessica changed her mind. She glanced at Kit, unsure of herself. She'd been to a two-day seminar about the technique, but she rarely used cognitive interviews because they typically took hours.

Her stomach tightened. "I will do my best. We're in a little bit of a time crunch, so I can't spend a ton of time talking you through it."

"Whatever," Jessica said miserably. "Just do it."

"All right, Jessica, close your eyes." The spirit's chest rose and fell with a heavy breath which Sarah Jane knew was just a habit. That expressed her anxiety. "All right. I need you to take me back to the day you died. What can you tell me about the room you're in?"

"It was small. Padded with insulation. Like, you know, the pink fiberglass stuff. I guess he thought it soundproofed it. He had me tied to a bed." Her voice dropped to almost a whisper. "And he made me wear this stupid diaper. I learned these spells, you know, when I was dabbling with witchcraft, and one of them was for unlocking things. I kept trying to unlock the handcuffs holding me to the bed. I got so tired from concentrating."

Sarah Jane leaned in. "That's good, Jessica. What happened next?"

"Somehow, my spell worked. And I was able to get my hands free. He didn't like to use handcuffs on my legs because it made it harder for him to..." Her face filled with disgust. "You know."

"You're doing great, Jessica." Sarah Jane glanced at her sister Susanna, standing next to her. A look of empathy on her face. Sarah Jane wondered how many women had sat in her office and talked about their rapes. Amy and Rainey both wore expressions of horror. Sarah Jane wished they didn't have to listen to this interview.

"And then what happened, Jessica?"

"Well, I was able to get out of the restraints on my legs. And unlock the padlock on the door."

Jessica's voice rose as she remembered her triumphs, her expectation of freedom.

"I was so elated the spell worked, and that it was real. I kept thinking when I get out of here, I'm going to dedicate myself to being a full-fledged witch. I ran out the back door screaming for help, but he pulled into the driveway. I guess he saw me because he came after me and chased me down in the backyard."

Sarah Jane exchanged an eager glance with Agent Spencer. "What does the backyard look like, Jessica? What do you see from your vantage point?"

"All the grass is dead. It's all brown. Rough and dry on my feet. But I don't care. I can see the house behind his, and there's a fence. And there's a woman looking out a window from behind a curtain."

"What happens then, Jessica?" she asked.

"She closed the curtains, and he tripped me." Jessica shook with fear. "He's on top of me."

"It's all right, Jessica. You're safe. He can't hurt you anymore." Sarah Jane used a soothing voice.

Jessica's voice turned into a drone, the shock of

losing her freedom returning. “He put his hands around my neck and just started to squeeze. It took forever. And I couldn't push him off. He wasn't that big. I should've been able to push him off.”

“Jessica, you did everything you could. He'd held you for days. You were probably weak. What happened next, honey?”

Sarah Jane wanted to embrace her, to comfort her, but she knew she shouldn’t touch her. Couldn’t touch her.

“My body. I rose out of my body. I just hovered there for a while, watching him drag me into the house. Once he opened the back door, that's when I heard all the screams. All their screams. It terrified me, and I ran or floated. I don't know exactly. I thought about someplace else, and I went there.”

“When you fled, did you notice anything about where you were? Any landmarks that stood out. I know it's hard, but please try.”

“There was this one thing. An old building, sort of stately, like an old City Hall or something. It had a clock tower.”

Sarah Jane exchanged a hopeful glance with Kit. “That's great, Jessica.”

“Gilroy's old City Hall has a clock tower,” Rainey said. “I'm forever picking up animals in Gilroy. I pass it all the time.”

“Jessica, can you tell me anything else?”

"No, after that, I went to my mom's house. I hung around there for a while until I don't know, I felt this tugging feeling in my chest. The next thing I knew, I was with my body, and you were there. And you could see me."

"Yeah, I could see you." Sarah Jane nodded. "I know that was really hard for you."

"I wish I could tell you an address," Jessica said softly.

"Jessica, do you remember the color of the house where he held you?"

"Sure, it was this pale yellow color. And it was in bad shape with paint missing in long strips. There was one other thing that was kinda weird."

"What?" Sarah Jane asked.

"I ran out the back door through this beauty salon. I mean it was old, really old, and I don't think anybody had used it in years, but it had sinks like for hair washing and a stylist's chair."

"That's very helpful," Sarah Jane said. "Thank you."

"Now, what happens? Are you going to keep me captive forever?"

"No, honey, I'm not. I think it's time. I think you've done everything you can to help me. Don't you feel that?"

"There's this heat on the back of my neck. I'm scared. What if I turn around, and it's hell?"

Kit spoke up. "It's not hell, Jessica. If you trust me, I'll take you there," he said.

"You promise it's not hell?" Jessica asked warily.

"I promise. It's where you're supposed to be. Where you would've been if that guy hadn't interfered with the natural order."

Sarah Jane eyed Kit and wondered if he would actually tell her if hell was real or not. Some part of her hoped it was because there were certain men she'd arrested during her career she'd like to see rotting in hell. Maybe when all of this is over, she would buy Kit a cup of coffee and ask for the truth.

"Do you want me to let her go?" Amy asked.

"What would you like to do, Kit?"

"That's completely up to Jessica. You can let her go, and I can continue to hunt her. But I think perhaps that's not a lifestyle she'd like to pursue."

"I'll go with you," Jessica said. "But if you take me to hell, I'll come after you," she threatened.

Kit chuckled and said, "Deal."

"Great choice," Sarah Jane said. "You can let her go, Amy."

Amy blew out her candle, stepped into the ring and blew out the candles around the Cardinal points. This freed the spirit.

Jessica approached Sarah Jane. "You're going to catch him, right?"

"Yes. I am. I couldn't have done it without you. I really hope you find peace."

"Thanks. Don't forget to tell my mom that I'm okay."

"I won't." Sarah Jane wished she could throw her arms around the spirit. She'd come to think of it in a strange way as almost a second daughter.

Kit stepped forward. "Are you ready?"

The spirit shrugged, just like a typical teen. "Yeah, I guess."

"Why don't we step around the corner to the side yard. It will be easier on the humans."

"Sure," Jessica said. The spirit followed him to the small side yard that was really more of an alley, where Sarah Jane kept the garbage cans. Out of curiosity, she waited a moment, then walked around to peek into the side yard. But they were gone.

CHAPTER 33

Before retiring to the dining table to discuss the best way to proceed after summoning Jessica, the family helped Amy clean up the backyard, removing the candles, crystals, and matches.

"What about your partner Mia," Cass suggested, helping herself to a glass of Amy's ice tea. "Could you call her and just tell her about your conversation with Jessica."

Sarah Jane rubbed the tiredness from her eyes with the heels of her hands. This kind of work was harder than running a half-marathon. She sat back in her chair and considered the pros and cons of Cass's suggestion for a moment.

"Yes, I suppose I can do that. But we still don't have an exact location. And I have to be very careful. I don't want to get her in trouble. I'm not supposed to be working this case, remember?" Sarah Jane fidgeted with one of the smaller black Tourmaline crystals.

"What about the beauty salon? Wouldn't he need permits for that sort of thing?" Susanna asked.

"Yeah, absolutely." Sarah Jane nodded her head. "But tracking that sort of stuff down takes time. What we need..." Sarah Jane tossed the tourmaline into the air and caught it.

"What you need is a location spell," Gran declared from the kitchen. "I know it's not popular, but do any of you girls still have paper maps?"

"Of course." Sarah Jane straightened in her chair. "We should've thought of that before."

"I don't think any of us were thinking along those lines before," Rainey said.

"What you need is either some hair or nail clippings." Gran took a seat on one of the barstools. "Do you have any of those things, Sarah Jane?"

"I don't know. Let me check her bathroom," she said.

From the time she was a little girl, Sarah Jane had cleaned her own hairbrush diligently and had made sure to burn the hair and any nail clippings. Something her grandmother had taught her. "If another witch gets hold of your hair, they can cast a spell on you. Best to just get rid of it."

And while she had kept up her own ritual, she'd never been strict with her children about it. She rifled through the Jack and Jill bath that Larkin and Selena shared when she was home. She whispered a little prayer to the universe, begging for Selena to have left some hair or even fingernails behind.

Sarah Jane found a boar's hair brush in the bottom drawer of the bathroom vanity with long dark strands still wound through the bristles. She tugged all the hair into a tangled mass and ran down the hall to the family room with her bounty.

"Found some."

"You sure it's hers, not yours?" Gran asked.

"Absolutely. I've never seen the brush before."

"Wonderful. Now we just need a map. Preferably not one of those electronic ones."

"I'm already on it, Gigi," Dalton said. He had pulled out his laptop and attached it to the wireless printer Sarah Jane sometimes used for work. A minute later, it spit out several pieces of paper. His aunts cleared the table of teacups and glasses and began putting them together to create a detailed map of the town of Gilroy.

"Thank you, honey," Sarah Jane said as she studied the complete map now spread on the dining room table.

Gran pushed to her feet and smiled her approval, tousling Dalton's hair. "Thank you, love. Now, we need a small dish, a black candle, and a box of matches." She bent over the dining table, taking a better look at the map. "We'll also need a small vessel of some sort to hold some energy. Preferably something glass or ceramic."

"I'll get something," said Amy. She headed to one of

the cabinets and returned with a small empty jelly jar. "Will this do, Gran?"

"Yes, it will, my dear. Put it on the table, please, near the edge of the map."

"Yes, ma'am," Amy said.

"I'll take the hair, Sarah Jane."

Sarah Jane placed the soft mound of Selena's hair in her grandmother's outstretched palm, a gasp of pain for her daughter threatening to drop her to the ground. She summoned every ounce of strength to swallow her fear and put her faith in Gran as she watched her rub the hair between her hands until it became a very tight little ball.

"Bring me the candle, Amy." Gran pointed to where she wanted it. Amy set a black candle in a quartz crystal holder down in front of her grandmother.

"All right, girls. I need you to lend me some of your energy. Focus your attention on Selena's face. Then set an intention to find her."

"Yes, ma'am," echoed throughout the room.

Gran closed her eyes. "Thank you, universe, for your perfect energy. Lead us to this child, lost to us at the moment."

Ball of fire, burning bright, lead us through the shadowy night

Ball of fire, glowing red, lead us to the owner of this hair.

Gran chanted the spell four more times before she set the hair on fire and dropped it into the jar. Sarah Jane watched as it turned from a red flame, to dark embers and ash. Gran put the lid on top of the jelly jar and shook it. A tiny ball of pale yellow energy burst forth from the embers and hovered in the center like a lantern.

"Just take this with you, and when you get close, it should glow bright red. And don't forget the map. It's infused with your intentions too."

Sarah Jane took the jar in her hand and stared at the flickering ball of light. She blew out a breath, feeling as if she held her daughter's life literally in her hands.

"I don't think I can drive," Sarah Jane said.

"That's okay, Mom," Dalton said. "I can drive. Maybe you should call Mia on the way there. Is your FBI reaper guy going to come back?"

"I don't know," Sarah Jane said. She glanced at her watch. He'd been gone for more than half an hour now. How long did it take to ferry a soul to the afterlife?

"I'll have Mia call him. I didn't get his card."

"Okay, who's riding with us?" Dalton asked.

Amy and Cass raised their hands.

"I'll drive," Rainey said. "Susanna, you can ride with me. I know Gilroy pretty well."

"Gran, will you be okay by yourself here?" Sarah Jane asked.

"Of course, I will. And somebody needs to be here when Larkin gets home from school, so he doesn't feel like he's been abandoned."

"Thanks, Gran," Sarah Jane leaned in and gave her grandmother a kiss on the cheek.

"I call shotgun," Sarah Jane said and headed for the front door.

❧

GRAN'S SPELL WORKED LIKE A CHARM. ONCE THEY GOT to the old City Hall building in Gilroy, Sarah Jane held up the jar in each direction. They turned down a street lined with vintage homes and a bright red light lit up the jar.

"This way," Sarah Jane said. "Selena is down this street."

After a few turns, the area became more derelict, and they found themselves in a rundown neighborhood of tiny wooden houses probably built in the 1920s.

"Keep driving, Dalton," Sarah Jane urged. "We're getting closer to your sister. I can feel it."

The jelly jar glowed brightest in front of a pale yellow house with peeling paint, just as Jessica had described.

Sarah Jane felt a dark energy hanging over the house. It reached out and wrapped around her senses. She could hear the girls wailing, terrified. Their souls trapped inside that building.

"What should we do?" Dalton asked. "It's not like we

can go knock on the front door, and you can flash your badge to get inside."

"I'm going to call Mia. Then we're going to surround the house to see if the back door is accessible. I'm not averse to an unlocking spell."

"Me, either," Cass said. "Dalton, you know how to throw an energy punch, right?"

"Yeah, Aunt Cass." Dalton sounded a little irritated. "Aunt Rainey taught me."

"Good. How are we going to handle this little weasel? Unless you want to call the Defenders of Light," Cass said.

"No, thank you. Defenders of Light will come in, scoop him up, and take him away, and we won't learn any of these girls' names. Or where they're all buried. These families need peace."

"All right. Then we'll just go in there with energy balls blazing," Dalton joked.

"If that's what it takes," Sarah Jane said. Her phone rang, but she didn't recognize the number. "Prentice."

"SJ, it's Kit Spencer. Where are you?" Sarah Jane filled him in and gave him the address. "I still have a dilemma. I don't have a warrant to just rush in there."

"I don't want you to worry. I told you I would shield you, and I meant it. I'll be there in less than five minutes. Have you called Mia?"

"I was just getting ready to," Sarah Jane said. She stared at the house for any movement. Suddenly, in the front window, she saw the sheer curtains move. "I definitely think he's home."

"I'll be there soon. Be careful."

"Careful's my middle name," she said and ended the call. She quickly made a call to Mia.

"I can't explain, but I've found Selena. And I believe I found his lair, if you want to call it that."

"How the hell did you do that?" Mia whispered.

"I have one advantage that the police don't. I can use magic. He's in Gilroy." Sarah Jane rattled off the address. "Mia, I need you to listen to me carefully. My sisters and I are going to breach the house. Along with Agent Spencer."

"Agent Spencer is there? Is he a witch too?"

"Something like that," Sarah Jane said. "He has a different agenda than I do, but so far, I've been able to count on him."

Mia growled, "I don't like this one bit. What if he has a gun?"

"We'll just have to subdue him before he can shoot us. It will be okay. You get a team together. Tell them that you got an anonymous tip. That someone saw something. Make something up that makes sense."

"All right. I'll talk to Stuckey. Besides me, he's probably the one who's on your side the most."

"Tell him, thank you for me."

"Sure. Be careful. This is so crazy."

"Tell me about it," Sarah Jane said and ended the call.

Agent Kit Spencer walked down the street in his dark suit. Sarah Jane would have to ask him when all this was done, how he had gotten here so fast. It had to be a reaper thing.

She got out of the car and raised a hand to wave at him.

"Are you ready to go in there?" he asked as he drew closer. He removed his sunglasses and folded them up before tucking them into the breast pocket of his jacket. The group of witches gathered in front of Sarah Jane's Volvo.

"Yeah. I think you should knock on the front door, distract him if you can. Cass, Rainey, you're with me. We'll head around back. See if we can get inside."

Kit nodded.

Susanna gestured to Amy, Dalton, and herself. "Where do you want us?"

"You hang back until Kit gets inside, then follow him in. But be careful. We don't know if this place is booby-trapped or not."

"Got it," Susanna nodded.

Cass reached into her pocket and pulled out a handful of black crystals. "It's all I have on such short notice. Black tourmaline. Should help protect us."

"Thank you," Sarah Jane said.

They each took a crystal and slid it into the front pocket of their pants.

"All right. Let's go get our girl," Sarah Jane said.

CHAPTER 34

Sarah Jane's fingers tingled with raw energy and anticipation as she studied the lock on the back door.

"Looks pretty flimsy for somebody who's trying to keep a hostage," Rainey said. "I don't even need magic to open that. Just a good blow with a hammer."

Sarah Jane nodded, but then said, "Often with hostages it's more psychological than the locks on the door. Of course," she explained, "his hostages are spirits so there must be a spell involved too." Sarah Jane waved her hand over the deadbolt and focused.

"Dammit," she muttered, "I'm so rusty."

"You want me to do it?" Rainey asked.

"No, she should do it. She has to practice. It's the only way she's going to get stronger," Cass opined.

Sarah Jane threw a dirty look at her younger sister

but tried again. She took a deep breath in and blew it out, her regime for getting focused. This time, she visualized the locking mechanism and tried to connect to the energy of the metal.

A slight sweat broke out on her forehead, but the lock clicked, and the deadbolt slid open. She turned the handle with ease. She pushed the door inward, cringing when the hinges squealed. She felt the heat of Rainey right behind her when she stopped to listen to the house. In the front room she could hear Kit trying to talk his way into the house. She glanced around. This was definitely the place Jessica had described. There were two hair washing stations, and the stylist's chair sitting in front of the cracked mirror. A solid door with two deadbolts on it caught her attention. She didn't think the spirits would care much about deadbolts. She put her ear to the door.

"Selena?" she whispered loudly.

"Mom?" Her daughter's muffled voice sounded relieved. "My goddess, Mom is that you?"

Sarah Jane rested her head against the door.

"SJ, don't just sit there. Let her out," Rainey whisper-yelled at her.

Sarah Jane shook off her stupor of relief and focused on the deadbolts. This time they opened more easily. Her magic was building. Cass was right. All she needed was practice. She opened the door and found Selena crouching behind the metal frame of the bed. Two pairs of handcuffs lay on the floor.

Selena launched on her as soon as she saw her, and Sarah Jane held onto her baby girl, hugging her tightly.

"Are you okay?" Sarah Jane said softly against Selena's ear.

"I'm fine. Hungry. Pissed as hell, but I'm okay."

Sarah Jane pulled away and brushed her daughter's hair out of her face. "Did he..." She swallowed hard. "Touch you?"

"No, mom. He didn't break me if that's what you're asking."

"Oh, thank goddess." Sarah Jane hugged Selena to her again.

"Can we just get out of here?"

"Soon, sweetie. Have you experienced any spirits?"

"There's this old lady who keeps floating in. And sometimes I hear screams. Knocking. Typical spirit stuff."

"Do you know where the trophy room is? Did he mention that or this old lady spirit?"

Selena shook her head. "No."

"No worries. We'll find it."

"What is it?" Selena asked.

"It's where he's keeping the souls of the girls he's killed."

Selena's eyes widened, and her mouth fell ajar. Her hand floated to her throat. The realization that it could've been her trapped in that trophy room shadowed her eyes.

"My goddess," Selena whispered.

"SJ, why don't I take Selena out the back door and to the cars. I can look her over and make sure she's okay," Cass offered.

"That would be great. Just be safe, okay?"

"Of course," Cass said. She held her hand out for her niece. "Come on, honey. Let's get out of here."

The door to the room slammed shut, and a loud voice screeched, "Darren!"

Cass shook the door handle and tugged hard. "That little bitch."

"Cass, try an unlocking spell," Sarah Jane said.

Cass tried, then Rainey.

"I can try," Selena said.

"No, I think she's holding it shut using her energy."

"Well, maybe we should just use her energy against her," Rainey said.

"I agree. I don't think she could keep that door closed if the three of us decided to blast it open," Cass said.

"Four of us," Selena interjected.

"You sure you're up to it? It takes a lot of energy," Sarah Jane said.

"Oh yeah, I'm ready," Selena said.

"Let's do this," Cass said.

The four witches squatted into an athletic stance and

held their hands in front of their chests. After several moments of manipulating the energy forming between their palms, glowing orbs of light and heat formed. Rainy breathed in and out through her nose before throwing the first blast. The door shook and a sooty stain exploded outward. Cass went next and the door cracked.

"Let's stand together, Selena. See if we can blast it all the way open."

"I'm ready," Selena said.

"On my mark," Sarah Jane said. "One. Two. Three. Now." Both witches assaulted the door with blasts of gold light and energy. The door exploded outward and another scream for Darren echoed through the house.

Sarah Jane rounded the corner into the defunct beauty salon. A reaper, wearing black robes from head to toe stood before her, and a sharp scythe in his bony hand slithered into the space. Sarah Jane's breath caught in her throat, and she couldn't look into his face, or at least where his face should've been.

"Kit? Is that you?"

"It is. Your sisters and son have subdued him in the living room. I see you found Selena. Unharmed, I hope."

"Yes. Apparently."

"I'm glad."

"You can't have me, reaper," the old woman taunted from a spot near the ceiling.

"Please, excuse me," Kit said.

He moved faster than any spirit she had ever seen. Before the old woman could open her mouth, he had hooked his scythe into her torso. She screamed, but Sarah Jane doubted it was pain. More likely, it was surprise. Kit and the old woman disappeared.

"Oh, my goddess," Selena muttered

"That was very disconcerting," Rainey said. "Not exactly how I pictured it."

"Come on, let's go see if Dalton and Susanna need help," Sarah Jane said.

When they walked into the living room, Darren was on his knees with a thin band of energy holding him in place.

"Nice work, Susanna," Sarah Jane said. She immediately recognized his face. How had she not seen it before? The security guard that had argued with her in the dorm. The man hanging around at the vigil. He'd probably planted all of those cameras.

"It wasn't me. Dalton did this," Susanna said. "I've gathered the things we need to strip him of his magic." She held up his silver name tag that he wore on his uniform. Darren Valentine. "This was the only photograph I could find of him that looked recent." She held up his badge for Chiron Security. "And I took a lock of his hair." She held up the small glass jar to show Sarah Jane. Then she dropped the name tag and the embossed work badge into it.

"What are you going to do to me?" he asked, his eyes wide with fright.

"We're going to make sure that the authorities take you to jail forever," Sarah Jane said. "But first we're going to take your magic away, so you can never do this again, and you can never ever break out of jail."

"You can't do that to me," he said, panic streaking across his face. "I need my magic. If I get to jail without magic, do you know what they'll do to me?"

"Yes," Sarah Jane said, nodding her head. "I have some idea of what they would do to you. And I can't imagine that it would be as bad as what you did to the young women you killed."

"I don't know what you're talking about." He pursed his lips together and stared forward.

"You can say that all day long, but I have a feeling we'll be able to find plenty of evidence in this house that says otherwise. And at the very least, we have you for kidnapping my daughter."

He glowered at her. "You can take me to jail. But you'll never find all those women. Not while their souls are mine."

"We'll find them. And we will free them."

Kit materialized in front of them still wearing his true form. He leaned in close and peered into Valentine's eyes. "You can never outsmart death, don't you know that?"

Valentine shook uncontrollably. “You can't have them.”

“It's too late. I’ve already sliced through your spell. Again, you can't outsmart death. Why is it you fools never learn this?”

The souls of the young women he'd collected, Ashlyn, Haley, and six others encircled him.

“You see, they're free. And now it will be my duty and honor to take them to the other side where they belong.”

“Kit,” Sarah Jane said.

“Don't worry, Sarah Jane. I'll make sure I have all of their names and where we can find their bodies.”

“Thank you,” she said.

He disappeared, taking the young women with him. This time their exit from this Earth was peaceful.

“Now, what will we do with you?” Sarah Jane said as she turned her attention back to Darren Valentine. “Oh yeah. We were going to strip you of your magic. Let's all form a circle.” Amy placed a small, clear jar in front of him. Then Sarah Jane, Rainey, Susanna, Amy, and Dalton formed a circle around him and held hands.

“Repeat after me: No more power through you shall pass, Magic move from man to glass.” Sarah Jane said. And the group repeated it along with her three more times.

As they spoke, a golden mist poured from his nose, mouth, and ears into the glass. When the last tendril of it left his body, Amy bent down and quickly closed it up inside the jar. She whispered a quick incantation.

I bind you now so you can do no harm

I bind you here with this charm.

That should do it." Amy slid the jar into her bag for safekeeping. In the distance sirens rang out.

"What should we do now?" Dalton asked. "Sounds like the police are on their way."

"You all should get out of here. I'll deal with the police. Just leave Selena with me. They'll want to take her statement."

"Sarah Jane, you should go too." Kit joined them in the living room, only now he wore his suit and his glamour again. "I told you I would shield you. I don't want you to get in trouble for this. You kept your end of the bargain. Now, let me keep mine."

Thank you," Sarah Jane said.

"Leave Selena with me, and I'll bring her home."

"Thank you, Kit. For everything."

"Consider us even. And perhaps we'll even get to work together again."

"Perhaps," Sarah Jane said. She smiled and shuffled her family out of this house of horrors.

CHAPTER 35

Sarah Jane poured herself a second cup of coffee and headed for her desk to make a couple of phone calls on the case she picked up this morning.

Things had gotten back to normal for the most part. She returned to work. Selena had fought with her about moving home when she suggested it, but of course, what else would she expect from her headstrong daughter? Somehow, Agent Kit Spencer had kept his word. There had been no evidence she had ever come close to the case, and she'd been allowed to come back from leave as soon as she wanted. Which didn't take long.

The strange part was that she missed Jessica and their chats on the way home. She hoped wherever she was that Jessica was at peace. Even Bernice showed up less and less now.

Darren Valentine was charged with nine counts of

murder in the first degree with special circumstances. They were still building a case against him, gathering evidence, but he'd been denied bail, and Sarah Jane saw that as a positive sign. If convicted, he would never be free again. And she had his magic in a jar, buried in her backyard to ensure that would never happen.

Sarah Jane rounded the corner from the break room and almost ran directly into Kit Spencer.

"Hi, SJ," Kit said. He looked debonair in his pale gray suit, pale purple oxford shirt. "I'm heading back to San Francisco today."

"I figured," she said. "I actually thought you might leave sooner now that the case is solved."

"I'll be honest, I dragged my feet a little." He smiled. "I hope Selena is doing well."

"She is. She's already back at school, and she refuses to move home so..." Sarah Jane shrugged. "What's an overprotective mother to do?"

Kit grinned. "You have to let them live their lives."

"I believe that's exactly what she said. Were you listening in?"

They both chuckled.

Kit paused for a moment, then said, "I just wanted to say I really enjoyed working with you officially and unofficially." He smiled warmly and continued. "You and your family are pretty special."

"Thank you." She felt a warm glow at the praise. "I don't always appreciate them the way I should. But you're right. They are special. And I'm very lucky to have them."

"Perhaps we'll have another chance to work together."

"I would like that," Sarah Jane said. They stared at each other for a moment shifting their feet at the awkwardness building between them.

"Well, I should get on the road."

"Okay. Drive careful."

He grinned, a twinkle in his dark eyes. "Careful's my middle name."

Sarah Jane groaned, then headed back into the squad room to get some work done.

OCTOBER 12

Sarah Jane and her kids hiked along the Lookout Trailhead in the Santa Cruz Mountains with Dan's urn in her backpack. They stopped every once in a while, to spread a few of his ashes along the trail. It was what Dan would've wanted; she was sure of it. To be surrounded by beautiful vistas of the mountains where in some places you could even see the ocean stretching out to the horizon.

When they reached the highest lookout, they waited until they were alone and took the bag holding the remainder of his ashes from the brass urn. They emptied it into the air, letting the ashes blow away with the strong breeze. Sarah Jane watched as his ashes swirled and spread and finally disappeared. She watched as her kids spread out, lying down on the grass to watch clouds, and a sense of tranquility spread through her for the first time in many months.

"So, what do you think?" a familiar voice said. Sarah Jane turned her head and smiled at Bernice. "Was all that anxiety about this worth it?"

"No," Sarah Jane blurted. "But his wishes have been fulfilled. And now I hope that he is at peace."

"He's definitely at peace, honey. But he still has an eye on you every once in a while." Bernice cracked a smile. "I just wanted to say I am very proud of you and to let you know I'm going to miss you. You have certainly been one of my favorite cases so far in my long life."

"Why are you going to miss me?" Sarah Jane chuckled.

"Oh, it's time for me to pester some other poor soul. I've done about all I can with you."

"Wait, you're going? Really?" Sarah Jane said. Stunned. "Just when I want you to stay you have to leave?"

"You don't need me anymore. I said from the beginning that I would be here as long as you need me."

"But what if I need you again?"

"I will always be here for you." Bernice grinned. "If

you need me all you have to do is call. Just remember, honey, to live your life."

"I know. Life is for living."

"Yes. Yes, it is." Bernice stayed for a few more minutes and when another heavy breeze whipped through the air, she disappeared.

THE END

CHAPTER 36

Thank you for reading *Witch in Retrograde.* Sarah Jane has quickly become one of my favorite characters to write. Maybe because she's close to my age and I can relate to her so much as she maneuvers middle age and all its unexpected (and expected) changes. As my first book in a new genre, it was a lot of fun to write, but different from my other series since I was exploring new characters, their tics, and a new setting. In the next book Witch on the Cusp, Sarah Jane encounters a spirit guide that has stepped right out of the eighties. She's faced with another murder, one that is too familiar, as it's exactly like her mother's. Family secrets will be revealed and we'll get to know her sisters better.

Click here to be notified of the preorder for Witch on the Cusp.

If you're interested in reading my other work, start

with Haunting Charlie. It's a little more suspenseful, but the characters are fun and lovable. And there are plenty of witches and ghosts!

OR YOU CAN SIGNUP FOR MY NEWSLETTER AND TO BE informed when *Witch on the Cusp* is available for purchase. https://wendy-wang-books.ck.page/482af1c7a3

CONNECT WITH ME

One of the things I love most about writing is building a relationship with my readers. We can connect in several different ways.

JOIN MY READER'S NEWSLETTER.

By signing up for my newsletter, you will get information on preorders, new releases and exclusive content just for my reader's newsletter. You can join by clicking here: http://wendy-wang-books.ck.page/482af1c7a3

You can also follow me on my Amazon page if you prefer not to get another email in your inbox. Follow me here.

CONNECT WITH ME ON FACEBOOK

Want to comment on your favorite scene? Or make

suggestions for a funny ghostly encounter for Charlie? Or tell me what sort of magic you'd like to see Jen, Daphne and Lisa perform? Like my Facebook page and let me know. I post content there regularly and talk with my readers every day.

FACEBOOK: HTTPS://WWW.facebook.com/wendywangauthor

LET'S TALK ABOUT OUR FAVORITE BOOKS IN MY readers group on Facebook.

Readers Group: **https://www.facebook.com/groups/1287348628022940/**

YOU CAN ALWAYS DROP ME AN EMAIL. I LOVE TO HEAR from my readers

Email: wendy@wendywangbooks.com

THANK YOU AGAIN FOR READING!

Printed in Great Britain
by Amazon